Praise for Sarah Lane's

The God
of My Art

Quarterfinalist for the Amazon Breakthrough Novel Award

"*The God of My Art* is at its heart a charming read. There is something about it that envelops the reader, sitting them right next to the tortured Helene. . . . But be warned: Lane's prose has a tendency to gently lure you into reading the book in one sitting."

—*The Ubyssey*

"This is a wonderfully written story, has a strong cast of lifelike characters and a gripping, quick-moving plot line. . . . This is a book that once you start it would be hard to put down."

—ABNA Expert Reviewer

"Really takes off during a high and naked moment in a self-made steam hut in the woods."

—*Publisher's Weekly*

The God
of My Art

A NOVEL

SARAH LANE

PURPLEFERNS PRESS

Grateful acknowledgment is made to the following for permission to reprint from previously published material. Éditions Gallimard: this author's translation of an excerpt from *L'Homme révolté* by Albert Camus, copyright © Éditions Gallimard, 1951. Faber & Faber and HarperCollins: excerpts from "Daddy," taken from *Ariel* by Sylvia Plath, copyright © Faber & Faber, 1965, and © HarperCollins, 1965.

Acknowledgment is also made to the following works. Excerpt from William A. Oldfather's translation of *Discourses* by Epictetus, 1928. Excerpt from Jeremy Collier's translation, 1887, and adapted excerpt from John Jackson's translation, 1906, of *Meditations* by Marcus Aurelius. Excerpt from J.H. Walter's edition of William Shakespeare's *King Henry V*, 1903. Adapted excerpts from Helen Zimmern's translation, 1906, of *Beyond Good and Evil* and Thomas Common's translation, 1909, of *Thus Spake Zarathustra* by Friedrich Nietzsche. Thanks also to Frank Sinatra, whose album title *In the Wee Small Hours*, 1955, is referenced here by a chapter title, and to Pablo Picasso as quoted by Paul Éluard in *Donner à voir*, 1939.

Library and Archives Canada Cataloguing in Publication

Lane, Sarah, 1976-
    The god of my art : a novel / Sarah Lane.

Issued also in electronic format.
ISBN 978-0-9916723-0-1

    I. Title.

PS8623.A5225G63 2013   C813'.6   C2012-906781-4

Published in Canada by Purpleferns Press. Printed and bound in the United States.

For more information, visit *www.purplefernspress.com*.

Submit to the fate of your own free will.

Marcus Aurelius

Contents

YELLOW

RED

O for a Muse of fire, that would ascend
The brightest heaven of invention.
WILLIAM SHAKESPEARE

June 2001: Two Sides of a City

Sunlight seeps through the curtain, shifting across the mattress with the fluttering of fabric and spotting my thighs with pockets of warmth. A shaft creeps across Matthew's freckled back to where an auburn wisp has escaped his ponytail and plays across his cheek. I reach out to tuck the strand behind his ear.

"What do you admire so much about Nietzsche?"

He laughs. "What? You haven't read him?"

I turn my face to the wall.

"What's wrong?" he demands, when I don't answer.

"Nothing." I wonder what made him recite me this line: *Man shall be trained for war, and woman for the recreation of the warrior.*

Matthew rolls off me and flops onto his back on the mattress. "Nietzsche," he explains, "encourages passion and truth in a world of tragedy and deception."

I reach across his chest for the wine glass on the floor and finish it off in one draft.

"Trust me," he whispers, lifting a hand to brush away a black curl that has fallen across my face. "Trust me, my ocean lover."

EARLIER THIS AFTERNOON, ON an inner tube in the ocean, my hair floated out behind me like ribbons of seaweed in the small waves. Matthew said my eyes reflected the bottle-green water. I said his reflected the sky. Now, as I pull up my shorts in his basement suite, he calls me his ocean lover and peels them off again: I can't say no, I don't want to say no.

Now here I am already letting myself out the door.

"My birthday's next week. June 30," I tell him, watching him stuff his face with sushi. "My boss is having a party the night before and invited me. Will you come? I have to go. Everyone from the restaurant where I work will be there."

He shrugs. "Why not? If I'm still here in Vancouver."

I climb the stairs into the backyard of his parents' house, leaving him sitting cross-legged on the mattress on the floor. Hopping onto my bike, I coast down Arbutus Street toward the ocean. Across the inlet, the downtown skyscrapers reflect the late sun. Here in Kits I turn at Eighth Avenue, along which pink plum and white cherry blossoms have given way to the bright foliage of June. I peddle past heritage houses with planters abloom and sleeping golden retrievers on their verandas. Here a yellow house with a white border surrenders to a facelift: bare-chested men hammer at the floorboards of a new porch, their backs a glimmer under the sun, tools and two-by-fours scattered across the lawn. Here at Cambie Street, I turn onto Broadway and coast past a cluster of mountain sports stores. A canvasser for Amnesty International tries to stop me outside of one, but I beg poverty until I remember Matthew's plan to volunteer abroad. I donate what change I do have: four dollars and sixty-two cents. Then I cross over Main Street into my own neighbourhood.

On a corner, waiting for the light to change, a strung-out street-walker dallies. Neon Chinese characters fizzle on the storefront behind her. A squashed soda can flutters against the base of an overflowing garbage bin as traffic whizzes by. Pulling down my shades, I ignore her outstretched hand and walk my bike across the street to the rack outside Kingsgate Mall. From there I swing through the mall doors past a group of snotty-nosed kids swinging their legs off the bench outside the liquor store. I climb the escalator through a waft of incense from the Indian store below and stumble blinking into the canary landscape of a grocery store, the yellow so bright under the fluorescent lights I keep my sunglasses on.

"Your card is coming back as having insufficient funds," the cashier informs me. I fish out another one from the back pocket of my shorts and the transaction goes through. In the parking lot, I wrap the plastic handles of the grocery bag around my handlebars and weave my way through the alleyways of East Vancouver to my building on Fraser Street. The elevator is broken. TEMPORARILY the sign posted on the door says, but it hasn't worked since I moved into my bachelor suite over a year ago. So I haul my bike and groceries up the four flights of stairs and run into the man from the second floor who stumbles when he sees me but insists on squeezing by anyway, his breath sharp with alcohol in the stairwell. I concentrate on Matthew; I clamp shut my eyes and conjure up his arms as shields to protect me against this drunken man's grime, against the impoverishment of this locality, against these human beings in various stages of waste and decay, and so diminish the significance of my own presence here to irrelevance.

Windeal

I met Matthew a month ago at university. Christine had asked me to help her study for her economics exam in the library. When we met up at the student union building, she wanted to return a climbing harness to the outdoors club in the basement, and this detour provided me a glimpse into her most recent obsession: extreme mountain sports.

I followed her into the club room, where behind two worn couches sat a guy snacking on pistachios at a desk covered in climbing ropes. He threw a handful of nuts into his mouth as we came in. The crest on his cap read *Cheeky*. Next to him, tucked in between the wall and the desk, a redheaded man leaned into the sloped ceiling and flipped through a magazine. His hair, a pale flame, was bunched up into a ponytail at the nape of his neck, and his translucent skin was tawny with freckles.

"Hey," Christine greeted them. "What have you been up to?"

"Just got back from climbing the Chief with an overnight bivvy," the guy at the desk boasted through a mouthful of green meat.

"Did you?" Christine turned toward the man leaning into the wall. "How about you, Matthew? Been out lately?"

He glanced up from his magazine. "Just got back with James."

"So how was the climb?"

The redhead shrugged. "It was all right. I was a bit worn out after climbing at Skaha last weekend and down in the States at Vantage, Leavenworth, and Red Rocks earlier this month."

"Lucky you to get so much climbing in," Christine said, tossing her blond braid back as she skirted a couch to stand between the two guys.

"What's luck got to do with it?" Matthew asked.

Ignoring his question, she turned back to James at the desk. "So are we still on for climbing in Squamish this weekend?"

Matthew's eyes wandered over to where I stood by the door.

"Helene!" Christine shrieked, drawing back my attention. She had lifted the brown *Cheeky* cap from James's head. She shook her fingers through his black hair, tousling it down over his dark eyes. "Help me!" she cried, attempting to toss the cap in my direction before he could grab it back. Matthew slid sideways along the sloped wall, away from them, reabsorbed in flicking through his magazine.

I turned toward the notice board. Pinned up was a photograph of three sunburnt men sitting in a snow bank outside an A-frame mountain hut. I tried to read the news clipping under the photograph about how the hut had been built by members of this club, but I gave up after re-reading the first line six times over. My senses were flying away from me, skimming across the concrete floor to swoop up the redhead's leg and torso, darting across his shoulder and down his forearm, flitting across a wrist of strawberry fuzz and a handful of freckles to alight on the thick fingers turning over the pages of *Alpinisme et randonnée* magazine.

James pulled his reclaimed cap back on and cracked apart another pistachio.

Christine turned to Matthew. "Hey," she cooed, pulling the elastic off her braid as she peered over his arm at what he was reading. She unravelled the strands, pulling her fingers through her hair. "The Garibaldi Lake trip is coming up," she said. She twisted around to James. "Hey, check the calendar, will you? I think it's the third weekend in June." James gave a nod, and Christine turned back to Matthew. "You going?"

He shrugged. "Why not? I usually ski the traverse every winter, but I didn't get a chance to this year." He tossed the magazine onto the desk and watched it slide off the ropes onto the floor. Pushing up off the wall and away from the sloped ceiling, he snaked around the end of a couch to head for where I stood by the door.

I feigned interest in the notice board again. His sandaled feet approached and came to a standstill. He smelled like rainforest, like moss.

"What?" the redhead muttered, and I realized I was blocking his exit.

"What kind of trip is it?" I asked, looking up, trying not to appear nervous. "You know, to that lake?"

"A hiking trip."

I must have given him a blank look because he walked two fingers through the air to demonstrate the concept of hiking. He paused to scratch at the rusty stubble on his chin. I let my eyes fall to where his pant leg was torn open at the knee. Still lower in his sandals, his big toes pressed against the smaller ones, gnarling inward like those of an old woman after a lifetime in heels.

"Climbing feet," he explained.

"What I meant was . . ."

"Ask Christine. She knows." With that he started to move around me like we were lovers, fighting.

"Wait." Somehow the word had escaped my mouth and, embarrassed, I squinted up at him. The bare bulb behind his head illuminated every wild red strand of his hair and shadowed his eyes black. Judging by the weathered creases under his eyes, I figured he must be ten or so years older than me. At his shirt opening, long, colourless hairs, almost invisible, curled around the top button. He started to move away.

"Wait, I mean, would the hike be hard? Would I . . ." I rotated my body with his to follow as he exited the club room. "I've never climbed anything. . . ." We were in the hallway now by another door decorated with a rainbow flag and a handwritten sign that read QUEER PRIDE.

He paused to study me. "It's an overnight hike not an expedition."

Christine's laughter spilled out of the club room as she burst through the doorway into the hall. "Helene! You're so—"

"What?" I demanded as she stepped between us. Why did I ever agree to help her study anyway?

Her back to me, she said to Matthew, "So see you in three weeks?"

"Yeah, sure."

After he was gone, I hissed, "What'd you do that for?" She made a face at me and strutted back into the club room. I followed her and said I was leaving.

"Oh, take it easy," she said, plopping onto one of the worn-out couches. "It's early."

I was about to insist, but then I saw his magazine on the floor. Skirting a couch, I bent down to pick it up. It was the February 2001 issue, only four months old, but already the centrefold had been torn out. On the remaining fragment, two weathered, bearded faces peaked out through the flap door of a tent encrusted with snow.

"So do you climb?" James inquired, digging through his bag of pistachios, now mostly shells.

Christine laughed like a maniac from the sofa. "Hah! *Helene?* Now that's funny."

I glared at her, but cold crept up my spine. In an advert for an ice axe on the back cover, a climber dangled off the inside edge of a crevasse, encased in turquoise walls that plummeted into darkness. With a shudder, I set the magazine down on the desk.

"What?" Christine laughed, bending her head back over the arm of the couch to check if I was still glaring. "Helene, you've never even been skiing."

AT OUR DESK IN the basement of the library, Christine glanced at her watch. "These concepts might come easy for you but—"

"Well, I guess they didn't give me a scholarship for nothing, then, did they?" For nearly two hours, I had been spinning circles around her with my dictation of the basic principles of international economics: home country has wheat to sell and wine to buy, blah, blah; foreign country has wine to sell and wheat to buy, blah, blah. My back ached from huddling over her textbook. I downed the last of a latte bought on impulse and stretched my arms toward the ceiling.

On either side of us, bookcases fell away into corridors, their grey tin shelves straining under the thoughts of a million intellectuals. Maybe Christine didn't remember that it was because of her words—*Get a grip on yourself! Do you want to end up working at A&W?*—that I'd finished high school in the first place. Maybe she didn't know I had graduated because, after I'd run away from the group home in Prince George, she had occasionally allowed me to crash on her futon. Maybe she didn't know that she had given me my first glimpse of university life, an alternative to clubbing with a fake ID, getting drunk, and sleeping around. Three years my senior, she'd chewed me out for the stupidity of hitchhiking down south, trying recreational drugs, and hanging out with shady acquaintances—but she'd never ratted me out to my mother and stepfather. She had compelled me to prove that I could be more than just another minimum wage slave; I could, like her, become someone cultured and educated.

Now here I am, tutoring her in the university library, where the arguments encased in these thousands of books have already lost their sparkle of novelty. They remind me of those interminable discussions of the men at my stepfather's Wednesday night Bible study on those long winter nights when I waited for my mother, Katie, to pick me up at the end of her shift at A&W. I think of my stepfather, Lyle, defending his interpretation of a particular passage until winded and sweaty, the thin strands of hair across his prematurely balding crown separating bit by bit as he shouted and pounded on the table. But it was always my mother who put aside dignity, when she came for me, to pick through the canned goods and used clothing at the back of the church basement.

"I have to pass this exam or I won't graduate this fall," Christine whined, bringing me back to the present. She shoved her textbook into a heap at the end of our cubbyhole and pushed off onto her chair's hind legs, chewing down the end of her pencil.

"You'll do fine," I reassured her as I gathered up my books and dumped them into my backpack. With my pack zipped closed, I sat there pondering how best to broach the matter of the hiking trip.

Glancing at me, Christine drew her brows together. "What is it?"

I set my pack down beside me. "Can I . . ." I began but faltered. My palms were sweating. I glanced down at my moist fingers laced together in my lap and realized that, prior to setting eyes on the redheaded man, I had believed I could do without reference. Now I felt anxious and slightly nauseated from my hunger to study him again. "I mean, I know I don't have any experience, but can I come on that hiking trip with you guys?"

She laughed, flinging her pencil down onto her textbook. "You mean with Matthew?"

I let my gaze flit up a corridor of books. How could I ever compete? She was, like him, an outdoors enthusiast. "What do you mean?" I asked as she stood up.

"Forget about him."

"Why?"

"Just forget about him, okay?" Her voice was gentle as she shut her economics textbook and tucked it, along with her notes, into her messenger bag. "He's a great guy, but he's not for you."

I closed my eyes. I tried to conjure up reddish, sweat-soaked hairs curling over a shirt collar. I tried to visualize a lucent skin darkened by freckles. I tried to smell him again ... that scent of pine needles and earth. Still, I was unable to shove from my mind that small northern British Columbia town—Windeal, population 4,000 and shrinking since the latest mill closure—with its Wednesday night Bible study, Christine's father the mayor, and my mother living down the hill in Lyle's trailer.

"Bye, Helene," I heard Christine say. When I opened my eyes she was receding down a corridor of books, and all around me the library was moving. As if a silent alarm had gone off, students were fleeing outward from the desks to the walls, spilling down the corridors and into the stairwells. As if I were the epicentre of an implosion of which I couldn't yet hear the blast nor see the destruction, everyone was running away. Until I found myself alone at that desk, alone with myself, alone in a bitterness blacker than space as I fell headlong once again into the poisoned well of my jealousy. Of people with a normal life. Of people with untroubled memories of childhood.

Wreck Beach

When Matthew called this morning to invite me to Wreck Beach, I assumed it was Katie ringing back to sulk. I picked up the receiver and barked, "What do you want now?"

"Is this Helene?" asked a male voice.

"Oh my god, *Matthew?* Sorry! I thought it was my . . . somebody else." It'd been six long days of silence since our return from Garibaldi Lake, and his voice flooded my ears like water over parched land. A twinge of guilt reminded me that my mother was getting the busy signal even as we spoke, but I ignored the pang. "So what have you been up to since Garibaldi? Been busy?"

"Nope, not at all. Why?"

"No, no reason." So why hadn't he called?

So now I arrive at the nude beach and lock up my bike. Behind me, the university campus is blanketed in the quiet of summer at midday. I start down the steps. The canopy of the temperate rainforest above blocks out the sun, and I shiver from the sudden change in temperature. I remember stories of a woman being attacked in these woods and give a start when a twig snaps nearby, but it's just one squirrel chasing another. The noises of the beach begin to reach me, and I catch the stench of the portable toilets blowing up the path. Emerging from the forest, I stand on the last stair and scan the crowded shoreline for Matthew.

Up and down the beach, vendors, stitchless under their money belts, wind their way through the picnickers and sunbathers. I am stooping to unfasten my sandals before stepping down into the sand when I spot James stretched out on a towel next to Christine at the far end of the beach. Just then, two naked women let the portable toilet doors bang shut behind me and come down the wooden steps. They sigh "ooh" and "aah" as their bare toes dive into the warm sand, the taller one bending to trail her fingertips through it and grab a handful, letting it sprinkle out behind her onto the driftwood. I watch the two of them stroll hand in hand toward the water, the shorter one lifting her free arm to wave a happy hello at a guy with a fro and a long Roman nose. Next to him, kneeling on a towel, a raven-haired woman rolls the contents of a small baggie with a sun-kissed toddler beside her who slurps on a pink smoothie—strawberry?—and has a sloppy pink moustache. I plunge my feet from the last stair into the sand and wrap my toes around its warm, coarse grains.

A sudden gust of wind.

Beside me, a shirt snaps on a makeshift clothesline in an attempt to free itself of two clothespins. Spread out below across a blanket, whose four corners are pegged down with rocks in the sand, are more wares from overseas: multi-coloured wallets and scarves that will sell for ten times their cost now that they've been dragged back to Canada to flap in the northern breeze.

From behind me, a sudden yell: "Vegetarian, chicken fajitas, only three dollars, vegetarian or chicken fajitas . . ."

A second burst of wind.

Surprised by the two women kissing, I lower my gaze to my toes that peek out of the yellow sand.

A man touches my shoulder with something ice cold that makes me jump away and rub my skin. He's proffering a beer from a backpack of melting ice. "Only four dollars, eh," he says with an accent that reminds me of gravel streets and northern towns and dirty snowdrifts melting in March.

"No thanks."

"Three dollars?"

"*No!*" I pull my shades down from the crown of my head.

With a shrug, he turns away.

"Homemade brownies?" asks a girl wearing nothing but a string of seashells around her waist. She stops beside me and pulls back the lid of a lime-coloured Tupperware to reveal a stack of dark, chocolaty squares.

I shake my head.

She drifts in closer, spreading the incense of her sweat, and murmurs, "Weed?"

They've stopped kissing. They've spread a large towel over the sand beside their friends. The taller, blond Caucasian one stretches out on her back with her hands tucked behind her head, her breasts slouching into her armpits. The shorter, raven-haired Asian one settles her head into the crook of her girlfriend's shoulder. They entwine their legs.

"No," I'm saying to the girl in the seashell belt, "no weed." I continue pushing through the sand up the beach toward where James and Christine sit on the shore with their backs to me. "Hi," I say as I come up behind them, but they don't hear me so I stand still and scan the water for Matthew. He emerges naked from the surf and ambles up the shoreline, his ponytail dripping a dark line into the sand behind him.

"Oh, it's you," Christine says as I step forward into the space beside her. In front of us, Matthew sprawls out on his back in the sand. Christine's greedy pupils dive down from his tresses, wet copper in the sunlight. My eyes follow hers like spies. We stare at the ginger curling out from under his armpits and over his chest, paling as it dries. We linger at the burning bush as long as we dare, before following the bunches of golden chestnut that blaze down the lengths of his legs to arrive at his toes, curled inward, over each other. *Climbing feet.*

Still standing, I lift my eyes to gaze out over the sparkling water. Do I take off my top but leave on my bra? Little puffs in the sky stain the water below with shadow and gather up over the broken islands and crumpled-up inlets further up the coastline. Do I bare everything?

"Anyone have a knife?" James asks, holding up a watermelon. "I forgot mine."

I don't want to be a disappointment. I don't want to be a prude. So off come my shorts and underwear.

Matthew props himself up on an elbow. "Got one," he tells James, eyeing me. Sand streams out of his hair and tumbles down his chest as he reaches into his backpack to fish out the blade.

I unsnap my bra. No going back now. As the cups fall away, one breast after another springs into view. Christine looks away. But doubtless she paid over a hundred dollars for that itty-bitty string thing from one of those expensive beach shops on Denman Street. I can't compete at that level—I don't have her blond tresses, her Barbie-doll waist, her bottomless wallet—so I go instead for overkill, competing with what I learned as a child: when you're uncomfortable, when you're out of your league, go overboard, go wild. But even as this line of thought puffs out my chest, I deflate again. Whatever becomes of me in this life, I don't want to end up like her, like Katie, so desperate for attention.

"Yeahhhh," James drawls with a twang, taking the knife from Matthew, adjusting his cap—a masked salute? He lodges the melon between his knees and takes to hacking at it with the tip of the blade, catching splattering chunks before they can drop into the sand, handing a piece each to Christine and Matthew. Then he reaches across Christine's ankles to offer me a dripping slice, sea green and coral red. I bite into the pulp. Crisp juice cools my teeth, dribbles down between my breasts. I try to discretely wipe away the stickiness, but James's pupils circle in from under the *Cheeky* logo of his cap—*Yeah, yeah, why don't ya stare, buddy? I'll cheek you*—but in spite of the bravado of my inner monologue, all I feel is naked. I steal a glance at Christine, hidden away behind her illusion-creating, hundred-dollar patches of cloth. My hand flees up from between my breasts to the rind at my lips, and James's eyes follow my fingertips as they settle at the edge of my mouth. I drop the melon rind in the sand and sneak a look at Matthew. Wiping juice from his chin, he too is staring. My knees start to buckle; I have to fight to keep my hands from crossing in front of my pubic hair and breasts in shame—don't magazines like *Cosmopolitan* imply in every issue that men are drawn to mystery?

"It's hot, I'm going swimming," I announce in a rush and step back into the surf. Turning my back on the trio, I focus on moving gracefully, extending one leg after the other until I can slide under a wave. With long strokes underwater, my arms pull me forward until I resurface on the other side of a breaker caused by a passing boat. Clothed now in liquid, I take a deep breath and let my muscles relax.

As I gain distance from the shore, I flip onto my back. The white puffs I noticed earlier streak along the horizon, worrisome thoughts on the sidelines, but otherwise the heavens are a vacant canvas. In Windeal, as a teenager, I used to lie on the strip of grass outside our trailer and stare up at the sky, waiting for a sign. For anything, for something to believe in. But the only response I have ever known to prayer is silence. So gazing up at the sky now, I don't bother to request an answer.

A splash behind me. I flip onto my front. With one arm wrapped around an inner tube, Matthew reaches for my ankle with the other.

"What are you doing?" I ask nervously, kicking at him, not wanting to hurt him.

He reels me in. He pins me to his chest. His thumb at my forehead, he tilts back my neck. His lips are brackish and cold, and I claw frantically at his back as we sink beneath the surface.

"You're crazy!" I yell at him between coughs, swimming back away from him. But I'm laughing. "You want to drown me?"

He grabs my wrist. Our bodies bounce and slide into each other, rebound and drift away. I struggle to keep a respectable distance, but his fingers pinch my skin as his grip grows tighter. Our legs tangle together. Gulping for air at the surface again, I manage to gasp, "Matthew?"

He clamps wet, salty lips over mine. I grab the inner tube. He motions for me to climb onto it, and when I do, he swims in between my thighs. He lifts my hips to the surface. I crane my neck to look at him, at this bodiless head floating in a glittering sea. Waves lap over my toes where they poke at the surface, wash up over my thighs. He spits out water and grins at me. I lie back. Overhead, a seagull circles, cocking its head. A wisp of cloud sifts across the sun. I feel Matthew's fingers and the nip of the sea. I push him away and float on the inner tube, crushed between this desire for answers, for direction, and the deafening silence of the sky.

"What's wrong?"

"The seawater stings."

He pulls me from the inner tube into the water. I let him wrap my legs around him. I let him push his way into me, the salt in the water knifing me with a thousand miniature razor blades. I cling to the round of his shoulder hooked over the inner tube. I struggle to stay above the surface, to not let him drown me.

FROM THE WATER, I watch Matthew's figure climb ashore and collapse on the sand. "I'm too exhausted to stay out here," he said with a quick peck as soon as it was over. I stared after him as he swam away.

I swim now with the inner tube toward shore. I try not to think about consequences. Maybe saltwater kills things. By the time I emerge from the waves, he is lying on his front in the sand, his face buried in a bunched-up T-shirt. I know those on the beach would have needed binoculars to see, but still my eyes sink low as I make to my towel, afraid to look up at either James or Christine, fearful that the words *easy*, *slut*, *used* will slip out of James's eyes to slide across Christine's lips in one deftly dropped allusion.

"Listen, love," James brogues to Christine in poor imitation of an Irish accent, "take off your bikini top, will you, and I'll buy you a pint."

"Bugger off," she mocks along with him. "You'll buy me water."

"Shite, girl, I'm an honest bloke. That's your man, there," he insists, pointing to an approaching vendor, the same man who tried to sell me a beer earlier. "Right then, two pints it is, mate," he tells the man. "To get the girl liquored up."

"You're getting to be a bad boy," Christine says, patting his leg. "Don't worry, I'm sure I can find you a couple of girlfriends who'll appreciate your bad boy qualities."

"It's ten bucks, eh, for the two beers," the man tells James.

James plants the beers in the sand, out of Christine's reach. "A real bad boy," he growls, retying the string of his shorts before paying the vendor. James grew up in a mansion in Shaughnessy, one of Canada's richest postal codes. *His big ambition?* Christine derided during our study session in the library. *To design videogames.* This from the girl who recently gave up ballet to pursue rock climbing, in line I suppose with her latest decision to pursue a career as a diplomat. Matthew grew up in posh Kerrisdale, and those in Christine's circle who didn't grew up in Kits or West Van (she grew up in the same northern one-stoplight town as me) still inevitably share, I am discovering, the same white-collar mentality of being one up on the societal hierarchy.

Adjusting his cap, James cracks open one of the Molson Canadians and guzzles down half of it. "Nothing like a brewski, eh," he mocks in the accent of the vendor, "on a fuuuuuuuckin' hot day, eh?" Something at the edge of his words begins to annoy me, something unfair in the way he imitates the accent of the reserve. "Eh," he elbows Christine, "want a beer, little girl?" He holds out the second Molson before her then snatches it away.

"Now you're just being obnoxious," she warns, grabbing his thumb to twist the beer out of his hand. She pulls at the tab of her beer. It lifts with a hiss, and froth sputters over her hand. She wipes her hand on his shorts and crosses her ivory legs away from him to squint at the sea.

Christine has previously told me they usually go to Jericho Beach with the yacht club, but the nudist Wreck Beach is a cool enough escapade so long as you leave before the whacked-out beach regulars and the Quebecois—*K'becers*, she calls them—on detour from the fruit-picking trail, with their long beards and underarm hair, start making their evening bonfires and tam-tam circles.

"What about that bikini top?" James asks, leaning his shoulder into Christine's, holding up his Molson can to remind her of their deal.

Christine rolls her eyes. She tosses her champagne hair back and leans onto her elbows, eyes closed to the sky.

An otter pops its head out of the water in front of us. I dig my camera out of my backpack, but the otter disappears underwater before I can snap a photo, so I set the camera down on the corner of my towel and lie back on my towel.

Turning toward Matthew, I watch his back rise and fall until the beach voices begin to fade, and I slip into that still place between awake and a dream. As the strict confines of consciousness lose their grasp, I start to visualize, as I always do, the colour of things: impervious yellow reflection of moonlight on water waning to a lucent aquamarine as it slides under the surface, cool liquid blue flowing down an underwater cascade, green plankton specks of self a whirl in the blackness where entire lives are nothing more than phosphorescent bursts in the dark—

Grains of sand prick my face as Christine leaps up to warn Matthew, "Don't you dare take my picture. I swear to god. . . ."

Matthew has my camera in his hands. He waves her back down onto her towel. "Just stay lying down. I'm not going to take one."

She tugs on his arm; he releases the shutter of the lens aimed at her bikini-clad body.

I sit up and rub my eyes. I wonder if poverty frightens Christine's friends or if they're too busy with their lives to think about it.

"What do you do with these pictures?" Christine twists around, still clinging to Matthew's forearm, to interrogate me. As if I am the one who has just taken her picture. Before I can answer, her fingers slide off Matthew's wrist as she turns to James. "Take off your hat."

"No, I like my hat."

"Take it off for the picture," she insists, flicking the brown cap off his head and into the sand. James's dark hair is marked with a circular impression. She laughs, messing it up for him. "Look at that hair." She shifts her legs into a longer angle for the lens, and Matthew finishes off my last roll of 35 mm film.

LATER, WHEN THE PINUP on her towel beside me is dozing—lying on her side, bikini top still tied across her back in spite of James's earlier efforts —I sit up and tuck my knees under my chin. James also appears to be napping and, to my right, Matthew's head is again buried in his T-shirt. Further up the shoreline, near the stairs at the entrance to the beach, two police officers wind their way through the sun worshippers with a dog that keeps its nose to the sand. The heat distorts their uniformed bodies into bulges of navy that dance above the wisp of tan fur.

A man passes by, following a narrow strip of sand between our towels and the ocean, his sex flapping free under a mustard T-shirt. He sits with his back to our group on a log on the other side of Matthew, whose shoulders are a splatter of freckles in the afternoon sun, whose sculpted torso is that of a bronzed god. *What does Matthew want with* me?

The shoulder of the man in the mustard T-shirt develops a rhythmic shake. As if sensing my regard on his rounded back, the stranger slicks back his greasy mop of hair and stands up. He wraps a towel around his waist. I grab my tank top and pull it over my head. I reach for my bag, as if in slow motion, dragging it across the sand. I tug at the zipper, reaching in for the rest of my clothes, but the stranger has come to a standstill in front of me, blocking out the sun.

I fling the contents of my bag onto the sand and grab at the first thing in sight: bikini briefs. I slide my toes through their leg holes and pull them up over my knees; they are stuck halfway up my thighs when the man opens his towel. Bloated red meat. I lower my eyes to my navel and finish pulling on my underwear. When the man is no longer in front of me, I glare into the ocean, its surface agitated now into whitecaps.

THE WIND PICKS UP. A mostly naked swarm of people gathers at the base of the stairs around the police officers. Christine sits up, rubs her pickled arms, and looks about for clothing. One of the officers directs the throng back, intermittently wiping his forehead on the back of his sleeve while the other writes in her notebook the details of whatever the dog has sniffed out. Between their navy blazers, I make out the woman I saw earlier with the toddler; from a distance she appears to be answering the officers' questions while distractedly tousling the hair of the little boy pulling on her skirt, who dances about her legs with his head thrown back and his arms upstretched.

A glance behind me places the man in the mustard T-shirt. He stares out from the shadows of the rock jetty at our back, hidden between two black boulders. He stares steadily at me as he works his hand back and forth under his mustard t-shirt. I turn back toward the shore.

Christine stretches then lifts James's cap to wake him. "Let's go. I've had enough sun."

Matthew stirs and sits up, brushing away the grains of sand lodged in his body hair. "Sure," he agrees, thinking she is talking to him. He doesn't notice me, shielding my eyes from the sand he is casting about. Nobody seems to notice the stranger crouching amongst the black rocks of the jetty. I strap on my sandals and roll up my towel. As I watch the others dress, I glimpse the mustard T-shirt through the frame of Matthew's upstretched arms as he pulls his pale blue T-shirt over his head. The man in the mustard T-shirt, clad now in tan shorts, slinks through the crowd past the police officers and climbs the beach stairs to melt into the anonymity of this city with its thousands of unwashed hands.

After the Beach

Do you want a ride?" Matthew asks me at the top of the stairs above Wreck Beach, already tossing my bike into the back of his pickup. I poke at the earth with my sandaled toe and watch him shut the tailgate. Christine backs out her car, with James in the passenger seat, and waves goodbye. "We can get some sushi takeout and hang out at my place," Matthew suggests from across the hood as he searches for his truck keys in the pockets of his shorts.

After he has climbed inside and pulled the lock on the passenger side, I clamber into his truck and stare out the passenger window. *Calm down. This isn't the man you're mad at.* As we drive through the forested Endowment Lands, the cedars on either side blur into hedges of green. I listen to the sound of my silence, to the consent in my absence of words. I could have snapped a photo of the guy, I could have pointed him out to the police, I could have yelled and scolded until he slunk away elsewhere.

From the driver's seat, Matthew is explaining that his parents are in New York for the summer. "On international business. Well, actually, more the regulatory side of international business." A nod on my part keeps him going. "The World Trade Organization for my father. My mom's with an aid outfit for children."

"Hmm . . ." Should have I woken the others? What would have I said? *Oh, look, some guy's jerking off behind us.* Isn't that what perverts want, attention? Anyway, the guys would have probably thought it was funny, and Christine would have given me a look like, *What'd you expect when you took off all your clothes?*

The cool breeze blowing in through Matthew's window wakes me up. I catch my head before it nods forward, thankful that my sunglasses hide my fluttering eyelids. What is it Matthew just said? Something about Japan, about climbing Mount Fuji?

MATTHEW LETS ME INTO the sunken basement of his parents' house in Kerrisdale and leaves me there while he goes out to get the sushi. I slip off my flip-flops and pad around his suite in my bare feet. The high window below the ceiling looks out onto overgrown grass. A ray of sunlight slants through it to play over the mattress on the floor. The sheet is half torn off; I bend down to tuck it back into place. Straightening, I notice boxes stacked in the far corner. Bare cupboards. The closet is empty except for a couple of shirts on the floor. Dishes teeter on the counter and table, everything encrusted with old food. How can someone live in such a nice house and care so little about cleanliness? I shake my head and give up on investigating further. Instead I pull the sheer curtain across the window to mute the heat and go into the bathroom—sink caked with the white chalk of dried toothpaste, comb knotted with red hair, toilet seat up, its base stained yellow. I turn on the shower and climb in, leaning against the soiled tile wall, clinging to the nozzle head for support lest my knees should buckle, lest the stream of grit that runs off my legs should take me down with it, a brown streak twisting into the drain. After a while, I turn off the water and dry myself off with a stale towel.

MATTHEW IS LYING ON the mattress. He has opened a bottle of sparkling wine and offers me a glass. As the bubbles fizzle at the back of my throat, I am happy to have something light and airy to pull me out of my moodiness. When the glass is empty, I balance it on the carpet. Matthew pulls me down beside him. His hands burrow deep into my damp hair, and his teeth sink into my neck. The sand caked into his chest hair sprinkles over the sheet as I wrap my arms around him and nestle my face into the crook of his arm. He swigs directly from the bottle. "Sorry," he says, resting his head back down on the sheet. "Do you want some?" He holds out the bottle. "You want me to refill the glass for you?"

I sit up to sip my new glass of wine. He undoes the tuck of my towel. I drop my arms to block his hands as he brushes them down my body. "Trust me, my ocean lover," he whispers. Like a hypnotic mantra his words wash over me, and I let him lay me down. He bites at my neck, his breath settling in circles of warmth against my clammy skin, and I shiver. In a way, having him call me his *lover* is exhilarating in that it hints of sophistication, of a grownup physicality. Yet, as his tongue sweeps across my skin, my gut churns with unease. Like Munch's scream passing through nature and shifting the colour of the clouds to blood red, Matthew's touch brings with it a quiet despair, and disconnection.

As Matthew slides back up my body and lowers his stomach over mine, he orders me to look at him. When I do, the icy tint of his eyes flows out and turns everything to blue: legs and arms like ribbons trailing off in the wash into unknown, pastel silences, bodies interlaced and composed of an infinite number of minute swabs of indigo, startling bursts of sapphire bleeding into these brush strokes that blur the end of his blue skin and the start of what should be mine.

Without warning, he rolls off me. "I'm used to older women."

His words reach me as from a distance. He shrugs. I turn away.

"What's wrong?" he asks, parting the veil of black curls covering my face. I am frozen up inside this watercolour of ourselves. He pulls me toward him. There is a shock of pleasure as our bodies collide. Colours begin to shift and blur, but then he rolls away again, and the used condom goes cold on my leg, and I am a white space with wispy contours on an as-yet-unfinished canvas.

When Matthew turns my head to lock my eyes, the intention slicing through my consciousness is perfectly clear: I want to tell him I am searching for the one thing that can give my life significance. But, before I can begin to negotiate this, Matthew bolts me down with his glacier-blue eyes. "*Man shall be trained for war,*" he recites, "*and woman for the recreation of the warrior.*"

"Are you a warrior?" I attempt to tease him, but I can't hold his gaze. I turn to stare instead at the wall. His laughter bellows through the basement as his chiselled stomach contracts above the softness of mine.

"What's wrong?" he demands, when I continue to lie still. He tugs at the condom. "Didn't you come?"

"It was okay."

"*Okay?*"

Yesterday I saw graffiti on the back of a bus bench that read IT'S NOT PARANOIA IF THEY'RE REALLY AFTER YOU. Matthew, do you know how it feels to be reduced? Knowing that in any dark alleyway they could be after you—do you know the taste of that fear in your mouth? But I stay quiet because I might be overreacting. The towel might have slipped. It was probably a mirage due to the heat, to the sun overhead. Everybody else was sleeping. What proof do I have?

Matthew stretches his foot toward the ceiling. "Only *okay?*" he insists, a touch of annoyance colouring his voice. The elegance of his long thigh muscle heightens my sense of dissatisfaction, as if he is holding out before me a beauty I can never possess. When I remain silent, Matthew drops his leg back down, sits up, and chucks the knotted condom in the direction of the trash can. Clearly it's time for his ocean lover to go home. I stand up and pull on my shorts.

"Don't you want any sushi?" He pops open the plastic lid of the take-out box and stuffs a tuna roll in his mouth.

I shake my head. I stand there in the entryway, watching him eat, wishing to tell him before I go about my twenty-first birthday coming up. As I twist my heel into the carpet, I notice the corner of an envelope sticking out from under his mattress. I point to the stamp on it with my toe. "What country is that from?"

"What?" he asks through a mouthful of raw fish, not following the line of my leg.

"This stamp," I say, bending down to pull the envelope out from under the mattress.

He rubs his hand down over his forehead and face.

The stamp is of a diamond and a diamond ring with Thailand written up the left side. "You have a friend in Thailand?"

"That's from Yoshiko." His mouth twists as he swallows. I watch him reach for another piece of sushi, this time with the chopsticks, his freckled forearm flexing as he positions the two wooden batons between his fingers.

"Yoshiko?"

He abandons the chopsticks and picks up a new piece with his fingers. "She's a woman I met two years ago in Bangkok." He pops the slice into his mouth. "She came to Canada shortly after for her doctoral studies. Now she's back in Thailand for some research on her way home to Japan." He points to a stack of envelopes and letters on top of the refrigerator. "Those are from her too."

I stare at him, waiting for him to go on.

"Have you ever been in love?" he asks, picking up a salmon roll. He holds it up in mid-air and examines the algae wrapper. Before I can begin to answer he declares in a voice drier than the driftwood at the beach this afternoon that he has never been in love before.

The sardonic undertones of his words haunt me as I peddle toward my bachelor suite. Still, by the time I arrive home, I've managed to re-shape their ambiguity to my advantage so that, when I flop onto my couch, I am able to bask only in what has already become in the storage spaces of my mind a sizzling afternoon spent making love.

After Happiness

A week ago, Katie called me up as I was packing for the Garibaldi Lake three-day hiking trip. It was our first conversation of the year not counting the obligatory Mother's Day call, which I had left as a message on her machine. I was stuffing my sleeping bag into a canvas rucksack borrowed from Christine, along with a lot of other equipment, wondering what I was getting myself into, when the telephone rang.

"You weren't sleeping yet, were you?" she asked. Her voice was edgy. "Thought you might be out or something since it's a Friday night."

"No, I wasn't sleeping." I cleared my throat. "It's only nine thirty."

"*Only*? How late do you usually stay up?"

Helpless, I watched the sleeping bag ooze out of the backpack, a lazy jack-in-the-box. "What do you want?"

"Honeybun, I . . ." Her voice wavered, and I began to imagine a slur to her words. "Just phoned to chat a bit . . . if that's*sh* all right."

"I'm going to bed soon." I forced a yawn into the phone. "I'm going camping tomorrow."

"*Camping*? Since when did you start doing that sort of thing?" Without waiting for an answer, she volunteered, "Lyle's fine."

Lyle. After marrying Katie when I was nine, he moved us out of our hotel room in Prince George and into his singlewide in Windeal's trailer park. He enrolled Katie in AA and another twelve-step program to quit smoking. After she had kicked those habits, he started in on her trademark ocean-blue eyeliner and bleached-blond hair, hallmarks, he said, of her previous trade. *Dear God*, he would pray at the dinner table, *thank you for this macaroni and cheese, and please help Katie get over her vanity.* Where he never got anywhere was with me: it took but a short while before I realized he wanted my mother all to himself. *Do you need your mommy to hold your hand everywhere you go?* he would mock me. So I did everything I could to defy him, and the more I did the more he struggled for control, until he managed to convince Katie to banish me to a group home in Prince George.

"Really? *Fine*?" I asked. "I heard his garage is going out of business."

"From who?"

"Christine—you know, the mayor's daughter? She said the only business he gets now is from those who won't go to the new native shop on the reserve."

"I don't care what people are s*sh*aying. I live with him. I should know what's going on, shouldn't I?"

I sighed.

"It's just like you," she continued. "Always looking for a new way to put him down. Don't you trust your mother? Don't you believe what I s*sh*ay?" When I was silent, she said, "Maybe I shouldn't have called."

"Yeah, maybe you shouldn't have." I reached for the water bottle on my night table, unscrewed the lid, and took a long chug. It's not that I wanted to be callous; it's that experience had taught me to never appear to care more than she did.

"I started smoking again," she announced.

"*What*? Why?" On the other end of the line, I heard her exhale. "You shouldn't be smoking, Mom," I said, trying to swallow my panic.

"Ha-ha-ha. S*sh*ince when do you care?"

"What are you talking about? I've always..." I hated the panic in my voice, the fact that I'd just called her *Mom*. I remembered ribbons of smoke weaving in and out of the light of our hotel room in Prince George, Katie perched on the edge of the bed and the stench of last night's binge hanging over the open mouth of an empty vodka bottle. She would ask if I had made her coffee, if it was noon yet—now here she was, exhaling again into the line. "Katie," I whimpered, "why'd you start up again? It's been twelve years since you quit."

"What's it to you?"

The sting of her words cooled off my concern. "Okay, Katie, I'd like to talk, really I would, but I still have to finish packing and I'm getting up at five thirty."

"All right." She breathed into the phone. "All right. If that's*ssh* what you want."

Her unhappiness unsettled me, as it always has, and so helpless I waited for her to go on, for the rest of her drama, and for the climax of the night's show.

All of a sudden her voice picked up, nervous. "Lyle's home. Got to go." The phone clicked dead, and there it was, the finale.

MY FEET TRIPPED ON the sleeping bag, flinging me out through the frayed sheet closing off my makeshift bedroom, out of the cubbyhole wide enough for a single bed and a dresser. I caught myself on the chrome edge of the table, and my hand glided across its blue laminate top on the way to the freezer. No need for utensils from the dish rack; I wolfed down fingerful after fingerful of raspberry sherbet. It melted on my tongue, sweet glissade into liquid cool until I was lost in ice sheets of candyfloss, my world blurred to slapdash smear of colour. But then there it was, tacked on the bathroom door, an obstinate photo. Resolutely in focus.

Not a photograph really, but a photocopy of one from *The Eyes of Montreal: 1989*, a black-and-white collection borrowed from the Vancouver Public Library with Lodi's name on the back cover. Of their own accord, my feet carried me across the wooden floor, avoiding out of habit the planks that creaked. In the shadows of the photograph, a young woman clutched a bouquet of wilted daffodils in her pale hands. Clouds huddled in the sky as if it might rain, and my aunt had darkened the woman's eyes to obscurity. I wished I knew some of my family, anyone. My mother's older sister and only sibling Lodi had titled this photograph "After Happiness." The annotation underneath it read: *Lost in the wastelands of self-despair.*

I was stuffing the sleeping bag into the backpack again when I remembered another photograph. Dropping the pack, I reached up for the blue shoebox in the closet. I flipped through its dog-eared contents: stray poems, drawings, photographs. In this particular picture, I was sitting on my aunt's lap at the train station in Montreal. Already at six years old I had her midnight curls, her translucent skin, her deep-set eyes of jade. The only family reunion to which my mother ever took me had just concluded, and with my mother I was about to board the train back to our hotel room in Prince George.

My mother doesn't know I salvaged this photograph from the bathroom trash can in our hotel room, that I found it lying underneath a letter written in a cursive hand I couldn't yet read, nor that for years I slept with it tucked inside my pillowcase, hoping that one day I might unlock the secrets within it to Lodi's unpretentious elegance and audacious self-determination, two qualities I couldn't yet put into words but already envied.

Tossing the photograph onto the dresser, I turned on the radio and returned to my packing. Over the airwaves floated a fuzzy grunge tune, distorted by a bad reception. Following the dark bass lines, I suffered the absence once again of other family photographs, ones of Katie's parents, my grandparents, or of Richard, my dad.

BY THE TIME I finished stuffing food, toiletries, clothes, and the sleeping bag into the canvas rucksack, the clock read quarter past midnight. I set the alarm and turned off the lamp.

The moment I climbed into bed, instead of sleep, images of my early childhood flooded my mind's eye: giddy with laughter as my father's thick arms threw me into the air, crying alone in a corner with my mother slumped over the table. These senseless memories ran faster and faster together into a crazy comic strip of screen stills. Still, I felt on the verge of discovering a punchline in the half-sleep swirl when instead a switchblade sliced through the funnies page.

Stumbling out of the blankets, I stood naked by the bed. I couldn't remember who I was or where I was. Then the phone rang again. "Hello?" I rasped, sleep having taken over my voice.

"Hi, honeybun. Lyle's in bed, ss*ho* we can talk now. . . ."

Panic stabbed me as I recognized my mother was slurring her words.

"You weren't ss*h*leeping yet, were you? You always*sh* were a night owl."

"Well I didn't have much of a choice, did I, given your line of work?" I grumbled. "Would you please let me sleep? Why are you calling me so much all of a sudden? What, are you drunk?"

"So you don't want to talk to me?"

Cradling the phone against my shoulder, I slid back under the covers.

"I had a fight with Lyle."

I moaned. "I thought you said he was *fine*."

"He is, he is. It's just that . . . he came home tonight and found me drinking, so he poured the rest of my bottle down the ss*h*ink."

I glanced at the clock—twelve thirty—and rubbed my eyes, frustrated that Katie had to choose this night of all nights for her latest drama. "Well, don't you think that was the right thing to do? Why are you suddenly drinking again anyway?"

"I promis*sh*ed him I'd go back to AA, but he won't agree to see a marriage couns*sh*ellor."

Marriage counselling?

"Katie, why don't you try talking to your sister? Isn't that what sisters, not daughters, are for?"

She let out a theatrical sigh. "Why do you always have to bring up Lodi? You know my parents paid her way through art school but never ss*h*ent me a penny. They wanted me to . . . You know, you wouldn't be here, or you would have been put up for adoption—"

"Spare me, please."

"You're the one who can't forget her! I always tried to protect you."

"That's why every time I picked up a crayon as a child, you told me not to bother?"

"I never said it *that* way."

"And you always threw in some gratuitous critique, like, 'By the time I was your age, I was already drawing in perspective,' or, 'I already knew proper shading technique.'"

"I didn't want to s*sh*et you up for disappointment. All you ever dwell on is how I never encouraged your artistic side. But I wanted more for you than—"

"So, rather than allow me to explore my talent, you thought it better to assume I had none?"

"Where's your loyalty?" she demanded, her voice rising up sharp and clear. "Haven't you ever considered that I might have had dreams of my own? That maybe how we were living wasn't like I'd anticipated?"

"Listen, Katie, it's nearly one in the morning, and I don't need you or anyone else yelling at me." Without waiting for her response, I clicked the phone into the receiver and pulled the cord out of the wall socket.

I settled back into bed but couldn't get comfortable. I kicked at the comforter wrapped around my legs and pulled at the sheet coiled around my torso, tossing and turning until the clock on the night table read quarter to two.

Memories of Prince George were keeping me awake. In one, Katie, feeling her way along the wall from the bed, her eyes squinted against the sunlight, came into our hotel kitchenette where I was drawing the cat asleep on the windowsill. I was seven, and it was early afternoon.

Make some coffee, she ordered.

I was bent over my sketch, concentrating on replicating the soft fur of my kitty.

Tying her bathrobe shut, Katie wandered over to the window, blocking my view of the cat as she stood there watching a dirty, unshaven man push a buggy of empties up the alleyway. *Hello ki-ki-kitty cat,* she purred, her hand swooping down to scoop up the cat from the windowsill. She turned and sat down with him in her arms, across from me at the table. *How's my favourite putty cat?* she cooed in his face, cradling him like a baby. Then, looking up, she announced, *One of the new girls downstairs has started turning tricks.* She gazed at me as though I was transparent and she was focused on a fly on the wall.

The cat, feeling ignored, began to squirm in her arms, clambering to turn himself upright.

Don't you know what turning tricks *means?* she demanded, drawing her eyebrows together, apparently not understanding the lack of reaction from her poker-faced daughter.

When she booted the cat off her lap, I bit my bottom lip. Poor kitty, woken up from his snooze and abandoned the moment something else grabbed her attention.

She shook her head at my silence. *What's your problem?*

My unfinished drawing slipped off the table, and I scrambled after it. She yawned and, glancing down at my sketch, gestured for me to go make her coffee. She reached for the pack of cigarettes on the table, took one out, and lit it. As she exhaled, a billow of smoke gathered over the table. *By your age,* she said as I poured fresh grains into the coffee maker, *I already understood the interplay between light and shadow.*

AT TWO THIRTY, REMEMBERING the sherbet left out on the table, I climbed out of bed, tossed it into the freezer, and sleepwalked to the bathroom. While unthinkable in the light of day, perched there on the toilet, my eyes closed in sleep, my thoughts were amazingly clear. I knew it futile, but still I imagined the life my mother might have had without me, if I hadn't been born: not coarse and debased but instead cultured and refined like Lodi's.

Garibaldi Lake, Day One

The next morning, I scrambled out of James's van through the sliding side door, yawning and blinking in the early morning sunlight. We'd arrived at the trailhead to Garibaldi Lake, after an hour and a half drive from Vancouver. Standing there next to the van, I shook out my legs and stretched my arms skyward. Christine jumped out of the front seat and strutted around to the back doors, where she tossed our packs out one by one onto the gravel and lowered herself into the splits.

I dragged my overstuffed rucksack out from under hers and sat down on top of it. Three other cars were clumped together at our end of the parking lot near a kiosk displaying the map of Garibaldi Provincial Park. Their occupants stood in a loose patch of sunlight further down the lot, the crisp outlines of their bodies fraternizing with the first early morning rays at the edge of the forest shadows.

"How do you do that?" James asked. I looked up to see him attempting to lift his leg past knee level to match Christine, who was standing with her leg drawn straight up against her body so that her ankle grazed her ear. James let his leg drop with a thud back to the ground and plopped his backside down onto the back edge of the van deck, where he fiddled with the shoulder straps of his backpack.

"Don't just sit there staring at me," Christine protested. Effortlessly, she set her leg down, shifted her weight, and lifted the other to her ear, leaning sideways to deepen the stretch.

Having seen her display of flexibility many times before, I returned my attention to the far end of the parking lot. My heart started pounding when I caught sight of Matthew emerging from the woods, zipping up his pants as he walked toward the group. He started chatting with a beefy guy who had a large zoom-lens camera hanging from his neck. As they talked, Matthew drew his arms across his chest and leaned back on his heels, standing out like Achilles against the Coast Mountains. The early light encircled his head with a golden chestnut halo, drawing out the fiery sheen of his ponytail and the stubble on his chin. I touched my knees together where I sat on my pack, feeling out of place as I dragged a boot across the gravel patch in front of me, clearing a dark square of earth out from under the jagged pebbles.

When I turned back toward the van, James was straining to reach down between his bent knees to touch his toes. Christine laughed at him as she stretched from side to side, popping bubble gum in rhythm to the sweep of her arms overhead. Behind the van, tall, thin conifers jutted up like paper cut-outs into the sky. Birds trilled from their branches as a slight breeze ruffled the foliage. I zipped up my fleece jacket, swatting a mosquito in warning to others that swarmed just out of reach. *Calm down,* I told myself. *What's the worst that could happen?*

SHOULDERING THEIR PACKS, CHRISTINE and James trotted over to the start of the trail. I stood and followed, half-dragging, half-carrying my rucksack over to where they had paused next to the trail marker. The marker stated that the lake was nine kilometres away with an eight-hundred-metre elevation gain: in other words, Christine explained for my benefit, nine kilometres straight uphill.

"How long will it take us?" I asked.

She glanced at me and shrugged. Her silence laid my desperation bare. What makes me go chasing after men like this? What would I seek from them? James disappeared into the woods for a pee. Still trying to buckle up my pack, I followed Christine as she began to hike up the path.

I finally caught up with her a half hour later at a creek. I stood panting on the wooden bridge, watching as she knelt in the creek bed below to refill her canteen. I threw off my pack and followed her example, dipping a recycled pop bottle into the gushing stream and gulping down an icy mouthful. The cold stung my teeth, causing me to catch my breath. For a moment, Christine and I were kneeling side by side over the angry torrent, our hands red from the glacier water. "I've been thinking about your sister," I yelled over the roar of the creek. "I wish she could have been here with us now."

Christine screwed the cap of her canteen back on. When she glanced up for an instant our eyes connected. I remembered the police had had to use dental records to identify Stacy's remains in the burnt shell of her boyfriend's car. A chill crawled over me. Brushing away a strand of hair from my eyes, I was surprised to find my forehead coated in a cool layer of sweat. At my touch, droplets rolled off my temples; beads slid down the slick sides of my cheeks. I wanted to tell Christine she was the sister I never had, that I knew she had tried, in her own way, to look out for me. "See you at the top," she said, turning to climb the bank back to the trail. I wanted to ask her if she had ever thought of me as a sister, if my being here had ever, in any small way, filled the absence of the one she had lost. Instead I watched as she scrambled up to the bridge and shouldered her backpack. "Come on!" she yelled down at me, still kneeling in the creek bed, before she disappeared up the trail. I scrambled up after her and, shouldering my rucksack, took to tearing up the path. But I was unable to catch up, and soon my lungs forced me to slow my pace.

The roar of the creek faded to a distant hum and then to a silence punctuated only by the steady shuffle of my footsteps. The Douglas-fir trunks repeated themselves on all sides as in a hall of mirrors, any hint of sky overhead kept out by their branches. A chipmunk darted in front of me, and I startled in turn as it retreated to the safety of a tree trunk before twisting around to shrill in sharp rebuke.

I turned another switchback and paused to catch my breath. I removed my pack and sat down on a fallen tree trunk, my face in my hands. The exertion of the steady climb was drawing up memories of Stacy. Like the time we'd fed her cat a jar of pâté, thinking it was cat food. Or the afternoon we'd played striptease, my idea, and lay huddled up afterward under her four-poster bed telling vampire stories. Stacy and

I turned twelve shortly after and, unbeknownst to her parents, she started dating an older boy. A year later, drunk, he drove his car into a telephone pole and staggered away uninjured before it caught flame and she burned inside. Kurt Cobain died the same week, heralding the end of something—nobody in our generation knew quite what. For three years, I wore black in mourning but also in anger, at Jeff the boyfriend of course, but also at something larger—perhaps, the injustice of death.

As I sat on the trail thinking of Stacy, a couple other hikers, including James, came up the trail and passed on out of sight. When Matthew reached me, he slowed his pace, lifting an arm to wipe his forehead on his sleeve before coming to a standstill at my feet. He kicked a twig from the path, stirring up the damp smell of earth and decayed needles. "Are you okay?" he asked. I looked up to see a bead of sweat trickling down his neck. With a nod I stood up, fighting the urge to sink my face to his chest and weep. He drank water and watched me. His gaze made me tremble.

"What's your name again?"

"Helene." I stared down at my feet. "You're Matthew, right?"

He gave a short nod. "Come on," he said, turning. His heels kicked up splatters of black mud on the back of his pant legs. I trudged after him as if in blinders, forgetting to see the forest, forgetting to feel the pain, focused only on placing my feet down where his had lifted off. An hour later, the trail finally began to flatten out as the trees thinned to an alpine meadow.

"Can we stop for a drink of water?"

Matthew obliged me and squatted on the trail to wait while I caught my breath, his blue eyes squinted against the bright rays of mountain sun behind me. I twisted around to see a snow-capped ridge and the valley out of which we'd surfaced. "I was about to . . ." I explained between gulps of water, turning back to him now to point out the meadow surrounding us, ". . . give up all hope that . . . that the trail would ever flatten out."

"We're in Taylor Meadows," he explained as we continued up the trail side by side at a more leisurely pace. "The trail here reminds me of a garden in Japan." He pointed to a clump of stunted, scraggy trees. "Nature's bonsai trees. Those dwarfed firs are older than they look."

I nodded and let him continue.

"In a Japanese garden, nature is a living work of art, tended to so as to design an atmosphere of perfect serenity. Here in this wilderness, there is a similar interplay of—"

"When were you in Japan?" I interrupted, squinting up at him.

"A couple of years ago." He listed off the names of cities and towns he'd visited, winding an incense of foreign syllables around me as I listened to the cadence and timbre of his voice. Nostalgia tainted the strange words on his tongue as well as a note of falsetto.

"So you speak Japanese?"

"I do." He paused on the trail as though seeing me for the first time. "And I got carried away with it just now, didn't I?"

I shrugged as if to say it didn't matter.

"I try to practice as much as I can." He sounded almost apologetic as we started up the trail again. "I'm lucky to have a private tutor."

WE CROSSED A WOODEN footbridge over a frothy green stream and after a few more twists in the trail arrived at our destination: the majestic Garibaldi Lake, tucked between forested shores in a mountain bowl. Its waters lay before us, opaque and turquoise, glittering in the sunlight and capped by small white waves. I dropped onto a boulder near the shore, rucksack and all, and pulled my steaming boots off my throbbing feet. Unbuckling the canvas belt of the pack, I eased it from my shoulders and took in the campsite: a small bear-proof hut that Matthew explained was for food preparation and eating, a scattered collection of wooden platforms for pitching tents amongst the fragile alpine vegetation, and a quiet, lapping shoreline of rocky beach that needed no explanation.

Walking to the foot of the water, Matthew undid his laces and pulled off his hiking boots. He peeled off his socks and rolled up his pant legs, stretching out his calves and wiggling his gnarly toes up and down. He pulled his T-shirt high over his head and flung it off. Unbuttoning his trousers, he tossed them off as well and splashed naked into the lake.

I slid off the boulder onto my feet, thinking I might join him. But my legs had already stiffened during this short rest, their newly discovered muscles knotted with pain, and my knees threatened to buckle. I glanced up to see Matthew leaping across the surface of the water back onto shore, his body reappearing with a shiver next to his pile of clothes abandoned on the rocks. "Is it that cold?" I yelled, laughing at him as I leaned back onto my boulder before the shake in my legs could give away my fatigue.

He grimaced as he tugged on a tattered pair of briefs. From his backpack he withdrew a ski toque with bunny ears, which he pulled over his wet hair. He hopped about on one foot then the other, rubbing his toes, and bent down for a dozen push-ups before leaping up for a dozen jumping jacks.

James came out of the eating shack and tossed his pack onto a blueberry bush, the berries still too green for eating. He looked, I noticed with some glee, as exhausted as I felt. He sank down onto the edge of a nearby tent platform and watched Matthew dancing around by the lake.

Christine, who had followed James out, yelled over to Matthew, "What took you so long?"

Matthew shrugged. From under his toque, his ponytail dripped a wet line behind him on the rock shards as he picked his way barefoot toward us.

"It's my fault," I told James.

Christine screwed up her face at me as she shook out her own wet hair and turned back to Matthew. "The water feels good after the initial shock, doesn't it?"

He nodded. "I pity those poor saps doing their nine-to-five right now." He selected a fat, flat rock and squatted down on top of it. From this perch he surveyed the lake, the glacier, and the surrounding peaks, looking like a wild sovereign sure of his natural right to a place at the top of the kingdom.

Christine plopped down next to James on the tent platform and stretched out her legs. James leaned into her. "Did I tell you about the game I'm designing?" he asked, stripping a sliver of wood from a plank in the platform with his penknife. Christine eyed him warily. I'd seen that smirk on her face too many times before not to feel protective now toward James. But James didn't take his cue, and it was too late to reroute him as, hapless, he launched into an explanation.

"It's a hard-core mountaineering game, you know? The challenge will be to climb the highest peaks in Canada without getting killed by grizzly bears, cougars, crevasses, hypothermia, rock fall, changing weather patterns, etcetera. Players will be able to choose their own routes, or they can climb in teams with other players."

Christine yawned. Leaning back on her elbows and tilting her face to the sky, she asked, "And why exactly would people want to sit parked in front of a screen playing a video game when they could actually be out climbing?"

"It's for rainy days," James persisted. "And think about the Rick Hansens of the world—don't you think they'd like to be able to climb Mount Robson from their wheelchairs?" He carried on to describe texture mapping, motion-path animation, and lip-sound synchronization before digressing to the pros and cons of 2D versus 3D animation. He expounded on computer code, input and output commands, programming languages, and the genius of fuzzy logic. I stared at him, surprised to see him so lit up, and his enthusiasm began to infect me. I imagined the mountains I would climb in his game, and then I imagined parallel games: one where you could become a Picasso or a Van Gogh or an Emily Carr and repaint the masterpieces of art history; one where you could start out as an unknown and finish up a household name—

From his stone throne, Matthew interrupted, "Hey buddy! *James*! Take a look around you—"

"We're here to get away from all that," Christine added, straightening up. A glacial wind blew over us from the icefield at the far end of the lake. I dug out my jacket from the bottom of my rucksack and pulled it on. "You used to be so down to earth," she continued to chastise James. "Now you're into all this high-tech stuff. What's up with that?"

James pulled down his cap, colour of terra cotta and moss, over his eyes, his whole persona bleeding now into the backdrop of wilderness. In the ensuing silence, Matthew and Christine drank in the profundity of our surroundings. James fiddled with the penknife in his hand, opening and closing the blade, but after an irritated glance from Christine dropped that too, in one of the numerous pockets of his cargo pants.

Restless, I looked around for an escape from their quiet self-absorption and noticed the beefy guy with the camera seated outside the warming hut, fiddling with his lenses. I wandered over in his direction. My shadow fell across his lap as I extended my hand. "Hi. I'm Helene."

He shook my hand. "Alex."

"So you're a photographer?"

He laughed. "Not a professional, just a wannabe."

"Well, that looks like one professional piece of equipment."

He turned the camera over in his hands, inspecting it as if it belonged to someone else. "Yeah, I guess it is."

A skinny guy with curly blond hair poked his face through the doorway. "Hey dude, where'd you put the fuel for the stove?"

Alex set his camera down on the bench and went inside the hut. I followed him in, temporarily blinded by the lack of lighting. After my eyes adjusted, I watched him kneel beside a small pack and pull out a red canister, which he gave to the guy. We watched the guy attach the fuel canister to a frail-looking camp stove, its legs spread out under a full pot of water like those of a daddy longlegs.

"First time up here?" the woman at the table asked. She leaned in to the guy next to her, fanning away with her open palm the fumes produced by her stove.

"Yeah," I answered guardedly. "Why?"

"No, no reason." She gave me a warm smile. "Christine said it was your first time out hiking, that's all." She held the saucepan to the side as she pumped the valve on her stove to relight it. When the flames were licking up around the bottom of her pot, she looked back up. "It's really peaceful up here, isn't it?"

"Yeah, sure." I sat down next to her, about to explain that this would also be my first night sleeping outdoors and did she have any tips, when I caught a glimpse of Matthew through the slightly open doorway. He squatted on his granite boulder, arms slung around his knees, his thoughts inaccessible, his eyes focused on the lake. The woman touched my shoulder and offered a hit from a joint. I took a small toke before passing it back. Looking up across the room to Alex, my eyes met his for a fraction of a second. The heat waves from the stove in front of him created a mirage in which his features flickered and danced. As the flames shifted from blue to hypnotic white, my heartbeats pounded out their rhythm with thousands of kilometres of silence between them, and, closing my eyes, I saw the infinitely large encompassed in the infinitely small and vice versa into infinity.

"Oh," the woman next to me giggled, "I think your hair is burning."

I swept my hair back and jumped away from the stove. The tip of one tangled lock curling under my chin smelled singed.

"Are you okay?" Alex asked, beside me now. I allowed him to lead me outside, where it was colder. We sat down beside the hut. Alex played with the settings of his camera and lifted it to his eye, taking a shot of me before returning it to his lap for more adjustments. "Did you bring a tent?" he asked me when Matthew moved to a nearby platform and began setting up camp for the night. I shook my head. "I'd offer you a place in mine," Alex said, indicating with a nod of his head the guy to whom he had given fuel earlier, "but Tim has already spoken for it. If I had known . . ." He searched out my eyes. "Anyway, I'm sure Matthew or James will have an extra space."

"Could you ask Matthew for me?"

He glanced over at Matthew stringing the poles through his tent and then back at me.

I shrugged. "You seem to know him better than I do. I would feel weird asking him."

LATER THAT NIGHT, I hugged the wall inside Matthew's tent and watched him roll a joint by the light of the headlamp balanced between his knees.

"So what do you hope to accomplish by twenty-three?"

"What?" I'd been watching him but painting out the events of the

42

day in the studio of my mind. I'd been thinking in the colours of things, as I often do, in reds and greens and earth-tone hues. So this question caught me off guard.

"Ever since my climbing partner died last year, I've often lain awake at night thinking about his death. He was a year younger than me—he would have turned twenty-two this week."

So Matthew is only *twenty-three*?

"What's wrong?" Matthew asked, sensing my surprise.

"Nothing. I thought you were older, that's all. I thought . . . oh, never mind." I shifted my legs into a more comfortable position, hooking my chin over my knee. I watched him raise the edge of the rolling paper to his mouth to trace the line of glue with his tongue before pinching the joint closed. "I'm sorry about your friend," I said.

He picked up the headlamp and, strapping it to his forehead, blinded me by turning it on me. "You're only twenty, right?"

"Almost twenty-one. How do you know that?"

"Christine told me. So what do you hope to have accomplished by my age?"

I shrugged off his question, still blinded by the light. He adjusted the focus of his headlamp so it no longer shone in my face. As my eyes readjusted, I watched him crawl around on all fours, lifting the edges of our sleeping bags. I watched him in silence. I wanted to ask him about his friend, about what happened to him, but before I could formulate any clear, any appropriate question, Matthew asked, "What are your plans for after university then?" He shone his headlight into the various compartments of his backpack and, still turning up nothing, paused, waiting for an answer as he scratched at the stubble under his chin.

"What are you looking for?" I asked him.

"My lighter." He sighed and sat down. "So what are you studying at university?"

"I'm doing a bachelor of commerce."

He snapped his head back up and blinded me again with the light. "*Commerce*? So you want money." He sounded disappointed.

I leaned further into the tent wall. Fiddling nervously with the edge of my sleeping mat, I discovered the lighter tucked underneath it. "I'd like to be able to get a well-paid job after school, wouldn't you?" I explained as I handed him the lighter.

Matthew stretched out on his back and turned off the headlamp. As darkness fell over us, I noticed the quiet of the mountain night outside. He flicked the flint of the lighter, bringing to life the small fireworks of sparks and then a yellow flame. A red ember climbed up the joint, casting a strange glow over his lips.

"So money," he observed as he exhaled, "is what motivates you."

"I don't want to be poor."

"What's wrong with poverty?"

You wouldn't need to ask if you had ever experienced it.

"The majority of the world's population is poor," he continued. "What makes you exceptional?"

"Is that how it works then? Rich people are in some way or another *exceptional*?"

He chuckled and passed me the joint. "So businesswoman is your dream vocation?"

I took a small toke to sidestep a foray into the economics of poverty and handed him back the joint. "I don't want to suffer."

"Ah ha! A life without suffering—does such a life exist?"

The night had grown chilly, and a light rain had begun to fall. I snuggled down in my sleeping bag and stared out of the hood into the dark. The glowing cherry of the joint bobbed up and down in the blackness as Matthew smoked.

"What about you?" I asked. "What do you hope to accomplish in life?"

He flicked the lighter above our heads, and in brief flashes I saw the jagged stains of raindrops dotting the roof of the tent. When he didn't immediately answer, I blurted out, "If I could study anything I wanted, without any thought for the future, I would study fine art and French."

"So you're an aspiring artist in a commerce program. Do you have any artistic talent?"

I shrugged in my sleeping bag.

"How does French play into that equation?" he asked.

"My father was French," I explained, happy to steer the conversation away from the question of my artistic ability. "From France."

"So you must speak French."

"No."

"Didn't he speak it to you growing up?"

"No. . . . He was a biker—here in Canada."

Matthew rolled toward me in the darkness. A sudden flash of lightning lit up the sky outside the tent's thin walls, and I caught a glimpse of Matthew's face bearing down on me inside the shelter. "A biker," he asked, "as in, a gang member?"

I rolled away from him. A clap of thunder rumbled across the lake. "I don't know," I mumbled, regretting bringing up my father. "I was only two when he died."

I LAY STILL, SUSPENDED in the cocoon of night. The colours of my mind played across perfect darkness interspersed with flashes of lightning. Matthew stirred, drawing me back from the brink of slumber—from its fluid association of speckles, lines, and patterns, from its muted pastels and soft hues swirling me into another world, a world of my own making, a world in which external formal structures began to match my internal aesthetic.

"What a mess," he grumbled. As I floated back to consciousness, I become aware of him unzipping the screen door and turning on his headlamp to poke his head outside. "So much for weather predictions." He held out a palm to test the sky.

For an instant there was nothing but a few more scattered drops; then lightning flashed again followed by a clap of thunder as the downpour started. I feared the torrent might chase us from the lakeside in the dead of night. Another sheet of lightning shifted across the sky, illuminating the growing stains spreading across the fabric of the tent walls. Already water was seeping in through the mosquito netting. The night outside blackened again and Matthew crawled out the doorway, naked except for his fraying briefs exposed by another flash across the sky.

Outside, he threw a fly over the tent and clipped it onto the poles. "You're soaking," I informed him as he slithered back inside, bits of stick and weed clinging to his wet legs. "Aren't you worried that the tent poles could attract the lightning?" I watched him wipe his feet on a T-shirt by the light of his headlamp.

"It's happened. But why worry about it?"

"Because I don't want to die up here in the mountains."

He laughed. "Where do you want to die then? Courting death can be a pleasurable game. Nietzsche wrote that the man who climbs the highest mountains laughs at tragedy. *It is the surrender of the greatest to run risk and danger, and play dice for death.*"

"What about your friend? Aren't you afraid the same thing could happen to you?"

"Mountaineering is a lonely sport. Isolated, remote wilderness offers an arena to surmount man's primal fear of death. Completing a difficult climb is a thrill verging on ecstasy. It brings the same pleasure of relief and pride of conquest. I've spent most of this last year trying to put myself in Stephen's shoes, going over each detail of our last climb together. I keep seeing him fall over and over. Two-hundred metres to the ground. What if it had been me? What if it is me on my next climb? But I could never give it up."

"Why not?"

He chuckled. "I need the thrill of it. I need the escape."

"Escape from what? What are you running away from?"

"The mundane. The conventional. For the same reasons that I climb, I'm going to volunteer with Doctors Without Borders after I graduate."

"In what country?"

"In any impoverished country at war."

Lightning flashed outside the tent, illuminating the splatters of rain on the tent fly; sharp like bullet wounds when they hit the wet fabric, they immediately coalesced like spreading blood. "But you're not a doctor," I reminded him.

"Logisticians are also needed—people to organize the delivery of medical supplies and equipment and the like."

"But why would you want to risk your life in a war zone?"

"Civilians in conflict-ridden zones often live the nightmare of war for years. They don't have any other option. They can't just up and leave their country. Even when they do manage to obtain a passport to get out, they still can't get *into* another country."

"But what's the point of you joining them in that nightmare?"

"What's the point of a life spent pecking at a keyboard in a corporate office?"

"But you might be taken hostage or tortured or shot. You might lose your life—"

"Exactly!" Propping himself up on an elbow, he leaned over me with his headlamp still on. I reached forward to switch off the light. White circles floated between us in the darkness. "Working in a war zone, as in climbing, a man's instinct to survive surfaces," I heard him saying. "The difference is that climbing is essentially a selfish, self-centred act, whereas the idea of humanitarianism is selfless concern for others. When something goes wrong climbing a man's life is at stake, whereas in a war zone, a people, a culture, a civilization are at stake. I want to experience the freedom of true courage, of fearlessness tempered by responsibility for the welfare of others."

Garibaldi Lake, Day Two

The next thing I knew it was morning, and I was alone in the tent. I unzipped my damp sleeping bag. *Brrrr.* I quickly whipped the zipper closed again. My breath puffed out in clouds all around me. Frost sparkled on the ceiling of the tent; I lifted a finger and melted a line through the rime. Outside the world was a choir of birds that twittered and cheeped and bartered and squeaked and otherwise got on with their morning. I closed my eyes. Courage! *Brrrr.* Gathering my resolve, I exposed my bare limbs and scrambled into frigid clothes.

The others, already outside their tents, huddled together gripping spoons and bowls with mittened hands. I filled a bowl with two packets of instant oatmeal and, looking around, mistook Christine for a ghost—her and her younger sister always looked like twins despite the three years between them.

When I moved to Windeal, with birthdays a week apart, Stacy and I had instantly become *best friends forever* with matching broken-heart necklaces. Christine said they were tacky, said we were so immature. She said people from the trailer park were dirty and I had to wash my hands before I could touch her things. Or better, that Stacy and I stay out of her room altogether.

"Sleep well?" the ghost asked. Behind her outline, the horizon was streaked sea green and ivory. Above us, the morning sky was the pastel blue of a robin's egg. I shrugged off her insinuations and rubbed the sleep from my eyelids, turning to stare at the dark lake instead of at my dead friend's sister.

"The glacier is beautiful in the sunrise, isn't it?" Alex asked, approaching me from behind, camera in hand. He pointed across the lake. "Look at how the ice shimmers under the first rays." I stared at his broad back as he knelt to take a photograph, my mind on Stacy, on how she'd always said, *Don't worry 'bout Chrissie—when she farts, she smells dirtier than a skunk—*

"Need some hot water?" Alex asked, noticing my bowl of dry oats as he straightened. I followed him to his camp stove where he tested the water in the pot with his pinkie. "Do you want me to heat it up again?" The early morning light brought out the honey in his warm brown eyes. I nodded. When the water was boiling, he poured it over my apple and cinnamon porridge, stirring the flakes for me until there were no more dry lumps.

"Cheer up," he said. "We won't be trapped much longer in these shadows."

I glanced at him to see what he might mean. His eyes darted to the lake. A line cut across its surface, dividing the sunlit water from the mountain's shadow still covering our end.

"I'm cheerful," I said, forcing a smile, my eyes skimming the shoreline for Matthew. Nothing. *Why do I crave obsession? Why must I pursue a passion that leaves me no room to breathe, only the ethereal space of imagination in which I must sketch Him?*

I left Alex for a granite stool on the water's edge. From there, I finally spotted my muse. His ponytail glistened red copper in the early sunlight as he came up the shoreline, bowl in hand, his hiking boots lapped at by the lake. As he crossed the dividing line between sun and shadow, he saw me and walked up to the rock next to mine. Without a word, he squatted on top of it. I watched him eat from his bowl with his fingers. "We're in the shade," he informed me through a mouthful of granola.

Maybe so, maybe so. But here is where I am, painting you in my mind: your thick-veined fingers in a dry-brush flesh tone; your rose-madder lips, wet in wet, across a wash of raw-sienna stubble. As Matthew paused to scratch at the beginnings of a copper beard, the thousand and one nerve endings of my skin were overwhelmed with a biting urgency. *This is it.*

This was truth suspended here between us by a strand, hanging like a silver dewdrop on a spider's web, refusing to plummet, refusing to be shattered. I breathed; a wave slapped the grey rocky shore and sap-green trees bent under a breeze. Mist rose off the lake in a white veil and the first ray of sunlight blinded me. *I want to paint you into being, Matthew. I want to encapsulate your agonizing beauty, and I want to breathe into that portrait a soul.*

AFTER EVERYONE IN OUR group had packed lunches, James and Matthew strung the rest of the food between two trees, out of reach of any bears. The plan was to hike up the Black Tusk, a monolith of black volcanic rock columns. From Garibaldi Lake, we crossed a bridge and ascended steadily until we came upon a meadow patched with snow. I was at the back of the pack, nursing a blister on my right heel from the ascent into camp the day before. Only Alex was behind me, trailing at the rear to take photographs. Every once in a while I stopped to squint upward at the foreboding tower before us and wondered what I was doing there, slogging my way up that hillside, kicking up slush in muddy splatters on the backs of my pant legs with every backward-sliding step on the shale.

On one of my breaks, Alex caught up and touched my elbow. "Turn around," he said. My breath caught when I did. Spread out before us were mountains wearing toques of snow that dipped into saddles and plunged into meadows, their caps melting into furious creeks that spilled into the turquoise lake we had now left far below.

"Once these mountains were undersea," he explained. "People still find fossils." He pointed to a flat-topped peak. "That mountain there is called the Table."

I glanced back toward our destination, the Black Tusk. Matthew was leading the way, a small figure near the base of the monolith.

"Beside us is Panorama Ridge," Alex was saying.

Yeah, yeah. I nodded and urged him on. "We're pretty far behind."

"What's the rush?" he asked, adjusting the strap on his camera. Still he followed me as I returned to slogging uphill in the snow, sliding back on the loose shale underneath with every step. Soon I broke out into a heavy sweat, and it was only after what seemed like an eternity that we finally attained the saddle.

As I stopped to wipe my face, Alex asked, "Need a rest?"

I leaned against the cold stone wall that formed the base of the Black Tusk, attempting to catch my breath. Matthew was most likely already on top of this ebony colossus.

"No, I'm okay." I let Alex lead the way. He followed the footprints sunk knee-deep into the snow. I lurched after him, no longer caring as the ankles of my boots filled with slush. As we rounded a corner, I heard James explaining, although I could not yet see him, that the couloir was wet from last night's rain. Within seconds we stumbled onto the rest of the group picnicking in the snow at the base of a shale-strewn gap in the wall that led up between two columns of black rock.

I peered up the dark crack and felt nauseated. I didn't want to climb up that sinister black monstrosity. Matthew moved closer to investigate. "It'll be fine," he said, rubbing his hand over the brittle rock columns. Pieces fell away and littered the snow around his boots.

A ROCK SHOT OUT from under my foot. My heart rate skyrocketed as I slid down a half metre or so, my fingernails scraping at the shale shards. Below me, Tim jerked his shoulder out of the path of the rock I'd just loosed and yelled up at me to watch what I was doing. The muscles in my legs twitched involuntarily.

"Go back down before you kill yourself," Christine warned when I accidentally grabbed her foot. I ignored her and pulled myself higher.

"Look," she said, glaring down at me. "Don't be ridiculous. This isn't worth killing yourself for."

"She's not going to kill herself," Alex said calmly. From above Christine, he beckoned: "Come on, it's not much further to the top."

"She's shaking like a leaf," Christine informed him.

Alex ignored her. "Come on," he called down in a steady voice, motioning me up.

I couldn't move. Adrenaline was pounding in my ears, shouting for me to get back down onto solid ground. Above Alex, Matthew stopped and bent back around to see what all the commotion was about. "Try not to look down," Christine counselled, stifling laughter. To the two guys above, she announced: "I don't think she can go any further. It's too much for her first trip outdoors." She twisted back to survey my lack of progress.

One finger at a time, I removed my hand from the basalt to which it was attached like a suction cup. With my teeth clenched, I forced my hand upward to seek out a handhold higher in the rock wall. My fingers were so dulled I didn't feel the sharp edges of the rock. I didn't see the blood until I was at the top: three cracked fingernails and red seeping out where a stone had slit open my thumb.

ALL THREE SIDES OF the summit plummeted into empty space. Crouched down, I scrambled toward the middle, as far from the edges as possible. "Oh god," I whimpered as I fell on my knees. "How will I ever get down?"

"You did great," Alex reassured me. He adjusted the shutter speed of his camera and focused the lens on me. "When we go back down, just keep your eyes on where your hands are, check the rocks aren't loose, and don't look down."

His voice calmed me. I tried to smile for the camera but discovered that my jaw muscles were still clenched in terror. Alex inched closer and balanced his camera on a rock. Gently, he lifted my chin toward the horizon. "This mountain that we're on is molten lava crystallized into columns of rock," he said, patting the flat black rock shards under our feet. Even though I knew he was trying to distract me from my fear, his strategy was working. "First Nations people call it 'The Landing Place of the Thunderbird.' According to their stories, if the bird flaps its wings, thunder will boom across the valleys. If humans venture too close, the bird will shoot lightning from its eyes."

"Aren't we too close now?"

Alex laughed. I turned from the string of mountains on the horizon to his profile. He turned toward me with a smile, his jaw square and his lips angular, an unassuming dignity etched into his features. The adrenaline inside my chest shifted to euphoria: I'd clawed my way up here, I'd pushed beyond some barrier within myself, and now I was even forgetting my fear. I smiled into his bright, kind eyes, into the eyes of this artist and photographer, and then I twisted around, scouting out the area behind us for Matthew.

Perched recklessly close to the edge, Matthew chatted with Christine. I watched the loose strands of his hair flutter in the wind. I watched his gestures like those of an actor in a silent film: his lips moved and Christine chuckled. The fearlessness of Matthew's silhouette at the edge of the precipice unsettled me: I wanted to experience with him reckless abandon; I wanted to escape with him the mundane. I wanted him as my *homme fatal.*

As soon as we got back to the lake, Matthew lit a fire, ignoring park regulations. "Let's build a sauna," he said, slipping into a pair of shorts.

I glanced over at Christine. She smiled and, having caught my eye, sauntered over to where I was seated on the ground. "Want to go look for rocks to heat in the coals?" she asked. I nodded, and together we headed for the shoreline.

"What do you think of James?" she asked when we were away from the crowd. I shrugged and attempted to free a rock from its bed. She bent down to help me dig it out.

"He seems nice. A bit of a computer nerd maybe."

She laughed in agreement.

We lugged our rocks to the fire in time to overhear a couple of newly arrived hikers not with our group complaining about the fire being against regulations. Alex wandered away from them down the beach. He reappeared not long after with an armful of sticks. He tied the tips of four longer pieces together with a rope to create the skeleton of a wigwam. Matthew in turn unhooked the fly from his tent and draped it over the gangly wood carcass. Then he stood back to appraise the result while Alex snapped a series of pictures of the crooked structure.

Turning toward Christine, I wanted to tell her that although James seemed flaky at times in that casually arrogant way of the affluent—full of himself as a nonconformist while at the same time conventional—he also seemed passionate and quietly intellectual. But Christine stared into the fire and James sat next to her, so I said nothing.

After mashing my potato flakes with hot water, I shared them with Alex in exchange for some of his noodles. Circled around the fire, our group chowed down on refried beans, instant pastas, ramen soups, hot dogs, and veggie wieners. Slurping at my bowl of noodles and broth, I watched the last traces of light flicker across the lake, skim across the glacier, and fade down the horizon. When the day was gone, I turned to Alex to ask if he had any plans for the photographs he had been taking on the trip.

"I'll be showing them at the Eastside Culture Crawl, in an exhibition pairing poetry and photography."

"You write poetry as well?"

"I'm trying," he said with a laugh as he touched my knee. "Maybe you can help me out?"

I leaned into him. "You've been taking a lot of landscape shots on this trip. Is that what you'll be showing?"

"If they turn out. I've also been working on a collection of black-and-white portraits—"

"Oh Alex, you're so pretentious," Christine cut in to tease him from across the fire. "You started out with mountaineering photography. Now here you are, all into black-and-white portraits!"

Alex stopped talking about his project. He took his hand off my knee. I lifted my hand to touch his arm, to bring him back from where he had chased his thoughts, but I stopped before contact with his skin. Instead I slid off our shared log bench. I pushed past Christine and her group on the other side of the fire—James, Matthew, and the woman I met in the hut yesterday—to the shore where I stood alone, staring into the black water.

Alex helped Matthew roll the heated rocks out of the coals and haul them to the sauna on a makeshift carrier of twine and criss-crossed sticks. Returning to the dying fire where Tim, James, Christine, and I were the only ones left awake, they announced that the sweat lodge was ready.

Matthew lifted an arm to wipe perspiration from his forehead. Alex followed suit. They stood on the other side of the smouldering circle of ash, their arms darkened with charcoal, their feet planted wide apart, their chins lifted high, their naked chests rising and falling as they recovered from their exertion.

"Looks like you guys are already sweating," Christine teased them.

Neither Matthew nor Alex responded. Instead, they left us by the dying fire, their pale shapes discarding their clothes on the bushes and disappearing through the flap door of the sauna. Tim followed them. James said he was going to bed. I sensed hesitation in Christine, so I stood up. I picked my way through the shrubbery and rocks toward the wigwam. From inside came short bursts of masculine laughter: gruff voices rippling out through the seams of Matthew's tent fly and into the dusk descended over the mountains.

I peeled off my pants and T-shirt. I unhooked my bra and stripped away my underwear. I tossed my clothes onto a bush and crawled in through the flap door.

"Here," a voice said from inside the warm darkness. Tim flicked the flint of his lighter. A flash of light then blindness. Again a flash of light. The flame, when ignited, drew my attention like a moth's. Tim held the wick of a candle to it and balanced the lit candle between his outstretched knees. In the pale light, Matthew sat cross-legged, his back straight, his feet tucked in under his thighs. I crawled into the empty space between him and Alex. Trying for the best possible angle in the candlelight, I arranged my legs to hide my privates.

"So how do you guys know each other?" I asked Tim and Alex. Anything to keep the awkwardness of silence from falling.

"Tree planting," Tim said.

"We were in the Charlottes for two summers," Alex explained.

I nodded, hoping to encourage the flow of conversation, but Alex didn't expound further. Instead he slid an empty bean can out under the edge of the tent fly and scooped it into the shallow stream that wound past the strategically placed sauna. When he poured the cold water over the hot rocks, a curtain of steam shot up, snuffing out the candle. Tim flicked at the lighter again, but the flint was damp and wouldn't ignite.

A damp hand groped my hip, pulled back. Patted my thigh. Pulled back. Returned to my knee. "Sorry," Matthew's voice rumbled. His hand glided down my calf past my ankle, scampering spider-like across my sole. Tim finally got the lighter working again and showered us in luminosity, sending Matthew's hand dashing off my toes.

Matthew gave me a sheepish grin. "I have another lighter in here if that one gives up the ghost," he told Tim. "It's around here somewhere."

Tim relit the candle, sheltering the flame with his hands from the droplets of steam that dripped off the roof. The light glowed through his palms like through a fleshy jack-o'-lantern. On my left, Alex's shoulder brushed mine, warm and damp. On my right, Matthew's leg hair tickled my thigh. I drew my knees in closer to my chest to give both men more room.

"You okay?" Alex asked.

I nodded.

Matthew produced a joint and took the lighter from Tim. He had to suck on it a long time to get it to light in the dampness. Finally we heard him gasp, and a heavy cloud billowed out of his lungs. The smoke spread out and collected at the ceiling, fingers of it probing down into our nostrils. Tim refilled the can in the little brook and dribbled it over the rocks. Puffs of steam draped a snug silence around us.

I closed my eyes and inhaled the steam mixed with smoke. Rivulets of sweat rolled down my forehead and splattered onto my thighs. Matthew touched my arm. I opened my eyes. He handed me the joint.

"Thanks."

The grass sent me tunnelling into the galleries of myself. In one self-portrait, I'd taken refuge with three other runaways under a bridge. The rain was pouring down on either side. I was writing to my mother on a notepad stolen from a dollar store: *I love you and miss you so badly. You don't have to worry about me—I'll be fine.* Studying this portrait now of that fifteen-year-old girl, I saw how overworked it was, muddied by poorly mixed hues of anger and guilt, washed out and overbrushed until the paper had wrinkled and torn. There was nothing left to salvage; the painting was murky, with no real drama, and should have been ruthlessly trashed long ago.

IN THE SAUNA, THE bead welling at the corner of my eye rolled down my cheek before I could catch it. I wiped the perspiration from my face and, reaching forward for the can, poured water over the rocks. They had cooled somewhat so that, rather than hot steam, they produced only a lukewarm fizzle.

Tim stared into the candlelight, looking miles away. Alex's head was slumped over his chest. I turned to Matthew. He appeared to have fallen into a trance. Desperate to clear my head, I asked on impulse, "Anyone want to jump in the lake?"

Matthew turned his face to mine, slowly, as if he was drawing himself up out of a well.

Alex straightened up. "That was some strong shit, too much for me," he said. "I'm off to bed." He crawled out of the wigwam, and Tim followed him. Their footsteps dissipated into the sleeping night, leaving Matthew and I alone in a silence interspersed only by the plunking of droplets from the roof of the sauna.

I tried again to rouse Matthew. "Let's go jump in the lake!"

"It's cold," he protested, his eyes closed again.

"Let's go," I insisted, shaking his knee. I crawled out the flap door, pulling him after me.

I ran so I wouldn't change my mind. The rocks on the shoreline cut into my feet as I leapt through the water before stopping short. Only knee-deep but already my calves were twitching in shock.

Matthew didn't hesitate. He tossed himself in with a gigantic splash, sending a ripple of frigid waves crashing into my thighs.

It was now or never, so I let myself fall. The moon hung low on the horizon. Above us, a trillion sparks rained down through empty space to bathe our bodies in their indigo glow. First the water ate my hands. Then it ran up my arms. I fell in slow motion through the orifice swallowing up my breasts, its teeth at my nipples, stabbing, erotic. Its arctic mouth licked across my stomach, sucked in my hips, and slid its tongue across my back, drawing me down by the shoulders.

No way to stop it now: ice sank into my hair.

I was thrashing. I couldn't remember anything but this gasping—this clamouring of numb feet over a rocky lakebed onto shore.

"Shhh! Quit screaming!" From behind me, Matthew clamped his hand across my mouth. I lost my balance as his arm pulled my head back, and I fell against him.

"The tight asses are sleeping," he whispered into my hair as he let me go.

I turned to glare at him. He raised an eyebrow, as to an arrogant child refusing a scolding. I dropped my eyes. Like spotlights over the round of my stomach below, my nipples stood out at full attention. I fluttered my eyelids to rid them of water and gazed up at Matthew. He stepped toward me. The water had smoothed his body hair into needles. I wanted him to take one more step forward to take me in his arms, but instead we stared upward at the sky ballooning under a burden of stars.

"A shooting star," he said. "Make a wish."

At the sauna, Matthew directed me inside. "I'll be right back."

I figured he was taking a leak, so I wormed my way shivering back into the lukewarm wigwam. I relit the candle that Tim had dug into the earth. I tried to heat up the place by pouring more water over the rocks, but the steam jet had lost its sizzle. Teeth clattering, I resorted to warming myself with friction.

Matthew crawled in dragging a branch behind him.

"What's that for?"

He crushed the tip of the branch between his fingers and thumb and offered me the scent on his index fingertip. I leaned in to smell it.

"Cedar," he explained. "To stimulate the blood."

I rubbed the goose pimples on my arms. "What do you do, eat it?"

"Lie down on your stomach," he told me.

"What are you going to do?" I suppressed a giggle. "Whip me?"

"Lie down."

"Why?"

"Come on. Trust me."

I twisted around to lower myself onto the spongy moss of the cold, damp earth.

"Relax," he murmured as he hit me with the branch. "Relax," he repeated, when I rose up in surprise. He pressed me back to the earth with a firm hand on my spine.

Bits of cedar bit into my shoulders.

"Relax," he said.

The bow stung its way down to my hamstrings, drummed at the backs of my knees all the way to my ankles. The more I allowed my muscles to go slack, the more my body felt like a limp bag for a limp spirit.

Uncertainty had wormed its way to my core.

Such a simple question he'd asked: *Where do you see yourself at my age?* In other words, in two years. Yet, without a suitable answer, the question wouldn't let me alone.

A voice reached me from far away, its rough edges asking if I liked what he'd done. I pushed myself up to study the face of this voice, its features distant as through the wrong end of a telescope. I brushed a clump of dirt from my lips, biting back the words that threatened to drift into question: *Will you love me?* Ridiculous question, out of the question, so I swallowed down the four syllables and asked instead if he wanted a turn.

He shook his head. "It's getting too cold in here."

"Come on! It's only fair."

He said nothing. Instead, he clamped his thumb and forefinger around my jaw. With this lever he pulled me in until he could graze my mouth, not kiss me, just brush his moist lips across mine, cool and firm. With each pass, expectation jolted through me. His breath smelled mossy from the pot, and his lips were salty with sweat as we began to kiss. The night was silent except for the rhythm of our breathing. He pushed me down onto my back with his hand still at my jaw, just above the base of my throat. He slid the other down my body. I wanted to push him away but my spine arched up, betraying my dignity for the brutality of his hands.

But he stopped too soon so that I understood his work had come to an end too soon, an abrupt end with too many loose ends. I felt numb as, crawling out of the sauna into the darkness, I followed him through the shrubbery to his tent.

June Rains

The late spring rain ousts June with a roar. I slide open a windowpane behind my couch to let in some air, but the showers blow in, soaking my T-shirt, and I have to shut the window right back up again.

The phone rings. When I pick it up my mother says, "My life is shit."

Cradling the phone to my ear so I can pour a cup of tea, I tell her, "There's a storm down here, Katie. I can barely hear you. The power might cut out any minute. The connection too." I twist the cord of the receiver around my thumb, tugging a little on where it plugs into the wall.

"Helene?" Her voice is a quiver over the wire. "Did you hear what I said?"

I reach for the photo on my fridge that she sent me last Christmas. Other than the fact that Lyle has fewer strands to comb over his bald patch, he doesn't look much different now that he is in his mid-forties: he still wears the same yellow cardigan over grey pants, *slacks*, as he calls them, held up by a pleather belt. My mother, on the other hand, her hair streaked with silver and her collarbone jutting out, seems much older at thirty-eight than when I last saw her six years ago; her navy dress hangs off her bony frame. It strikes me as absurd that she could have aged when I've always imagined her ageless.

"Helene, did you hear what I said?"

"Yeah, I heard. Is that why you've suddenly started calling me again?" I ruffle through the kitchen drawers for a sketchpad and my charcoal pencils. I sit down at the table with them and the photograph.

"I've decided to see Katherine for counselling." She lowers her voice to a whisper. "Even if she is a . . ."

"Lesbian?" Using a regular HB pencil, I lay down a rough sketch of my mother, copied from the photograph. I remember the worried gossip at church when Katherine and her "lady friend" bought a house behind the combined elementary high school in Windeal back in 1993.

"I can't afford anyone else," my mother continues. "She's the only one free through family services."

Great. More welfare aid. I switch to a hard charcoal to pencil in her hair, alternating sharp lines for the darker strands with softer highlights for the greys.

"Helene, is this a bad time to be phoning?"

I ignore her question. For the soft texture of the navy dress, I use my pinkie to smudge the charcoal into smooth drapes and the eraser of the HB pencil to emphasize her bony areas. "How can you go to a marriage counsellor alone?"

She blows her nose into the phone. "I'm scared Lyle might leave—"

"Why? Because you were drinking the other night?"

"—but then I tell myself he's not like your father, you know?" The razor-sharp edges of these words cut into me before I can take guard. "He'd never just abandon me," she says.

I have but one memory of my father: a burly man calling me *petite* and tossing me into the air. My mother has told me he was stick thin from heroin addiction, that my memory must be mistaking him for somebody else.

"My dad didn't *abandon* you, Katie. People don't just choose to die." Using a kitchen knife, I scrape the tip of the charcoal pencil to sprinkle a fine dust around the contours of my mother's frame. "So what makes you think Lyle might leave, anyway?" I ask, rubbing the dust into the paper with a crumple of tissue until the background is a uniform grey.

"He's been seeing Elaine."

"Who's that? A lawyer or social worker or something?"

"She's his hairdresser. You don't know her. She just moved to Windeal last year."

It takes a moment for this to sink in. "You mean he's been cheating on you?" I ask, straightening up from my drawing, shocked another woman could find him attractive enough to bed.

Silence.

"How long has it been going on?"

"I don't know . . . a couple of months. Maybe more. He just came clean the other night."

"Oh, you mean the night you said he was *fine*?" I pick out my softest charcoal to shade in the features of her face.

She ignores my jab. "Since he told me, he's clammed up and won't talk about it anymore. He said he has done God's will by confessing his sin and now he can put it to rest and be healed."

"But what about *your* healing? He's obviously not thinking about that."

"The whole thing with his garage going out of business has been hard on him. I think he might be having a nervous breakdown."

"Oh, so that makes it okay for him to cheat and be completely insensitive to your feelings?"

"Why are you always so quick to judge, Helene?"

"Why do you always have to be such a victim?" I snap back. A bolt of lightning flashes across the darkening city sky outside my window. "Hold on," I tell her. I get up to rummage around under the bathroom sink for a bottle of hairspray, which, returning to the kitchen table, I use to seal in the charcoal lines of my quick sketch. A clap of thunder follows the lightning, and the lights flicker and go out. Fumbling around in the semi-darkness, I realize from the silence when I pick up the receiver that the line has also cut out.

Settling into the couch with my now cold cup of tea, I watch the wind gusting through the trees in the alley and wonder why, after any interaction with my mother, I feel flat and dull, like a sombre portrait muddied beyond repair.

Turning Twenty-One

The eve of my birthday, I pace my studio apartment, waiting on Matthew to show up so we can leave for my boss's house party. I stop in front of the photograph of Lodi and me that has been collecting dust on my dresser top since I dug it out of my blue shoebox two weeks ago.

Shortly after rescuing it when I was seven from the bathroom trash can, I asked my mother what she was burning in the bathtub.

Letters.

Who from? I implored, my imagination running wild with possibilities. Letters from unknown lovers, from Lodi, from my grandfather and grandmother, or . . . letters from the silent side of my family tree: my dad's relatives in France.

My family doesn't have a clue, my mother complained, holding the lighter to a sheet of stationery adorned with poinsettias and somebody's longhand. She shook her head. *They think I care to receive their stupid holiday letters? What about sending a little cold hard cash? What do they expect me to do—beg?* She paused as though suddenly remembering my presence. *They aren't for you anyway, so go mind your own business.*

Now, almost fourteen years later, I drop the photograph of Lodi and me back onto the dresser and check out my side profile in the mirror, sucking in my tummy and lifting my chest. I've inherited Lodi's emerald eyes and dark, unruly hair, but what doesn't show are these colours inside; I wish I knew, like her, how to distill the abstract, muddled hues of my private self into a public, palpable body of art.

* * *

I WAIT WITH MATTHEW in front of a closed convenience store on the corner of Fraser and Broadway. He strides back and forth in front of the grated windows trying to wave down a taxi; buses aren't running due to a transit strike.

"The name of this neighbourhood—Mount *Pleasant*—is an oxymoron," he says, hailing a passing cab. The driver ignores him. "Rundown buildings, empty shops, ghetto dry cleaning. I always forget how ugly East Van is. Even when it's sunny like now, no one is out on the sidewalks."

I stare across the street at the archways of the brick building of the Broadway Youth Resource Centre, thinking of how they helped me find my current apartment. "Not everyone can afford to live on the Westside, you know? But that doesn't mean it's the only part of Vancouver with character. There's a whole world beyond Main, and not all the residents here are dumpster divers."

"I didn't say they were. But seriously, there's no excuse for poverty in this country. If you want to see human misery, travel to India."

"You think poor people in this country are that way by choice? Or, maybe you think poverty is only about not having enough to eat?"

He hails another taxi, and this time the driver brakes. Matthew throws open the rear door and hurries me into the cab.

I hesitate at the open door. "That's a rather harsh statement, isn't it? I mean, we don't exactly choose our lives, do we?"

"Ah ha!"

"What do you mean, *ah ha*?" I demand as I climb inside to the far seat, digging through my pockets for the scrap of paper with my boss's address.

"So what's our destination?" Matthew asks as he slides in beside me.

I read out the Westside South Cambie address to the cab driver, and Matthew leans back in his seat, a satisfied upturn to his lips. I twist sideways to face him. He zeroes in on me for a moment then tilts his head back and stares up at the ceiling of the cab. "I suppose we don't choose everything. I had planned to climb the Chief a second time this year, but now it looks like that isn't going to be an option."

"Why not? What's stopping you?" I demand, still annoyed.

"James is down in Oregon for a month, climbing at Smith Rocks with Christine."

"And so?" I turn to stare out my side window. She didn't tell me. Maybe Matthew didn't go with them because of me? "Well, can't you climb it when he gets back?" I ask, warming a little.

"I'll be gone already."

The shabby blocks of East Broadway fly by: barred windows, gritty murals, unsolicited graffiti, the odd pedestrian. I catch the taxi driver's eyes in the rear-view mirror; she flicks them away as is the habit in this cool city. Out across False Creek, the night glitter of the downtown penthouses is gaining on the light of day.

"I thought you knew," Matthew says.

The taxi driver has her foot to the pedal. There's no stopping her, not even for yellow lights turning red. My breath catches. In a passing window, cryptic neon Chinese characters flash in red; I wonder, why do I always end up in these culs-de-sac? Why do I never see the NO EXIT signs? *I'll be gone already*, dripped so casually off his tongue, *gone already . . . gone . . . gone*, bouncing back and forth, mumbo-jumbo in this taxicab leaping up Broadway.

"Helene, everybody knows." His voice is gentle. "Helene, I assumed Christine would have told you."

I REMEMBER WATCHING MY grandmother's reflection in her bedroom mirror when I was six. Katie and I were staying at my grandparents' house in Montreal for the duration of the family reunion.

I want to be beautiful like you, Grandma, I told her, after watching her twist her silver hair up into a chignon, line her delicately creased eyes with kohl, and fill in her thin lips with cerise.

You already are, sweetheart. She lowered her voice as she bent down to confide, *All this stuff is just smoke and mirrors.*

Can I dress up with you? I whispered back. *Pleeease.*

Of course. She dabbed a dot of red on my lips. *Look*, she said, helping me climb onto a chair to gaze at my reflection. *You look like a geisha.*

What's a geisha, *Grandma?*

A beautiful Japanese dancer. She smiled in the mirror as I stared at the strange girl with the round red lips.

My mother burst into the bedroom. *What are you doing?* she yelled. Her rough hand descended on my shoulder and pulled me off the chair.

We were only playing. My grandmother beseeched me with big round eyes. *Weren't we?*

I nodded fervently in agreement, but my mother's hand, pinching into my shoulder, cut my enthusiasm short.

She's too young to wear makeup. I don't need you transforming her into some exotic Japanese whore—

Honey, my grandmother's words fell softly, almost silently so that we had to strain our ears as if to catch the footfalls of a deer, *there's only ever been one of* those *in this family.*

MATTHEW'S ANNOUNCEMENT HAS SHATTERED my festive mood. "Where are you going?" I ask, my throat tight.

"Japan," he says buoyantly.

"When?"

"In a little under four weeks."

"What for?"

"I've arranged to do my third year there on a student exchange."

"But isn't your major in Latin American politics?

He grins. "It took some smooth talking."

"So that's why you've been studying Japanese all spring."

He shrugs. "I learned the basics on my trip to Tokyo two years ago. The pronunciation is very close to Spanish."

I stare at him, dumbfounded, remembering the boxes stacked in the corner of his basement suite. The letters stacked on top of his refrigerator. "How old is she?" I ask.

"Who?" He studies me carefully then shrugs again. "*Yoshiko*?"

What do I care? What can it matter if he's leaving?

The corner of his mouth twitches. "She's thirty-one."

My eyes settle on the upright palms of his vacant hands, curled up in his lap. I wish I had pen and paper on me now to pour myself into a scumble and crosshatch sketch of those hands.

"Didn't I tell you I've always dated older women?" I hear him ask as the taxi pulls to the curb.

Out on the sidewalk, I stare up the street as Matthew pays. As soon as he has climbed out of the cab, I take off up the block in search of my boss's house.

"Wait up," he yells after me.

I cross my arms as I turn around. When he catches up, he holds out his clenched fist. "Open it," he says.

With a sigh, I peel back his fingers one by one to discover a chunk of tinfoil.

"Happy Birthday," he says.

"Is this a joke?"

"Unroll it."

Inside, I discover two misshapen lumps of chocolate. "Drugs," I sigh.

"Shrooms," he corrects me. He chomps down on one of the pieces. Between his teeth, the coating slides away to reveal a grey mushroom stem speckled with an electric-blue fungus.

The last time I did magic mushrooms, I was fifteen. I ended up skulking about on all fours in Deer Lake Park pretending to be a cougar. Tracy, an acquaintance of mine at the time, had promised to babysit me should things get out of hand. So, high as she was, she managed to get me out of the park and into a 7-Eleven for a Slurpee; maybe, she thought it would calm me down. When I peeked into the enormous paper cup, the icy molecules swirled around in a spiral that opened its blue mouth to scream at me: *We are alive!* I dropped the cup on the floor. Slush slid out in a layer of transparent blue turning the tiles into a skating rink, which made me double over in hysterics. I was laughing even as the store clerk stepped out from behind the counter and threatened to call the cops. I worried they would send me back to the group home, so then I started crying—hysterical, like a baby, holed up in Tracey's arms until the morning came, on her tired purple sofa, feeling jittery and old.

* * *

MATTHEW AND I MAKE our way through the cars piled up outside my boss's house. I experience a slight whooshing in and out of distance—the house is tiny then omnisciently large as I reach the front door. Someone puts a Kokanee in my hand.

Giovanni, the owner of the restaurant where I work part-time on Commercial Drive, takes my face between his fat hands and kisses my cheeks with an exaggerated smack, smack. "That is what we do in Italy," he says as he always says, giving my cheek a gentle pinch before turning back to the crowded room. "Now we sing Happy Birthday to my youngest waitress!" I try to back away, but he leads his guests in an a cappella. He gesticulates like an orchestra conductor while he leans in to whisper, alcohol thick on his accent, "You okay? You don't look like yourself tonight."

"I'm fine," I whisper back as the performance ends and I'm dragged into the crowd of cheering hands. The familiar faces of coworkers and clients from the restaurant take on a distance and mix in with the many faces I don't know, all grins and friendly stares from drinking wine and beer. Clink, clink all around, their drinks accost my beer can, making my beer foam up and spill out over my hand. My fingers feel sticky. I unlace Giovanni's arm from my shoulder and grasp my beer can with both hands. I lean over it to sip away the leaking froth. The beer fizzes at the back of my throat, trickles down into a pool at the pit of my stomach. The noise level as everyone resumes their chatting is overwhelming: voices clamouring all at once in English and Italian, confounded with the tired Led Zeppelin booming over the radio. Now that they've forgotten my birthday, I find myself alone in the crowd, hedged in on every side by somebody's back. I swim through the throng in search of Matthew. Olivia, my boss's daughter, tries to stop me—she places a string of balloons in my hand. Her laughter is giddy. "Please," I say, pushing past her, "please . . . I need some fresh air."

I find Matthew in the entryway, leaning into the doorframe, his arms folded tightly across his chest. "All these drunk people," I comment, giggling at the way my syllables bubble out of my mouth and bob against the balloons in my hand. Matthew opens and closes his mouth like a fish underwater. I can't make out what he's saying, but it doesn't matter. We are by the door, Matthew and I, my face upturned to his, caught up in the cocoon of silence Olivia's balloons have wrapped around us.

Outside in the backyard, Matthew climbs an arbutus tree with peeling red branches. I totter at the top of the steps that lead down onto the lawn. People are coming up the drive, saying hello. They seem too friendly—what do they want from me?—as they kick out pebbles from under their clumsy, drunk feet. I sink onto the top stair, a bare spruce plank twisted with multiple knots, and slide over to let them pass one by one as they enter the house. My fingers circle the knots in the wood, dark spirals bleeding into the lighter areas.

Arms raised in victory, Matthew comes back from the peeling arbutus. He motions for me to come down the stairs. I'd forgotten all about him. Looking down at the spruce plank again, I see that its knotted rings are like the spheres into which I have been born—language, race, culture—spheres over which I have no control. Matthew has come up the stairs and is tugging at my arm, but I refuse to look away. *Anglophone, Caucasian, Canadian.* I shiver.

"You're cold." Matthew throws these words out into space, and I watch them slip across my mind like a suave rose martini. "Here, take my coat."

I brush it away. He too is *Anglophone, Caucasian, Canadian.*

"Let's go for a jaunt," he says, hopping down the stairs one by one. But I don't want to leave. I am a pale-skinned North American speaker of English. But I am not of his class. I am not of his sex.

Someone opens the door of the house behind me. A flood of music rushes out, its notes piling up against my backbone before bouncing down the stairs to float out over the night air and burst with sad *poufs* on the damp grass blades. Matthew paces the lamp-lit gravel of the driveway. I heave myself from the steps to lurch after him lest he abandon me here to the remains of the music. I grope my way over the electric pebbles, blinded by their luminosity under the cold streetlamp. I wander about in a maze of trucks piled haphazardly around cars, losing my sight.

I've lost sight of Matthew. Solitude settles onto me with a stranglehold, and I sink under its weight to the curb of the street.

When I open my eyes, I see Matthew. Standing there on the other sidewalk, legs shoulder width apart, arms crossed, gazing back at me and my human chaos. The self-possession of his stance unsettles me. I can't reach him; he can't reach me. We are alone, utterly alone, separated by this divide of an empty street.

So why am I going to you, Matthew? Why are my feet lifting off the sidewalk to settle onto the black asphalt, why do they cross the dividing line? Why are my arms stretching out to uncross yours, why are they wrapping around your waist, why is my face pressing against your chest?

Matthew loosens my grip and holds me at arm's length. "Let's get lost!" He grabs my hand and drags me down the street, racing around corners, through dark alleyways.

"I have a good sense of direction," I yell as I stumble after him.

"In here," he shouts, letting go of my hand to sprint into Queen Elizabeth Park.

Under a tree with a bitter-orange bark we sit, our backs to the scaly trunk. A streetlamp glows like a distant moon from outside the park, and we sit staring at the dark lawns spread out under its luminescence.

"I've never been lost before," I tell him, enjoying this game of disorientation, all the while aching for more—for the distraction and perdition of being in love.

"It's good to get lost sometimes," he says.

HOURS GO BY. MOVING from this spot under the tree seems needlessly complicated. Matthew starts laughing at his thick fist, which he weaves back and forth in front of us. I giggle, too, until he puts it right in my face. I push his arm away. His skin is clammy. All around us, the grass is growing damp with dew. I wrap my jacket tighter around me, shivering. He lets his hand drop to his lap only to start up again a moment later, zigzagging his hand in front of my eyes.

After countless repetitions of this, I manage to ask, "What are you doing?"

"Rock, paper, scissors."

I push away his hand again. "What do you mean, *rock, paper, scissors*?"

Matthew stands up. I jump up after him. He races deeper into the park, snaking around shrubs and bushes.

"Matthew! Matthew!" I chase after him, terrified of being left alone at night in the park.

He freezes all of a sudden, one foot in the air.

When I reach him, I grip his arm.

He flings me away. "Shrrr! Go away!" he shouts into the bushes. "We're lost and we don't want to be found."

His foot falls and he is off again; this time, I'm right on his heels.

WE STUMBLE OUT ONTO the street on the other side of the park. Matthew leans against a lamppost; I double over to catch my breath.

"Rock, paper, scissors?"

I spring upright.

"Why such a poker face?" he asks.

The pads of my feet press into the pavement as I rotate away from him. I don't want him thinking I don't know how to have a good time, but a chasm has sprung up between us, the same divide that has separated our realities since we entered puberty, the same rift that made our park escapade a game of tag for him while I ran for fear of the nightlife. On one side of the chasm is his easy access to adult pleasures—strip joints, porn, and prostitution; on the other, my childish fear of monsters stalking me in the dark.

He pulls me back under the streetlight. "We'll play best out of three."

"No, Matthew, no!" I extract my upper arm from his hand.

He lets me go and reaches out instead to tilt up my chin. His retinas are seeping pools of ink in seas of blue ice. I try to shake his gaze but his fingers tighten on my jaw. As if my words were unheard, he explains: "If you lose, you have to reveal your deepest, most secret desire."

I'm coming down, strung out and jittery as if overly caffeinated. Time seems distorted; day is now beginning to light up the streets.

"What if the loser lies?" I slide down, out of his grasp, before he can answer. I take a step backward, careful not to land on any of the cracks in the pavement, suddenly aware of the gridlines around me, tunnelling away on all sides toward the horizon, boxing me into this megalopolis, stringing my nerves along their razor-thin edges.

Matthew grabs my hand again. He reels me in and plants his lips over my mouth. An elderly Chinese couple is crossing the street from the opposite sidewalk. They pointedly don't look at us. I try to catch my breath between his kisses. I feel like I'm underwater and drowning. *Please don't look at us—not now, not like this.*

I manage to twist my mouth away from his. "Okay," I relent. I glance at his watch—just after five. The Chinese couple steps onto our side of the sidewalk. They enter into the park and, not far in, begin to move through postures of Tai Chi. The woman floats across the grass, her arms sliding through the cool air. The serenity of her movements highlights my angst. *Did I say goodbye to my boss last night? Will wasting my birthday sleeping off this hangover jinx my twenty-first year? Do I even like Matthew—his Nietzsche quotes, his views on poverty, his casual arrogance, his daredevil sports, his crude lovemaking?* A cold sweat trickles down the nape of my neck, under my hairline. I push him away and start walking. All I want is to be alone, to lose myself in a painting or drawing at home.

He follows. After twenty or so blocks, I stop for a rest on a bench at a bus stop on the corner of Main. "Show me what you've got," he says, and we shake our fists three times. Each time his paper covers my rock or his scissors cut my paper. "Don't be shy, ocean lover," he croons in my face, his tone dirty. "You can tell me anything."

I gaze up the gum-stained sidewalk, away from him.

"You're very determined," he whispers.

I don't want to be pegged. I don't want to be square or round or triangular and shelved with a big fat nametag.

"Secretive," he adds.

I glare at him. Dark circles have formed under his pale eyes, and wiry strands have escaped his ponytail to twist around his ears and poke under his chin. "What am I *determined* about? What am I *secretive* about?"

He raises an eyebrow. "You tell me."

I try to outstare him but lower my gaze when he refuses to look away. My line of sight falls to his hands in his lap. The grace of the fingers curling there on his blue jeans is astonishing. It is this secret I would divulge: it is his beauty I would capture. It is his agonizing otherness I would make my own. The grace of Matthew's gesture is torturous in that it is still out there, it still belongs to him, and I do not know how to recreate it as my own.

Matthew leans forward over his knees and rubs his temples, breaking my concentrated study. Now I turn instead to his tousled hair, to the translucent orange strands that stray in the early sunlight, to the burnt umber of the freckles darkening his fingers that blend into the disarray.

"I'd like to paint you, Matthew."

He straightens, studying me with an incredulous look. "That's your most secret, deepest desire?"

I nod. "Yes—to be a painter."

"But do you know how? Do you have any ability?"

I shrug and gaze at the sidewalk.

"Why aren't you in an art program then?" He frowns slightly as he adds, "If that's what you want to be doing?"

"Commerce is a sensible career choice," I tell him, even as I admit to myself that, like this city waiting for the alarm clock to ring and fill up her streets, I am sleepwalking through my life. "Don't you get it?" I turn on him. "Don't you get it yet? People like you and James and Christine can afford to follow your dreams. People like me—"

"In this country, it's as simple as choosing what you want to do with your life."

"Is it?" I think about what it means to be a man versus a woman, to be from a middle-class family versus raised on welfare, to be white versus First Nations, to be Canadian-born versus an immigrant. I open my mouth to argue, but then I think how different my life and Katie's could have been if she hadn't been so passive: if she'd *chosen* to return to Montreal after my father died, if she'd *chosen* to seek help for her drinking.

I think about the different person I might be now if only she'd *chosen* to take my side rather than allow Lyle to banish me from their life.

An Unfinished Study

Late in July, the evening before his flight to Japan, Matthew arrives dripping wet at my door. "It smells wonderful in here," he says, pulling a bottle of chardonnay from his sopping backpack and handing it to me.

"I made a Japanese curry. I thought it appropriate," I tell him as I set the bottle of wine on the table.

Little rolls of mud fall out of the tracks in his hiking boots as he kicks them off. I bring him a towel from the bathroom. Bending over to shake out his hair, he showers my bare toes with wet as I gather up his boots and arrange them on a newspaper by the door.

"I rode my bike because I thought I could beat the storm," he says, peeling off his socks. "Big mistake!"

I retreat to the stove to stir the curry. Matthew marches barefoot toward me. He takes the wooden spoon out of my hand and leads me into the bathroom. "You don't waste any time," I quip as he pulls off my dress. My underwear follows suit and his black jeans and MEC T-shirt shortly after.

He turns on the shower and guides me into the tub. Outside, rain pounds against the tiny stall window; I press my cheek against the cool glass pane.

Chills flush out across my skin as he joins me under the water and pulls me against him; his hands are ice cold. "Look at me," he growls, shaking me by the shoulders. My eyes settle on the determined line of his jaw. "Don't be sad," he says. "I didn't come here for that."

A flash of lightning outside the window startles us both. *One, one thousand; two, one thou*—Matthew's grip on my shoulders tightens. In spite of the roar of the water in the shower, the thunder when it comes is a boom that weakens me at the knees.

A draft blows in through the open bathroom door.

"Shrrr," Matthew says. "Don't tremble." He draws my cheek to his chest and strokes my hair.

I remove his hand and pull away. I deserve more than his pity.

"What's wrong?"

"Is this all there is then?"

He bends down to turn off the water. "You are an only child without much of a family." Reaching for the towel, he dries me limb by limb. "It's only natural that you want to fill that void."

"You're sidestepping the question." I search out his eyes. "Don't you believe in love?"

He shrugs as he begins to towel himself. *"Ah, women. They make the highs higher and the lows more frequent—"*

"Don't!" I put my finger to his lips. "I didn't ask what Nietzsche said about women or whatever. I asked what you believe."

He shrugs. He walks out of the bathroom, flops naked onto the bed, and watches me slip into my dress. I toss him his boxers, collected off the bathroom floor. He glances at where they fall on the mattress by his foot.

Rolling onto his side, he perches his head in his palm. "So when are you going to paint me?"

I turn to study the naked man lying on my unmade bed, locks darkened with wet to an Indian red dangling over his cerulean-blue eyes, the fuzz covering his body giving off an earthy orange glow, one bent knee resting against the lemon-yellow sheet, the other pointed at the ceiling.

"I would need time, a few days. Or a photograph."

"Take a photo, then."

I bite my lower lip. He is the one who finished off my film at the beach, with photos of Christine and James that I may never bother to develop. "I'm out of film," I tell him. "But I could do a quick study to use later as a guide for painting." When he shrugs in agreement, I walk over to the closet to take down the blue shoebox from the top shelf.

"What's that?" he asks as I pull out a brown leather-bound journal.

"It's my diary. But it also doubles as my sketchbook right now until I get a new one." I flip to a blank page near the end. Grabbing a ballpoint pen from the table, I return with a chair that I position kitty-corner to the bed.

I scan the background of the cubbyhole bedroom to help with scale as I lay down the first few strokes to outline his basic figure. Then, with a quick glance down at my journal to check the proportions are correct, I begin the more difficult job of trying to capture in a few strokes the essence of Matthew, the entirety of his being, his shape, his form, his expressions, his emotion—

"Smile," he says, breaking my concentration. "You look so serious."

"Wait, don't move!"

"You've been staring at me like that for over twenty minutes. My arm is going numb."

I feel the desperate slide of time as it slips away from me. *Don't move!* I want to scream, but it's too late as he sits up on the bed. I try to memorize the v-line of his collarbone, the length and width of his torso, the ribbon of his abdominals disappearing into his pubic hair, the sharp angle of his elbow, the few spots on his body without hair. I try to meld these various parts of him into a whole portrait that I can store in the catalogue of images in my head. But already he has left the bed and is peering over my shoulder; as he invades the intimacy of my squiggles of ink on the page, all the minute details of the picture I had hoped to capture shatter apart.

I snap shut the journal, slide it back into the shoebox, and slip on the lid. "So much for that," I say, trying not to let my frustration show.

"I'm starving. Let's eat," he says. He starts to pull on his boxers but changes his mind. "Come here for a second," he says, pulling me down with him on the bed. "We don't have much time left." He rolls on top of me and kisses my neck. He pulls my dress up over my head. The rain lashes sideways at the windowpane over the couch in a frenzied rhythm. He licks the hollow of my breastbone, his tongue tracing outward to a nipple. He kisses my face, one cheek at a time. I kiss him back. The wet of his lips tastes like tears, or maybe they are my own. As he enters me, slowly, gently, he holds me down by the wrists, anchoring me; only my neck and back can arch up as I billow out across the night sky and into the storm clouds, weightless, held down only by the mass of his sweat-soaked body.

THE SILENCE AS WE eat salad, curry, and rice is that between lightning and thunder: expectant, waiting to exhale. "I've been meaning to ask you," Matthew says when his plate is empty, "what's with that weird photograph on your bathroom door?"

I clear the dishes from the table and begin to wash the plates. "It's by Lodi Baker. She's an artist and photographer originally from Montreal, based now out of New York. She's done some funky stuff, like an oil painting of a broken teacup that I like, and"—I point toward the bathroom door—"that photograph. She's a role model for me in many ways."

"Looks like the woman in the picture got both eyes punched out."

I bend over the sink, scrubbing at the pot.

He gets up from the table and leans against the counter beside me. "Why don't you try to get into an art school then, if you want to be a painter?"

I shrug.

He fingers the stem of his wine glass. "Who is your favourite artist?"

Again I shrug.

"What artistic movement do you prefer? Romanticism? Impressionism? Fauvism? Futurism? Constructivism? Cubism? Minimalism? Conceptualism? The anti-art Dada movement?"

"Who cares about all that?" I snap, scrubbing harder at a black bit of curry burnt on the bottom of the pot. "I mean, does everything need a label?"

"All artists have their influences."

I open my mouth to explain that I know little of art movements or influences, other than what I've managed to chance upon in my random explorations of the art section in the public library, where I first discovered and fell in love with the works of Frida Kahlo and Amiet Cuno, but then I close my mouth again because Matthew doesn't want to know me —he wants to provoke me. I am the anthill he has overturned, raw and exposed; he is the boy with the shovel. Now that he has dug me up, he stands back to watch me scurry about to protect my eggs, all these hidden, private aspects of self. He stands back to watch as I try to drag them back underground, away from his overly educated spotlight.

"Or you could at least take an art history course as one of your electives," he offers as he strokes my back, his voice gentle now that my naïveté has been forced onstage to dance for his entertainment. "In any case, I'd like to see you again. Perhaps in a year or two circumstances will allow us to meet up. I'd like to see how you mature and develop."

Leaning into the sink, I close my eyes. *Hush.* I don't dare ask what will happen in the meantime. He seems to have written the script, elsewhere, without my collaboration. Tomorrow, I will leave for work in the morning, leave him sleeping in my bed, and in the afternoon I will return to these four white walls hugging the emptiness of his absence.

"Shall we exchange addresses?" he asks.

In a daze, I walk to the nightstand and take my journal out of the blue shoebox. He writes in tight, controlled letters on the page I open for him. When he's finished I hand him a scrap of paper with my address. I close the journal and wind the string that holds it shut around its leather buttons. He watches as I place it in the shoebox, as I slip the lid over the box's fraying corners, and as I toss the ensemble onto the top shelf of my closet.

Still he's watching me as I settle onto the edge of the bed, and still I don't know what he wants from me.

BLUE

When I run out of red, I use blue.

PABLO PICASSO

A Petty Theft

My thighs peel off the dry ceramic walls of the bathtub as I shift position. I pinch a dark hair on my calf with my tweezers. The skin doesn't want to let go and pulls up like a tent. I give a short tug and—there it is! The glistening black eye of the root quivers at the end of my tongs.

I lean back against the cold rim of the tub, the energy inside me shifty and dark, my shoulders stiff from hunching over my legs. The sound of feminine laughter drifts up from the street below through the open stall window. I pull myself up and press my face through the small opening. The city skyline wavers against the distant mountains, warped by the August heat. I cock an eye to peer down at the two teenagers in flip-flops and shorts who stride arm in arm up the street, toting straw beach bags on their tanned arms and wearing large sun hats over their sunglasses.

I stumble out of the tub stall and catch myself on the sink counter. In the mirror, a stranger in a white T-shirt encrusted with tomato sauce and orange juice stains stares back at me with wild eyes: pupils tiny black flecks, irises vacant and large, sockets denting the surrounding bluish skin.

"I'll give you the week off," Giovanni conceded, "but only because I'm nice. You'd better come back with a smile. Jeez, the way you've been moping around this joint, I'm thinking I might have to start looking for a replacement."

His kindness expires tomorrow when I'm expected back at work.

I mouth the words into the mirror that Matthew preached to me over and over this summer: *Everyone is mortal. You can't live in fear.*

So what are you supposed to do, wise guy? Pretend you aren't afraid?

The stranger in the mirror doesn't react to my question. Below her tuft of pubic hair, her thighs are cut off by the countertop, no legs to stand on.

Why don't you do some solo travelling? Matthew asked. *It might change your vision of the world and your life.*

Because, I told him, *travelling alone my days would be spent avoiding philandering men and my nights confined behind locked doors. No hitchhiking, no exploring red-light districts, no accepting strangers' offers of hospitality. All of which are more or less risk free for you.*

Matthew, who had smoked opium in a thatch-roofed hut in Laos and received a full-body massage to top off his experience—with a happy ending?—responded, *You can't live in fear.*

I asked about his previous travel to Japan.

I ended up in Japan by accident, he explained. *I hitched a ride on a yacht from Australia to Indonesia and then flew from Jakarta to Bangkok, where I met Yoshiko. From there I rode by motorbike through Thailand, Laos, and Cambodia before scraping together enough money for a ticket to Tokyo. I was planning to return to Vancouver the same week because I was out of funds, but then I met a forty-something American woman who offered me a job teaching English, and so I stayed in Japan six months.*

And Yoshiko?

He laughed. *You've got to be open to life and experience everything while you can—while you've still got time, while you're still in the game!*

He spoke of openness while I searched in vain for a way in. We'd make love, and he remained impenetrable even in his moments of ecstasy. Enigmatic, mysterious, an unsolvable riddle. *Matthew, Matthew, who are you behind your mask?* Behind the stunning, hypnotic blue of his eyes, his internal composition remained a secret. He'd whisper my name; I'd wrap up within the folds of myself, burying this unspeakable desire to ravish him, and over and over I fed his narcissism with my silence.

Didn't you come? Didn't you come?

Time after time, I nodded, biding my time, postponing truth for the moment he'd let his guard down and allow me to gaze at his naked soul.

* * *

I STAGGER OUT OF the bathroom and in through the hanging curtain door of my makeshift bedroom. There on the night table is the baby-blue shoebox that betrayed me. My foot sends it flying across the room with a smack to the wall by the dresser. It collapses in a heap on the floor, its cardboard sides splitting open and its guts spilling out: a spray of photographs, a roll of drawings, letters from long-lost friends, a half-heart pendant from Stacy, a recently purchased anthology of Nietzsche's works.

It's no use. The more I read in that anthology—*A man who strives after great things looks upon every one whom he encounters on his way either as a means of advance, or a delay and hindrance, or as a temporary resting-place*—the more I despair. Such words cannot replace those Matthew has stolen from me.

I fall back onto the bed. Staring up at the ceiling, I consider what Matthew now knows. He's had four weeks to read about the Beatleman Hotel in Prince George where my mother lap-danced for the loggers downstairs. He knows that Christine and Stacy's home was the quintessence of luxury to me. He's read that he and his yuppie friends can afford to sneer at consumerism precisely because they spent their formative years swimming in its materialism. He knows that, while he unwrapped matchbox cars or Lego bricks, a BMX or a Superman comic, I spent more than one Christmas Eve making wishes over the toy section of the Christmas Sears catalogue.

Worse, he's seen the sketch I made of his genitalia after he fell asleep that last night, next to which I so stupidly penned the word *beautiful* coupled with his name.

Four weeks. Of waiting. Descending and re-ascending the stairs to stare into the mailbox, but nothing, nothing. No journal, no apology, no explanation.

THE DAY MATTHEW LEFT, I came home from the lunch rush at the restaurant to find that my pillow still held the shape of his head. I sank my face into it, inhaling the woodsy scent that lingered of his hair. Like that

I fell asleep. As I napped, I dreamed that Matthew was showing me a map of the world. He pointed to France and explained, *Language is everything. Language is the medium in which we dream and create.*

I awoke much later, as dusk was settling across the day. Lost for a moment, I sat up in bed and glanced around the quiet apartment, trying to recall the events of the past twenty-four hours. As I remembered Matthew was gone, rather than give into my melancholy, I got up to pull down the blue shoebox from the shelf in the closet. I would cope as I always had: by dumping my mumbo-jumbo mix of emotions and expectations into my journal and letting the yellowing of the paper with the years sort them out for me.

In the shoebox, the furled roll of my childhood drawings was on top. I slid off the elastic and examined each sketch, seeing them now through Matthew's eyes as clumsy and adolescent. Thank god I'd had the sense not to show them to him. Underneath the sketches was Stacy's fifth-grade photo with her inscription to me on the back. . . . What was I looking for again? I lifted out a pile of photographs, the half-heart pendant Stacy had given me falling to the floor. I left the shoebox to rummage through my dresser drawers, scour the bookshelves, and check behind the couch, even peeking into the kitchen sink and the garbage can, every light in the apartment on now, until there was no doubt: my journal no longer belonged to me.

With his petty theft, Matthew had taken from me the narrative of my past; he had taken multiple studies for later paintings; he had taken his address in Japan and the addresses and phone numbers of all my other ex-boyfriends and scattered friends; he had taken a wish list of everything I had hoped to accomplish over the course of my life, from the first item *learn French* to the middle item *sketch ~~Stephen~~ ~~Doug~~ Matthew* to the last item *paint a masterpiece.*

I sat on the couch in a state of shock, telling myself that things don't happen in random, unrelated events, telling myself that life must be more than chaos, that underneath the apparent randomness there must be a thread of meaning tying it all together.

Katie Is Lonely

The hanging clock at Pacific Central Station reads just after five o'clock when I arrive. I grab a cup of coffee to wake myself up and take a seat on one of the long wooden benches, twiddling the strap of the camera hanging from my neck and feeling like a tourist. Katie is due to arrive in fifteen minutes on the overnight Greyhound from Windeal.

When she told me she was coming to visit the first weekend in September I was so stunned I didn't know how to react. She has never been to Vancouver. The last time she visited a large city was when she took me to Montreal when I was six.

"Why?" was all I could manage to ask.

"I want to see where you live," she said. "Besides, since Lyle moved out, the trailer feels so empty."

Now, as her arrival approaches, I leave the hall for the bus platform out back, the chill of the morning air passing through me as I push open the station doors. Zipping up my jacket, I wait with a few others near the gate for the buses arriving from the North.

When the bus pulls in, its tinted windows impenetrable, I feel queasy. In fact, my knees feel a little shaky knowing she can probably already see me. I stare down at the concrete under my feet and wait for her to disembark.

The first passenger off is a rugged, handsome guy about my age. The girl waiting next to me rushes forward to throw herself into his embrace. He lifts her off the ground and kisses her until they are asked by the driver to move aside to allow the rest of the passengers to exit the coach.

My mother is one of the last to step off the bus. I lean forward just enough to reach her, giving her an awkward hug; she reciprocates with a few light pats on my back.

"How was your trip?" I ask.

"Long," she says hauling her blue suitcase from the luggage area of the bus onto the platform. "Sixteen hours with a two-hour stopover in Prince George."

I reach to take the suitcase for her, but she waves my hand away. "I can handle it."

Whatever, just trying to be nice. "I was thinking that since you're only here for two days, we could do some sightseeing this morning before heading back to my place."

"No way. I'm pooped. I didn't sleep a wink on those twisting roads with that bus driver leaning into every corner."

"Are you sure?" I lead Katie out the front station doors into Thornton Park, where the early sunlight beams through the catalpas branches to form a shifting patchwork on the grass. "We could grab some breakfast in historic Gastown and then head to the beach for—"

"What's wrong with that woman?"

I look around the park. An Eastside waif, whom I hadn't even noticed, is shouting obscenities from the centre of the slain women's monument—a tribute to those women killed by a gunman in 1989 in Montreal and dedicated in its inscription to ALL WOMEN WHO HAVE BEEN MURDERED BY MEN. The image is so striking I lift my camera and snap a photo.

"Vancouver's skid row is just a few blocks that way," I tell Katie, pointing north up Main Street. "Don't worry, we're going the opposite direction."

My mother stares back over her shoulder at the woman as I steer her toward the bus stop on the other side of the street. "Are there a lot of people like that here?" she asks.

I shrug.

"You don't care?"

"Do you see that bar over there called the Ivanhoe Hotel?" I point up the street to the five-storey brick building bordering the far side of the park. "I spent almost eight months living in a squalid room above that skid bar. Beer was a buck a glass, and Welfare Wednesday was the busiest day of the month. Cockroaches and bed bugs were rampant in all of the rooms. That was after a few very rough months on the streets, which I managed to escape thanks in part to social services, thanks in part to Christine."

"What is your point exactly?" Katie asks.

"My point is that all it would have taken is for me to have tried heroin or crack one night instead of acid and ecstasy, and that could have been your daughter over there, across the street."

"You've always had a flair for making up your own stories, haven't you?"

"That is the truth. That is exactly what happened, whether or not you want to hear it," I tell her as the bus rolls to a stop in front of us.

"Want some tea?" I ask Katie as I unlock my apartment door. I want to distract her before she can start inspecting my apartment. I remember the way she criticized the family who had us over for Christmas dinner when I was eight, the one year we didn't need to get a turkey from the food bank. *Did you see the grime in their house? Did you see the mess they live in?* All I had noticed was the abundance of toys scattered about their house and trailing down the basement stairs toward the foosball table, the rooms upstairs full of bunk beds and bright thematic bedspreads and, outside the large windows, a swing set beckoning under the snow.

Katie follows me inside and lugs her suitcase to the couch. I watch her eyes sweep over my bachelor suite, across the collection of pens and papers on my chrome-rimmed laminate table, past the tied-up sheet that separates my bedroom, and onto the photocopy of "After Happiness" tacked to the bathroom door. At the foot of the bed, I kick under the skirt dirty clothes overlooked in my earlier efforts to erase all evidence of my holing up like a rat in here for the past five weeks.

She plops down on the sofa and leans into her suitcase. "So this is your place."

"Yeah. Do you want some tea?" I ask again.

"Sure," she answers in a tired voice, gazing out the window behind the couch into the alley below. "I'll have some tea."

I walk to the kitchen nook and heat water on the stove. "I put fresh sheets on the bed if you want to take a nap after."

"No," she answers, without glancing my way.

"No, *what*?" I hear the change in my tone as if my voice belonged to somebody else.

She looks over at me. In six years, crow's feet have grown around her eyes. Soft greys have appeared along her hairline. Her once full lips have grown thinner and sag now a little at the edges.

"Are you saying I *didn't* change the sheets?"

"I'm not going to take your bed!" She pats the couch. "Here will be just fine."

"Whatever." I notice how weak my voice sounds, as if straining to reach us both from afar. "It's lumpy. It'll give you a backache. But go ahead—if that's what you want." After I pour the water into the teapot and place it on the table, I settle onto the end of the couch opposite her, the big blue lug of a suitcase between us.

"Why are you doing this?" she insists. "I just got here. Can't we try to get along?"

You haven't come to visit me. You've come to hide from the fact that Lyle has moved in with Elaine.

Behind us, on the outer windowsill, a broken leaf flaps against the windowpane, a first sign of coming fall. In three days, classes will start up again, and I will begin the second year of my commerce degree. The leaf flits up from the wooden ledge, only to be clamped against the pane by a gust of wind. It flaps against the glass. I stare past its helpless gesticulations into the slanted showers that have overtaken the short sunny break of this morning. I wonder if freedom is possible in this world of necessity, if it isn't just an illusive ideal to which we all blindly aspire.

I get up and pour tea into two mugs. I hand Katie one and hug the other between my cold palms. Katie's eyes are glued to the hangnail she's biting. "It's Lodi's, isn't it?" she asks without looking up, her teeth tearing the translucent skin along the edge of her nail.

"What?"

She jabs a finger in the direction of the bathroom door.

"Oh, the photograph."

She sighs. With a sudden boredom, her mouth abandons the hang-nail. Her hand falls with a thump onto the suitcase where it lies on its back, its ring finger curling up over her wedding band toward the ceiling.

"Don't you know her art?" I ask.

She doesn't answer and asks instead, "Mind if I smoke?"

"Not in here, please."

Her hand jerks back to life. It pushes at the window until the pane screeches open. Dampness creeps into the room, climbing down my neck to settle in the small of my back. "It's been a long trip, Helene. I'm exhausted." She reaches into her purse and pulls out a pack.

I get up and push open the window above the sink: four panes of glass on a wooden cross. Below on the street, crisp bits of debris flutter about on the wet asphalt. I reach into the cupboard beside me and pull out a ceramic bowl. "At least use this as an ashtray," I say as I hand it to her.

"I'm lonely," she says, words that crawl out over the hardwood floors and creep up into the unwilling pores of my skin. "I thought you would understand," she says when I say nothing.

I slump into a chair at the table, overcome with the ache of famili-arity as I watch the cigarette in her hand dwindle to a stub. I could tell her about the cavity where a family should be. I could tell her I feel be-trayed in some profound, unforgivable way. *You never gave me my father.* I could tell her I've sought out Lodi's artwork as a way of gathering up the courage to contact my aunt, who will initiate me into the milieus of family and art. *All I ever wanted is to be an artist, but you discouraged me in every possible way.* I could tell her how absolutely and fiercely in-dependent I had to become to protect myself as a child from her, and about the lonely person I have become as a result.

But she beats me to it by repeating again that she's lonely, more to herself than to me this time, as if discovering the truth in her words by the saying of them.

I laugh at her. "So you had to feel lonely to come visit me?"

She butts out her cigarette on the outer windowsill. "You make me sound awful. Am I really such a terrible mother?"

I don't let her eyes search me out; I rise from my chair and lean over the kitchen sink, my back to her. Outside the window, a gust tunnels down the alleyway and knocks over the beer cans on a neighbour's back porch. I shut up the window.

"In your books, I'm always failing, aren't I?" she asks. "Well, you should give me some credit that I haven't gone back to drinking even if I did slip up once when I found out about . . ."—she hesitates then spits out the name like a bad taste from her mouth—"Elaine."

I turn from the sink and count the steps until I am towering above her. "But you're smoking, aren't you? In my home after I said no. You know what your problem is? You have no self-respect so you don't respect anyone else. You let whatever man you're with control your life so you don't have to take responsibility for it." I sway on my feet. Catch myself on the bookshelf. Pause to exhale. A single tear streaks down her cheek. I return to the chair at the table in an attempt to cool down. I grind my elbows into the tabletop until their bones feel like tiny white shards of kindling ready to go up in flame.

"Helene, please, I came here to—"

"You came for company in your misery. But you've come to the wrong place. You should have come when I needed you. Now it's too late."

"You should have stayed at the group home," Katie says meekly. "We were going to visit you. It was your choice to run away. Maybe you need to take some responsibility too."

"I was fifteen, Katie. *Fifteen!* Do you think I wanted to be housed with a bunch of juvenile delinquents?"

"The screaming matches with Lyle couldn't have continued. It wasn't healthy."

"I hated him, I agree. It made me sick how you let him control you and never stood up for me. I mean, who was supposed to stand up for me if you didn't?" The room blurs under the tears that line my lids, but I don't let them fall. One by one, I swallow them down, stinging acid at the back of my throat. "I still question authority and I still rebel. But I didn't deserve to be sent to live with a bunch of kids whose parents didn't want them. One girl's anger was so out of control she stabbed another girl in the leg the first week I was there. So my question is: Why, Katie? Why didn't you stick up for me? Didn't you want me anymore?"

Katie starts crying. "I was only sixteen when I got pregnant," she sobs. "But I couldn't give up my baby. My parents left me with no choice but to run away. Lodi's life is what mine would have been if I hadn't met your father. They paid her way through art school. They gave her a big wedding. I'm sure they're still close; she's been the perfect daughter. But they left me with no choice. I've always wanted you, Helene. If I failed you it's because I didn't know how to do any different."

A Chance Encounter

The next morning, I tilt my head sideways to peer up through my kitchen window at the high cloud cover. Another grey, overcast Vancouver day—so much for my plans to take Katie downtown to Denman Beach. With a sigh, I lift a sudsy hand out of the water in the sink to flick on the radio on the windowsill. I bend over the basin to scrub at the oatmeal stuck to the bottom of the pot.

Ken Lum is a local conceptual artist from East Vancouver whose new work appears on the exterior roof of the Vancouver Art Gallery, the Sunday anchorwoman reports. *The title of the rooftop exhibit is "Four Boats Stranded: Red and Yellow, Black and White."*

The porridge pot clangs against the steel of the sink as I drop it to turn up the volume.

The exhibit calls attention to the influence of colonialism on Canadian immigration policies. Each boat is painted in one of the stereotyped racial colours of the children's hymn, "Jesus Loves the Children of the World."

I rinse the soap off the pot and place it on the drainboard, thinking of the passion and dedication it must take to achieve the recognition necessary for the fourth largest art gallery in Canada to display your artwork on its rooftop. Pulling the plug from the drain, I watch the water snake downward in a dirty spiral.

Lum, whose grandfather immigrated from China to work on the Canadian Pacific Railway in 1908, is currently head of the graduate program in studio art at UBC. He previously taught at the École nationale supérieure des beaux-arts in Paris and—

I flick off the radio. I wonder if it is too late for me. A life without art seems like no life at all, and every single day that I don't create in some way seems not fully lived. Yet how do you become a professional artist with a successful career like Lum? I don't want to be just another starving artist, worn down by the struggle to pay the bills, with neither time nor energy left over for art. Am I to be nothing more than hobbyist, then, for the rest of my life?

I wipe the last bit of scum from the bottom of the sink and turn off the tap. The apartment is silent. I cock an ear toward the bathroom door, straining to catch a splash, a sigh, a spritz of hairspray.

"Want to go see a new exhibit at the art gallery?" I shout in the direction of the bathroom.

No response.

I've always been afraid of Katie dying on me, keeling over unnoticed. When I find the body, I'll regret not being a better daughter. But wait. . . . *Flip-flop flip-flop* over my hardwood floors, she is circling my bachelor suite in her slippers, a waft of copycat perfume swirling after her. An alien presence, this body, picking at an orange scab of food encrusted on the blue-flecked tabletop, poking at my Chinese lantern in the corner, saying she'd rather go see the new Nicole Kidman movie—I want to yell at her to get out of my apartment, out of my life.

"Why do you hate art so much?" I ask instead.

Katie laughs. "You judge me because you are a dreamer, but I am a realist. Art doesn't mean anything to me anymore. A stiff drink or trashy novel can make you feel and forget just as much as any sculpture or painting."

"That's escapism, not art."

"Honeybun, all I want out of human creation is escapism. Give me thrillers and soap operas. I don't need any deeper meaning—God gave us the Bible for that."

"So you're saying fine art is for the godless."

She parks herself in front of the bookcase. "Where's the tiger figurine I sent for your birthday?" she asks, ignoring my question as she dusts the ceramic animal knickknacks on the shelves with her fingers and realigns them in front of the books. She started giving me these trinkets when we lived in the hotel room, when we made it a game to give small gifts because we had no space for larger ones. I must have nearly all of Noah's ark by now, but still she manages to send a unique miniature twice a year, one for my birthday and one at Christmas. I loved those animals as a child and spent hours playing with them, until I discovered in Windeal the joy of real toys at Stacy's house.

The tiger is tucked away inside the little box it came in, buried somewhere near the bottom of my sock drawer. "It's in the bedroom," I mumble, as I consider how I might rummage through my mismatched socks to sneak the figurine onto the dresser. Instead, I put away our breakfast bowls.

With a sigh, she resumes her cleanup of the dusty bric-a-brac. I pull the dishtowel through the handle of the fridge door and grab the dishcloth to wipe the table. Dusting off the last of the figurines, a baby seal, she inspects the rest of the bookcase. She reaches up on tiptoe to pull down the edge of one of the many warped sheets of paper stacked on the top shelf.

"Don't," I say, tossing the dishcloth into the sink and drying my hands on my corduroy pants. Most of my artwork is housed in the old suitcases under my bed, but these I forgot to hide.

She reaches up with both hands to take down the pile. The top sheet is a watercolour in the single shade of burnt sienna of a nude man lying on his side. After a brief glance, she moves on to a rendering of the same figure in sepia-tone pastel pencil.

"Don't," I beg.

She lifts a third, a fourth, a fifth, and still another. She flicks through them and stacks them up like dominoes against her chest. She turns to me, her eyebrows drawn together. "Helene?" She unfolds her arms to reveal the evidence. A gust of wind whips in through the cracked window, and the sheets fall like autumn leaves, each in a single shade of red ochre, terra rosa, scarlet lake, or rust earth. My red period.

The pages flutter to the floor at our feet.

"Helene?"

"What?"

I know his hair is a melange of raw umber and ochre, but his eyes refuse to be captured: under my hand they are always frog-like and dead.

"Who is this guy?" Katie demands. "Who do you keep trying to paint?"

I stare at the floor, counting the sheets of evidence: eleven, thirteen, nineteen. My hands find solace in the back pockets of my pants, but the traitor is my throat, which allows the single word "nobody" to scale its dry tunnel and sound in the air.

She bends down to sweep the drawings into a heap. "Well, there's over a dozen sketches here of whoever *nobody* is. I wish you would tell me if you have a man in your life."

I lean back against the table, removing my hands from my pockets to grip its chrome edge. With downcast eyes, I watch my knuckles turn white and force myself to swallow. *She can't just waltz in here and expect me to open up.* "He's nobody," I repeat, trying not to think about the journal afloat in the world, no longer mine. "Nobody!"

She stands back up and steps toward me. I slide away from the table and back up. She points toward the bathroom door, and my eyes follow the lead of her finger. "You're still dreaming of being an artist, aren't you? That's why you pinned up that photo of Lodi's, isn't it?" I back into the refrigerator and press my palms against its cool skin. She sighs and turns away from me. "Just don't give up your accounting," she warns as she settles into a chair at the table.

The floorboards under my bare feet are full of slivers. I glide a toe over the rough edge of a plank. "Commerce, Katie."

"What?"

I'm ashamed, so ashamed. For her. For us. "I'm doing a bachelor of *commerce*, Katie."

"Whatever." She brushes at the air with her hand as if to wipe away the word. "Commerce, accounting, whatever—that's not the issue here. Anyway, it's all Greek to me," she says with a dismissive laugh. The huskiness of her voice reminds me of her drinking days. "I'm just saying you need to stick with something sensible."

I slip past her to scoop up the sketches from the floor.

"A few of them aren't bad," she says as she watches me from the table, "but some of the proportions are off and you've got the eyes all wrong. So are we going to the movies, or what?"

"BOY, YOU'VE PACKED ON a few, haven't you?" my mother remarks as she stops to tie her shoelace in the stairwell of my building. She's bent over like a hissing cat, squinting up at me as I zip up my raincoat.

"What'd you expect?" I snap, thrust into the grips of a memory: Lyle caught me puking in the bathtub and yelled, *You'd better not clog the drain!*

"The last time you saw me I was fifteen," I say. "I was bulimic, and I hadn't finished growing yet."

"You've inherited your father's build," she pronounces, straightening up. "My family's all small-boned like me."

"But you've always said he was thin."

She waves away my remark as I lead her through the exit onto the street. "Drugs can make anybody scrawny, but he had a large frame. I never met his folks, but they couldn't have been, as they say in French, 'petits.' Oh, don't look at me like that. I'm just saying, you can't fight your genes."

"Katie, I'm quite happy with my body and genes, okay? So quit trying to make me feel bad."

"Oh, don't be so sensitive."

Outside, the sky is pale. Sharp gusts speckled with rain snipe at us; we have to squint our eyes against the dust blustering in the air. As we fight our way toward the bus stop, I wonder if she remembers her words to the school counsellor when I got caught smoking pot on the school grounds: *She'll only wear black. It's creepy. We try to talk to her, but she yells at us to leave her alone. I don't think anybody can get through to her. Have you seen what she wears? Studded chokers and drain catchers and spiked dog collars. We wanted to confiscate them, but she bit Lyle when he tried to take them off her. Yesterday, she came home wearing an upside-down cross. We're at our wits' end. We don't know what to do. . . .*

On the bench at the bus stop, sitting next to me, my mother stares up and down Broadway, taking in the closed-up shops and traffic whizzing by. "What are you brooding over?" she asks, her feet shifting impatiently on the sidewalk.

THE FRASER BUS ROLLS to a stop in front of us. Katie grabs my sleeve and points to the back window. "Look! Isn't that Christine?"

Indeed, it is. Sitting next to her is James.

Christine waves from the back as we board. Katie lifts her hand in return and checks me over when I don't follow suit.

The driver pulls out from the curb, sending us lunging for handholds. I fumble through my pockets for the correct fare, taking stock of the threadbare knees of my corduroy pants and peeling laminate of my blue rain jacket. This was supposed to be a private outing with my mother to the movies, not a meet and greet with everyone I know in Vancouver. What are Christine and James doing here on an East Van bus anyway? These gritty streets are hardly their territory.

Katie snakes her way down the corridor toward the back of the bus. I take our transfers from the driver and follow after her. It's the first time I've seen either Christine or James since they returned from their climbing trip together down in the States. They are seated on the back bench, their elbows looped together and their hands entwined—apparently now a couple.

As soon as my mother reaches Christine, she says, "I can't believe we ran into you like this—Helene was telling me only yesterday how much you helped her out here. We're going to see *The Others*, you know the new Nicole Kidman movie? I'll have to tell your mother that I bumped into you when I see her working next time at the Royal Bank—"

"Katie's first time in Van," I cut in, shrugging to excuse her excitement. "I'm taking her to Tinseltown and then for a stroll up Robson—it's what she says she wants to do."

"We're coming back from a visit to James's grandmother in Mountain View Cemetery," Christine says.

"Oh, that's nice of you," says Katie.

"Robson Street is a tourist trap," Christine tells her. Her tone is slightly condescending. "Wouldn't you rather walk around Stanley Park or see the library or visit the art gallery?"

"No." Katie laughs. "Helene asked me the same thing. I want to do some window-shopping in the famous shopping district everyone always talks about."

Trailer trash. That's all we are.

"So how was your summer?" I ask before Katie can embarrass me any further.

"Mostly uneventful. Some good climbing in the States, and then we took a trip to the Skaha Bluffs. It was too hot to climb, so we mostly just swam in the Okanagan Lake. That's how I got this great tan." Christine pulls back the sleeve of her jacket to show off a tawny forearm. "All in all, good times. How was yours?"

I shrug. "Equally uneventful."

"Oh, by the way, I was going to call you," she adds. "Matthew sent a postcard to the outdoors club. Have you heard from him?"

I turn to stare out the window. "No, I haven't," I hear myself admit. Outside the bus, Eastside buildings flash by, some boarded and closed, others with barred, cracked windows, and I wish I could be alone right now to mourn their disrepair.

"Well, I pinned it to the bulletin board outside the club room," Christine explains, "in case you want to read it."

"Who's Matthew?" Katie butts in. "Wait a minute, wait a minute," she says, "he's not the guy in all those sketches you've been doing, is he? The ones painted in various shades of red?"

"Katie . . ." I whimper, turning from the window to face off the three of them. Christine's eyebrow crooks as she lets go of James's hand and leans forward in her seat, staring up at me.

"What?" Katie glances from me to them and back to me again. "Did I say something wrong?"

Clinging to the overhead handrail, I turn to stare back out the bus window. The same waif we saw yesterday outside the train station shuffles down the sidewalk in a miniskirt, one of her heels broken, pushing an empty shopping cart and cursing no one in particular. I knead the front of my neck between my fingers. Beads of perspiration gather at my collarbone and drip down between my breasts under my raincoat. One block. Two blocks. We are in the heart of the downtown Eastside now, and the homeless people on the streets have swollen to a crowd. Like all the abandoned buildings at their backs, window cavities boarded over and pasted with the flyers of has-been concerts and shows, I am crumbling inside, slowly, in the corners where no one can see.

"Matthew posed for me this summer," I say, turning back toward James and Christine, meeting their eyes with a look I hope will pass for honesty. "Unfortunately," I turn to articulate to my mother in particular, "none of the sketches turned out."

WHEN I DROP OFF my mother later that evening at Pacific Central, the screech of train wheels on rails reminds me of our parting with Lodi in Montreal when I was six. I find myself wanting to jump on that train and return to that moment, to that station, to ask my aunt to adopt me and save me from a life without art.

I stand waving goodbye on the platform as my mother's bus pulls out from the gate, its windows opaque so that I can't see if she is waving back. I wonder when, and under what circumstances, I will see her again. Guilt for not listening more to her problems with Lyle tinged with nostalgia for the time when it was just the two of us accompanies me home, along with relief that she is gone.

Desire and Discontent

I'm about to hit the snooze button again when I awake with a jolt, realizing I'm running late for my first class of the day. Yesterday, a week after Katie's departure, the university opened for the fall semester and reestablished a routine in my life.

I already miss the leisure of summer. Yesterday, I struggled to remain conscious all morning as the instructor for my Capital Markets class droned on about the equations scrawled across the chalkboard. In the afternoon, the professor for Business Statistics woke me up at the end of his lecture. "Perhaps," he suggested, "you're not interested in my course?"

Grabbing a granola bar now on my way out the door, I steel myself for another day of monotony, which yesterday was at least broken up by a visit to the outdoors club to read Matthew's postcard. Now, on my way to the bus stop, I whisper the haunting name of the woman he mentioned on the back in his message: *Yoshiko*.

Does he love you? Did he write and call you all summer? Were you faithful while he cheated? *Yoskiko, Yoshiko.* Has he told you about me?

AT THE UNIVERSITY, THE professor of my elective class, Introduction to Philosophy, jostles his way to the front of the classroom, an overstuffed briefcase swinging at his side. A slightly stooped man, he plonks his case down on the table and pops the latch by the handle, scratching at a receding hairline as he pauses to slurp his coffee. When he begins to sort through his papers, his eyes slip over his glasses in our direction, and he stiffens in the hunched position of a bear staring into headlights, as if shocked by our presence. Then, after a series of coughs to clear his throat, he straightens. He points to a girl in the front row and demands, "Who are you?"

"Me?" The girl throws a glance back at the rest of us.

"Yeah, you. What are you doing here?"

The girl turns back to the professor and mumbles, "Linda Chow, chemistry major. You know, like, I registered and everything. . . ."

"Yeah?" the professor challenges. "Well, I hope to make you question everything you are and believe by the end of this term: the nature of meaning, identity, reality, etcetera." He flaps his hand to emphasize *etcetera*.

"In fact, I'm writing a book. . . ." He pauses as if fearful of giving too much away. We stare at each other: the learned and the unlearned. He lifts his coffee cup to take a sip. As he slaps the mug back down on the table, black liquid sloshes over his hand and onto his papers. He glances down at his soggy notes. "But I suppose," he mutters, more to himself than to us, wiping his hands on the front of his trousers, "we won't get to those themes until later on in the year." He blows out a sigh and re-adjusts his spectacles. "For now, I want you to consider the role that philosophy plays in your life, a question which may, if I'm so inclined, turn up later on the final exam. All righty then, enough about me." He points at the girl directly behind Linda Chow. "Your turn."

"Hi." The voice is smooth like jazz, velvety like peanut butter on hot toast. The owner of this voice glances around the room as if to ensure she has our complete attention. She does—I'm holding my breath, we all are, and I can hear nothing but the pounding of blood in my ears amid the hush that has followed her one word.

"I'm Hana," she continues. "I'm in theatre." She tucks a straying strand behind her ear, a streak of blue in the otherwise black bob that frames her porcelain face. "I'm in this class to discover what theories we have come up with to explain birth and death . . . and everything in be-tween."

The class is silent, as if pondering this *in between*. Hana, with a flick of her wrist, indicates to the professor that he should now continue around the room. He stirs as if from a trance and points to the student beside her. Her friend bobs his head up and down, the tight curls of his caramel-brown hair dancing in and out of his eyes as he sputters, "I am Laurent"—*bounce bounce*—"I am foreign student from Paris"—*bounce* —"I take this course because I like to study the philosophy."

They make for a beautiful couple, artist and muse. Hell, I'd be in fine arts, too, if I had a family's support to fall back on if my studies didn't work out. A spoilt Asian kid, that's what she is, and I bet her posh French boyfriend will be earning six figures by the time he's thirty.

I shouldn't be here. I'm not some bored bourgeois kid seeking to give my life meaning.

"*Hello*. Earth to whoever you are," the professor is saying.

"Sorry," I mumble and bow my head. "I'm Helene," I manage to stammer. "Commerce student. And the reason I'm here is to . . ." As I search around for a suitable explanation, the truth rolls off my lips without premeditation: ". . . discover who I am and why I am and where I might be going."

I think of what my mother once said and it scares me. *Artists are by nature inward-looking and self-centred. That's where their art comes from. But rarely are they happy.* I don't want to be like her. Whatever it takes, I don't want to end up so full of poison.

AFTER MY CLASSES, I take the bus down Broadway to the restaurant where I work on Commercial Drive. I slip into a seat next to a man in his mid-thirties, unshaven, short wavy hair, dusky skin, perhaps of Iranian or Spanish descent. As he shifts a leg to give me more room, he raises an arm to brace himself against the bar of the seat in front of us. The veins running down his thick forearm and over his hand bulge slightly from the skin, and he smells of freshly rained-upon earth.

His scent evokes a memory of a flash rainstorm this past July, a bouquet of raindrops splattering onto hot, dusty asphalt. I was waiting for Matthew outside a bakery on Fraser when I felt the first drops. It had been sunny when we'd left my place three blocks up the street, so I was in flip-flops and shorts. While Matthew chose from the selection of fresh-baked goods inside, outside the sky darkened. Through the window, I watched the Korean girl place four cookies in a brown paper bag.

As Matthew stepped out with the grease-stained bag in his fist, the rainfall turned torrential. He hesitated under the eave then pulled me in under the overhang. Rain ran off my bare arms in rivulets; my hair stuck to my cheeks.

"Even the monsoon rains in India give you more warning than this," he grumbled, letting go of my arm. We stood there watching the water gush from the sky, splashing up off the sidewalk and streaming in small rivers toward the storm drains. He offered me a chocolate chip cookie. The moisture in the air and the wet on my hands dampened it to a mess of melted chocolate and mushy dough.

"So," he asked, when the cookies were gone and the rain was still streaming down, "do you know any poetry?"

I was about to recite Sylvia Plath's "Daddy," which I had obsessively memorized in high school, when Matthew crumpled up the paper bag into a tight wad and tossed it through the rain into a nearby trashcan. Most likely, he wouldn't recognize Plath's poetry anyway, those words I had made my own as a teenager—*Daddy, I have had to kill you*—and realizing this distanced me from him. Standing there in silence in the doorway, his damp arm brushing mine, I sensed once again the chasm separating our experiences.

Now that seven weeks have passed since that rainstorm, Matthew's features and contours have begun to slip toward obscurity in my mind. At best, I can paint him in the doorway of that bakery with features muddied by slanted showers, standing there, but not fully there, a blurry figure bleeding into the background wash. What I do remember is that the rain stopped shortly after and that, as we picked our way through the puddles back to my place, the sky cleared up to a patchy blue. The more time passes, however, the more I confuse which scenes with him were real and which I've since composed solely for my own artistic needs.

In stark contrast, the image of this stranger on the bus beside me, whose scent reminds me of rain on hot earth, rises up sharp and clear:

him I could paint with crisp and hard-edged lines. I could highlight the thick brows and dark shadows of his face, its right angles, the lean contours of his body, the veins swelling over his musculature, the lack of anything soft in his pitch black eyes. I long to invite him home, tell him I desire him—desire to capture his anguish, his hardness, his sensuality, and to magnify those qualities on canvas into a man who captivates not only me but all of his viewers.

Matthew did what he wanted with my body, but he never did enough. He always hung back; he was never fully there. I fantasize now about inviting this stranger back to my place to seek out the satiation Matthew's haste denied me, to undress this stranger and scrutinize every inch of his body until I can replicate its enigma. I turn to him, longing to propose that we meet after my shift. He meets my gaze, and all I dare ask is the time. After he answers me, I mumble thanks, and when the bus lurches to a stop on Commercial Drive, I carry my body to work in agony, that of a restless hunger and unsated desire.

Terror

I check my mailbox first thing in the morning, as I do every day. Its emptiness makes me feel discarded, left behind in the brackets of a summer, deposed to a forgotten corner of Matthew's mind, whose affection now centres, I imagine, on Yoshiko.

Back upstairs, I heat water for my morning tea, listening to the wet glass pot sizzle on the burner as I butter my toast and skin a banana. I leaf through yesterday's paper, the September 10, 2001 *Vancouver Sun*. As I decorate my toast with slices of fruit, a headline catches my eye: UGLY RACISM CONFERENCE ENDS: CANADA STAYED AT UN MEETING, BUT VOICED "STRONG OBJECTIONS" TO FINAL DECLARATION. I bite into my toast and continue reading, crumbs spraying over the newsprint and onto my lap. I read that, after the USA and Israel withdrew from the UN World Conference Against Racism in South Africa, Canada objected to the classification of slavery as a crime against humanity and to any reference of Israel's treatment of Palestinian refugees as racially prejudiced. Brushing crumbs from my lap, I twist in my chair to check if the water is boiling. Inside the transparent walls of the pot, the water spins languidly around, like a bird circling under a storm about to break.

AT THE UNIVERSITY, FINGERS of early sunlight play across the tables of the coffee shop. "Looks like it's going to be a sunny day," I chirp at the barista as I order a chai latte. She smiles feebly and passes me my change.

"Haven't you heard?" the man in line behind me scolds.

I turn to face him. He meets my eyes but doesn't offer anything more. I turn back to the counter and pick up my chai latte. As a trickle and then as a stream and finally as a torrent, the noise of the radio in the background begins to penetrate my consciousness. I hear the tremor now in the reporter's voice: *The second tower has fallen. The mayor is calling for an evacuation of lower Manhattan.*

"What happened?" I turn back to the man behind me. His ear is cocked toward the speakers. "What happened?" I tug at his sleeve.

I TAKE A SEAT near the windows in the university café. On the radio, the anchorman announces that a fourth plane has crashed at an unknown location. I wrap my palms around my steaming mug and stare down at my arms crawling with goose pimples.

All my life I have been waiting for something significant to happen and reveal my destiny. Now I wonder, what needs to occur before I say to hell with a mediocre, ordinary life?

Something terrible could have happened the day Matthew took me cliff jumping in Lynn Canyon Park. Each line drawing on the billboards in the parking lot read like a horror story of death by treacherous under-tows, entrapment by rotating debris, failure to clear outcrops of rock, hyperthermia-inducing temperatures, and fatal impact with water.

We'll start by going down this waterslide, Matthew shouted over the steady roar, pointing off the suspension bridge to where the river snaked between the cliffs underneath us before shooting out in a mad spray to plunge into a swirl of white spume in the canyon below. *The drop off the falls is only about thirty feet,* he said, sensing my fear. *From there we can continue on down the circuit if you're game for higher jumps.*

As I followed Matthew to the other side of the bridge and scrambled down after him to the river's edge, I wondered if he was an insane dare-devil or if I was overly cautious. Standing there on the rocks above the falls, where the river was transparent and calm, I watched Matthew wade out into the pool to where the water narrowed. Climbing over a lip of rock at the top of the slide, he sat down and, with a whoop, let the river carry him twisting and turning with the bends of its channel into a milky spray where he disappeared over the top of the falls.

It's not that I wanted to die; it's that a colourless still life shaded in with regret for risks not taken seemed the worse arrangement. Without warning, I found myself standing thigh-deep in the river at the head of the natural pipe. The current was so strong I could barely keep my footing, and the frigid water numbed my feet so that I had difficulty feeling underfoot.

In a moment of hesitation, I imagined allowing the river to pull me downward with it on its centuries-old journey. I imagined plummeting off those falls to spin about in the mad white water as if in a washing machine, around and around, over myself, head banging into my knees and against rocks, having no idea which way was up, which was down, what my life was worth other than that it had been beautiful because it had been mine.

I climbed out of that river, back over the rocks and onto the path. As I waited shivering on the suspension bridge for Matthew to climb back up the cliffside, I pondered my reasons for pursuing financial security at the expense of self-realization. The adventure of being thrown over a waterfall was one I could do without, but what would it take for me to risk the plunge, I wondered, into the unknown of a creative life, surrendering to the overwhelming currents of my artistic impulse?

Sipping on a warm chai latte and listening to the news reports of the tragedy in New York, I am reminded yet again of the transience of my life. So I ask myself the same questions as I did in Lynn Canyon that afternoon, only to find I still don't have the answers. Do I put everything on the line to be an artist? Or do I continue to carve out a comfortable life of conformity?

Hanako and the Cherry Blossoms

The days that follow are a haze of graphic images and reports—people hurling themselves from office windows, towers aflame and perforated with planes. Page by page, report by report, the tragedy is disseminated for digestion. I find myself wandering amidst the burnt smell of coffee beans in the university café, hovering over expectation, trying to get a handle on what has happened and what has not.

"You're in my philosophy class." The theatre student has set her cappuccino down on my table and is pulling out a chair. "Freaky, isn't it?" she asks, indicating with a nod the front page of a newspaper next to me on the windowsill.

"So how . . ." I begin but lose my nerve. Why is she befriending me? "So who do you think is responsible?"

She shrugs and picks her teeth with the corner of her napkin. "They're saying there might be links to the Taliban."

"Who?"

She flicks the blue strand of her bob from her eyes and leans across the tabletop. "It's a sad fact but true—different lives have different values. You shoot a woman in the head in a country where she has no rights, and even when Afghani women risk their lives to film a public execution, no international news station will broadcast it. Not BBC, not CNN. It takes Americans getting killed—people whose lives have a perceived value—to get the world indignant." I stare at her as she continues. "All this talk about justice is a bunch of meaningless words. The United States has the highest rate of incarceration in the world. The only time the American government worries about justice is when it needs to find a plausible excuse to try out new war toys. Now, you see, human rights atrocities in Afghanistan are suddenly making headlines. . . . What? Am I shocking you?"

"But what can we do about it?" I edge my chair forward. *"Huh?"* I demand, the accusation in my voice surprising me. "What can we do?"

She sips her cappuccino, leaving behind a bit of milk foam on her top lip. I watch her tongue lick it off. I watch her mouth dance over her chin. I realize she is explaining something, but I can't follow because I'm seeing her death. I'm seeing that she will grow old and die. With her demise, all of her cherished memories will dissolve. I see that everything she fights for now is for the benefit of future generations. I see that she breathes and yet already she is dying. I see that life is despair and that hope is but an illusion to mask the unbearable spasm that is being born, enduring, and giving way to the inevitable.

I ask her to repeat herself.

"It's a decision we all have to make," she says softly.

What decision? I want to ask her. No matter how we flail against the coming darkness, against the injustices of this world, our mouths screaming out against the absurdity of pain, in the end worms creep into our windpipes and stifle our cries.

"We have to fight back," she explains. "In every way possible. We have to stand up for the right and never back down for fear, or out of sorrow."

"But why bother? What's the point when life is brutish and short?"

She smiles mischievously and withdraws from her bag a dog-eared copy of Albert Camus's *The Rebel*. The first chapters are this week's assigned reading for our philosophy class, homework I have yet to complete. With a silver-ringed finger, she beckons me to read out the sentence she indicates. I follow her blue-painted fingernail that prances from word to word, my words barely audible: *"I cry I don't believe in anything and everything is absurd, but I cannot doubt my cry, and I have to at least believe in my protestation. The first and only evidence thus given me, inside this absurd experience, is revolt."*

I look up. Her eyes meet mine, penetrating my consciousness, assessing all that is in my mind and explaining it back to me. She returns the manuscript to her bag. We lean back in our chairs. We lift our mugs in unison, our mouths opening at the same time, surging and swelling, throats rising and falling. Small and lost amongst the atoms of the planets, we swallow. My chai slides down cold, snake-like, into the pit of my stomach. I try not to fidget and break the spell, but the edge of my chair has numbed my thighs.

I shift my legs and, outside the café, a woman yells at a man. The glass pane blocks out the sound, but we can see the man throw an embarrassed look our way. I glance down at my fingers where they twiddle the hem of my sweater.

"You make a strong argument," I admit, tucking my hands under my hips. "I mean, how do you put it into words? The injustice lying like a worm at the heart of the world, and then the choice everyone is forced to make: to care or not to care." My eyes meet briefly with hers again— Hana, I've just remembered her name is *Hana*—but I don't know what else to say, so I look out the window at the woman who has begun to cry.

"Relax," the theatre student says, reaching out to stroke my arm.

From her fingernail at my wrist, my eyes climb up her arm to settle at her throat. The hollow there swells and falls away again, her breaths slight rasps that lift a strand of hair that has fallen across her cheek. Here is someone following her ambitions in theatre without fear, it would seem, of the multiple possibilities for artistic failure.

"Okay, enough about politics already," she says. "I'm Hana by the way."

"Yes, I remember from our introductions in class. I'm Helene." I cross my arms. "So where are you from . . . originally?"

She looks at me briefly but doesn't answer. She tears open a sugar packet and, dumping its contents on the table, forms a white pile with her blue fingernail. The man outside the window walks away, and the woman sinks to the curb with her face in her hands.

"He's not coming back," I remark. "They never do. . . ."

"I'm so sick of people asking me where I'm from," Hana says, ignoring my remark. "It's like this overwhelming need to classify, and the easiest category after sex is ethnicity."

I stare at the mess she has made on the table. "Sorry, I don't mean to pry. I'm just curious about your background and where you grew up."

"I grew up in Cranbrook, in the East Kootenays. Been there?"

"No, but I know where it is." I want to ask how her family ended up in that remote Southeastern corner of British Columbia but don't dare.

Hana picks up her spoon and coaxes the sugar into a pyramid. Bent over in concentration, she shapes and reshapes the mound. Without looking up from her pile, she explains, "My grandparents, on both my father's and my mother's sides, were forced into a camp in New Denver for Japanese Canadians during the Second World War by the Canadian government. They were living in Vancouver at the time. They lost everything. Furniture and heirlooms and photographs and souvenirs—everything except for what they could carry in their suitcases. Once they were released and the war was over, they resettled in Nelson. They made sure to speak only English to their kids so that people would see them as good Canadians. So neither of my parents speak much Japanese. When I was born, my dad named me Hanako, after my great-grandmother. It means *flower girl*. The short form I use, Hana, means *blossom*. The cherry trees were in full blossom in Nelson when I was born. That's where I grew up, before we moved to Cranbrook for my dad's job—" She falls silent all of a sudden, shutting off the flow of her words like a faucet.

"My dad named me too," I tell her, regretting my previous snap judgment of her as a spoilt rich kid the first day of our philosophy class.

She stares down at her sugar pyramid.

"My dad," I repeat. "He must have. Because my name is French, you know? He was from Lyon in France. He died in a motorcycle crash when I was two."

"I'm sorry," Hana says, looking up at me.

"I'm sorry too. I mean, for what happened to your family. And for my dad too. My mom won't even talk about it."

Reaching across the table, Hana brushes the back of her palm across my cheek. Her touch makes me want to spill out the tale of Katie's sorrow drowned out at the bottom of so many bottles over the years, but instead I tug at the bottom of my sweater and clamp my elbows to my ribcage in silence. Pulling back her hand, Hana licks her pinkie and stabs it through the peak of the sugar pyramid. White granules spray away from her violence. "Don't worry," she says, "I hate talking about my family too. Other than my dad, who phones me on the sly,"—she pauses to lick her baby finger—"I try not to think about them. About all those black scenes of my teenage years."

Living in Doubt

I scrub my apartment floors listening to the news streaming in from the radio, a steady flow of on-the-hour reports and commentary. Much of the coverage paints a picture of an unsafe world where mass surveillance and *humane* methods of torture could become necessary to safeguard freedom. A few detractors argue civil liberties and human rights have become such a joke there is no longer any freedom to safeguard. Between these poles, various experts debate the universality of democracy and freedom, the historical achievements of Islam, the possible sources of the anthrax letters, and the reopening of the New York Stock Exchange.

I feel like I've lost my faith.

I feel numb.

Since my encounter with Hana in the coffee shop, during which she spoke with ease about current events and the Taliban, I've been trying to stay informed. I leave the radio on, a constant purr in the background, a white-noise soundtrack for what feels like a hamster run on this North American trajectory of school, metro, drinking, sex, dating, recreational drugs, sleep, marriage, traffic, work, kids, affairs, prescription drugs, divorce, remarriage, kids' graduations, kids' marriages, retirement, RV camping, nursing home, death. The more I listen to the news, the more everything seems meaningless; everything seems like chaos.

Is there no definite, absolute truth?

Kneeling here before the bathtub, scrubbing soap scum off the walls, I listen to the anchorman speak of loved ones lost in New York, these tragic victims and heroes of our time. Accompanying this refrain is a silence: there is no coverage of the Nigerian riots between Christians and Muslims that have claimed a thousand lives over the past ten days—a story I found digging online. *You're editing history*, I want to write to the station. I've been listening attentively. I've been following all of your reports, as they happen. You've told me about mouldy public housing, you've told me about the collapse of a major airline in Australia, and you've told me about Osama bin Laden being wanted dead or alive. So why this vacuum of words in which other casualties—in this case, African—remain unreported? Where is the collective grieving and memorial for those loved ones, also mourned over by their families, their lives cut equally short?

THE UNIVERSITY CAMPUS SEEMS deserted; the two students I do cross on the way to the computer labs keep their eyes cast low. Sliding into a seat in front of a free computer, I sign into my student account and click on REGISTER. For the past two weeks, I've been lulled to sleep by Financial Accounting, Capital Markets, Labour Negotiations, and Business Statistics. I select these courses and click DELETE, deregistering myself from a bachelor of commerce degree.

Only the philosophy class has survived.

I stare at the computer screen, my heart pounding. What have I done with an impulsive click of the mouse? I feel queasy as I realize there is no going back: admission to the commerce program is competitive, and the classes have waiting lists.

I scroll through the French courses, feeling like my mind has gone blank. My hands tremble on the keyboard as I register in the first available grammar class and conversation lab. Then I browse the fine arts section. All the studio classes are closed, so I scan the art history courses until I find one with a spot left.

The breeze as I leave the lab is nippy with the damp, woodsy smell of fall in the air. A squirrel cheeps at me, and I jump. The sky overhead is brooding and threatening rain. As I head toward the bus loop, I recall the classes I have just dropped, the life that was within my reach that I have just thrown away, and I feel short of breath. Waiting in the line-up for the bus, I shift my weight from foot to foot. My legs are restless, and I have got to move. With no bus in sight, I take off up the sidewalk toward home, some twelve kilometres away on the other side of Point Grey and the Shaughnessy mansions.

A few kilometres into my walk, scattered raindrops begin to fall as I'm waiting for a pedestrian light. I flip up my hoodie and continue on, determined to outpace the surge of panic on my heels. Soon the downpour begins in earnest, and I'm forced to take refuge under a bus shelter. Pacing back and forth, hands thrust deep into my pockets, I peer through the showers at the church across the street. The billboard on the front lawn reads: YOU'RE NOT ALONE. JESUS LOVES YOU. Those bright plastic letters, a burst of yellow under the rain, confront me with the godlessness of my life. Waiting for the cloudburst to peter out, I stare out into the rain feeling detached and unreal.

When the shower has tapered off, I step out from under the bus shelter, and the tires of a passing bicycle spit muddy water at me. Pant legs soaked, I slog onward under the fine mist, reflecting on those rare moments when I manage to lose myself in a painting, letting the image wash through me and over me until I become one with the shape and the colour. The more I get caught up in the flow of mixing pigment and working the palette, the more the world fades away until I experience the ecstasy of complete absorption. In this state the hours escape me. Engrossed in transcribing my mind's image onto the external canvas, I forget to eat or sleep. When the painting is complete and I emerge from this trance, it is to the sensations of timelessness and connectedness. I am exhausted yet filled with clarity. It is then that I see most clearly that, at the end of every analysis, the only definite answer is a question mark and so living in doubt is, for me, the only honest way to be in this world.

Thunder grumbles in the sky. The rain picks up to a steady drizzle. I arrive at my apartment drenched. Peeling off my sodden hoodie, I strip off my jeans and the T-shirt plastered to my skin. I wrap up in a blanket, my skin clammy and cold, for some reason remembering a flu that kept me home from school as a teenager and how, half awakening from the fog of the fever, I found Lyle reciting a prayer over me. I remember realizing as if in a flash that the Christian Father, the Jewish Yahweh, the Muslim Allah, the Hindu Vishnu, the enlightened Buddha, and the prophets Moses, Jesus, and Muhammad were all revered as male beings. I knew in that moment, in becoming a woman, I could never be a believer.

Settling onto my couch now, I flip on the radio. The force of the rain falling outside my windows dampens out the city lights. I wrap the blanket around my shivering body, my teeth chattering and my feet like ice. They are citing Bush's speech again: *Make no mistake, the United States will hunt down and punish . . .* This proselytization of the goodness of violent retribution makes me feel like an outsider, like an ant marching against the mowing of the lawn with a sign that reads YOU'RE DESTROYING OUR WORLD, and I feel like my voice, for or against, carries no weight at all.

Unable to warm up, I search out a pair of thick wool socks. Still, no matter how many layers I pull on—flannel pyjamas, an old sweater, my winter parka—I can't shake off the chill that has settled deep inside.

WARMTH FINALLY COMES AFTER a third cup of tea. I doze off on the sofa in the semi-darkness. I dream I am alone in Matthew's room in Japan, which consists of a cot, a bookshelf, and a chair. The door opens and he strides in. He drops a stack of philosophy, French, and art history textbooks onto the chair and meets me at the foot of the bed.

I want to ask him about my diary and insist he return it, but when I lift my tongue to speak, it lies like a thick, drugged worm inside my mouth.

It seems I am also invisible. A book slides off the chair and smacks the floor. Matthew flops onto the short cot and closes his eyes. A voiceless, unseen ghost, I bend to pick up the book. It is Milan Kundera's *The Book of Laughter and Forgetting*. Matthew recommended it to me this summer, but after ploughing through the anthology of Nietzsche's works, I didn't have time to read Kundera's novel before classes began.

So now I crack open the novel for a browse, but in this dream the pages are blank. I bend over Matthew's sleeping figure. *What have you done with the words?* I demand, my voice ever elusive as my lips move in the soundless shapes of a mute. *More importantly, what have you done with my words, my memories, my journal?* I pound his chest with impalpable fists. A look of apprehension flashes across his face as he begins to realize someone, or something, is in the room with him. *With what diabolical cruelty have you violated the privacy of my inner world, brought me under your surveillance, and bared me wide open like a blank page on which to inscribe the manifesto of your will?*

A feverish laughter wakes me up. I break out in a cold sweat, not daring to move until I can locate the source of the mirth. Staring up at the ceiling, I don't recognize my apartment until, after a long silence, I turn onto my side and float back down into the body curled up on the sofa. As I regain consciousness, I grasp that I am the one who has been laughing, and I realize that I must be running a temperature.

I get up to find some fever medication. The clock reads slightly after midnight. I haven't eaten since breakfast. I've dropped out of my degree program. I've walked home twelve kilometres in the rain and caught cold. I stagger to the bed and fall into an anxious half-sleep, weighed down by a feeling of impending doom: I don't understand men. I've never understood men.

Confession

For the second time this week, I scan the bulletin board outside the climbing club room. I find Matthew's postcard tucked under a posting for a used pair of skis. The photograph on the front features a red bridge spanning a fishpond. I pull out the thumbtack pinning the postcard to the board and flip over the card. The words on the back, penned in a tight cursive hand, are like a secret code into which I have not been initiated; I can only imagine the connections linking their symbols to reality.

> *Hello everyone:*
> *I hope this finds you in great health and spirits. We just got back from an amazing trip to Gunma, where we did a bit of climbing. Other than that, we're settling into our new routines and training for Mont Fuji this winter. My Japanese is improving rapidly now that I'm forced to speak it everyday. Come and visit if you can! Yoshiko sends her love.*
> *Keep in touch,*
> *Matthew.*

I'm still staring at the postcard when Hana comes out of the adjacent club room, whose door is decorated with a rainbow flag and a new sign reading QUEER STUDENT ASSOCIATION. "Helene!" she says.

Keep in touch, I'm thinking. *Visit if you can?*

"What's wrong?"

I force a smile. "Nothing. I'm fine."

In the otherwise empty hallway, Hana reaches for the postcard. The authority of her tiny stature—she barely arrives at my chin even in three-inch heels—unnerves me, and I hand it over. Her eyes scan back and forth across Matthew's slanted lines, and I recall them one by one as she is reading. When she is through, she looks up and shrugs. I stare down at the white strip of floor between us, sliding sideways along the wall away from her, feeling like a distended balloon about to blow.

"Who is Matthew?" She searches my face. "Who is Yoshiko?"

I take the postcard back and pin it to the bulletin board. Ever since Matthew stole my journal, my innards keep falling out at the most inopportune of moments, in the most public of places. Although I try to hold my peace now, Hana is a bother, pecking and cajoling me like a mother hen until I find my sneakered feet following the path of her stilettos. After a stop in the cafeteria for coffees, we sit on the bottom step of the stairs outside the student union building under a greying autumn sky.

"Hana!" Out of the ebb and flow of the crowd climbing up and down the stairs, a woman has come to a standstill at our feet.

Hana hugs her in greeting. "Amani, this is Helene. She's telling me about a *guy* she dated this summer." Hana tilts an eyebrow upward at Amani and kicks away a yellowed leaf with the toe of her stiletto.

Amani has dark almond eyes, light brown skin, and a ribbon of black hair that falls to her waistline. "That's cool," she says. "I'm a sucker for relationship talk, no matter the orientation." She sits down on the other side of Hana and helps herself to what is left of Hana's coffee.

Hana recaps my story, but I don't follow her account as I get caught up in the flutter of the leaves shifting across the square. The lateness of the afternoon and the year have snuck up on me. The day is dying; darkness encroaches on all sides, waiting in the underbrush and the shadows of the buildings.

Hana grabs my wrist. "Don't allow yourself to get hung up on someone who doesn't care about you. Respect yourself enough to let go."

"Now we're talking," Amani says with a laugh. "Now we're getting somewhere." She covers her mouth in mock remorse when Hana gives her a sharp look.

"What?" I ask, missing the point.

Amani shrugs. "Hana can explain. Unrequited love is her area of expertise."

DUSK GATHERS. WE MOVE away from the student union building so that Hana can smoke. Amani leaves to catch her bus home. On a mossy bench under a maple tree, I watch the blue flame of Hana's lighter eat into the end of a cigarette. Clouds of smoke puff up around her, dispersing into the foggy evening air. "It's so gloomy," she murmurs, the cigarette hanging off her bottom lip as she drops the lighter back into her handbag, the fingers of her free hand splayed out on the damp wood of the bench.

My lips part, and words trickle out. Soon they gather into brooks and flow out as a river, images and feelings sloshing and slapping together. I want to float everything out before Hana, arrange the currents into some sort of order, talk her through this deluge of passion, get all the undercurrents outside of me, outside this cramped tank in my head—so that I can find the source from where the trouble first sprang, the moment when everything went sour.

"Sorry, what's that?" she murmurs as she exhales, smoke escaping in two blue wisps from either side of her lips.

"Nothing."

"Oh, I thought you said something." She laughs and gives her cigarette a twirl and flick, knocking its ash to the gravel at our feet. "I can tell you what you are, Helene, and I hardly know you. You're a real sucker for mulling over your disappointments. But we're going to fix that with a little fun. I'm having a party at my house this weekend and you're going to come."

Desperate Lives

Twenty minutes early for my philosophy class, I wait in the hallway for another class in the same room to let out. Spotting two payphones by the pop dispensers, I realize with a twinge of guilt that I never called Katie to see if she made it back to Windeal. I walk over to the closest phone.

When she answers, I hear the drone of television in the background.

"Sorry, honeybun. *Days of our Lives* is on. Can you call back later?"

"Are you kidding me? With everything that's been going on in the world, that's all you've got to say to me?"

"All right, don't preach at me. Did I tell you Lyle and I have legally separated?"

"I mean the terrorist attacks, the anthrax letters. The Americans invading Afghanistan and now—"

"*Days* is on, Helene. Can't you phone back in twenty minutes?"

"—that plane crashing into a building in Milan."

"Honeybun, I don't feel like going into all of this today, all right? I'm going through enough as it is."

"Don't you ever think about anything other than yourself?"

"*Please*, Helene. I can't do this today."

"I'm a freak and it's all your fault," I spit into the receiver. "You never taught me a thing about culture. Just a bit of country music during your dancing years and then *Jesus says* ever since you married the control freak. But I know you know art. You had a private school education."

"Oh, quit badgering me about all that. You know I didn't have the money for art supplies or private lessons. I did the best I could—"

"I've dropped out of the bachelor of commerce program."

She is so silent I can hear the dramatic tears of a soap actress in the background.

"I dropped out because—"

"I should have known you wouldn't stick with it. You're just like your father in that way."

If I were to sketch the figure at the payphone, I would trace the horizontal line of her arm braced atop the telephone box. Using a graphite pencil, I would draw in the shadow of her body cast by the natural light streaming in through the hallway's floor-to-ceiling windows. I would complete the sketch with her oval head bowed down, its outward curve where hair meets neckline, the vertical line of her rib cage, the rectangle of pelvis, the angle of her knee.

I hang up the handset, confused as to why I allow Katie to hurt me. I should know better by now than to seek her approval. I make my way into the empty classroom, taking a seat near the back. I am so tired of carrying these bitter childhood memories around. If only I knew how, I would brush them clean and clear, so that I could paint on top of them new works, recycle them into new paintings, leaving only the faintest ghosts of residual line and colour to peek through my new compositions.

THE PROFESSOR YANKS A yellow notepad out from under a pile of text-books on his desk, the top page of which catches on a book cover and tears. He looks up and shrugs. "Sleep deprivation.

"But seriously," he continues a few minutes later, once he has flattened out his notes with a smooth of his hand, "what if we have no control over what we do?" He holds up the torn sheet of his notepad as an example.

"The old dilemma of free will verses determinism," smart aleck in the front row interjects. I've been dying to throw a book at the back of that guy's head ever since I joined this class. Still, the professor's question has me wondering: what if Matthew had no choice but to fall for Yoshiko when he met her in Thailand? What if he didn't want to cheat but it was written that for six weeks he would betray her trust and raise my hopes?

What if it was my destiny to be smitten by a globetrotting daredevil of a thief who trotted off in search of new adventure at the end of a summer?

After digging masking tape out of his briefcase and, with some ceremony, knitting his notes back together, the professor peers up at us over his spectacles. "So," he repeats, signalling for smart aleck to keep silent, "what if we have no control?"

I look at Hana. Does she believe in destiny? She flips a pen around her fingers in a tight, fast circle, back and forth, back and forth. Her French friend slouches at her side, doodling on the back cover of a spiral-bound notebook. I keep waiting for Hana's pen to clatter to the floor, but smart aleck draws back my attention before it can fall, as he blurts out, "If we have no control, then there must be a master plan—"

The professor puts up his hand, signalling for smart aleck to keep quiet, and nods at Hana, who has set down her pen and raised her hand. "Maybe," she says, "there's no plan, only the limitations of our genetic make-up and cultural development. Maybe we all start out free, but then our education, our nationality, our language, our sex, our social class, etcetera, wear down what initial freedom we had into non-existence.

"For example, imagine there was only one person in the universe and nothing else. That person could occupy any space he or she wanted. But what about if we add a chair? That person is still theoretically free, except now he or she can't occupy the same space as the molecules of the chair, so somehow this person's liberty has been diminished. If we then add a second person, the first person is no longer even free to sit on the chair when it is occupied by the second. Imagine now that we add many more chairs and many more people—"

"Over six billion people," her French friend cuts in, looking up from his doodling.

"Exactly." Hana smiles at him. "Our free will gets very small indeed."

I find myself thinking of Matthew and his favourite philosopher, Nietzsche. What would they think of what Hana has just said? They would certainly agree that, for this very reason, freedom is the privilege of the few, those strong and driven enough to throw off the shackles of their given culture and language, its values, its mores. Yet is this possible,

Matthew? Is it? Tell me, no matter how far you roam on this planet, will you ever escape these unchosen yet tenacious aspects of self?

OUR PROFESSOR IS NOT a good-looking fellow, but gossip has it he is nevertheless quite successful at seducing young men. Gawking at him now, I wonder what his secret is. He has a pockmarked face, skin as worn and tired as a battleground. His crown emerges smooth as an egg from tufts of brown hair. In spite of the rumours of his unscrupulous exploits with some of his students in Germany two years ago, he is still here teaching, even flaunting what is to others a scandal by publishing a collection of short stories about his numerous conquests. While I, on the other hand, am still mortified at the thought of Matthew reading my far less scandalous diary. Staring at this professor, I wonder if I will ever have the courage to conduct my affairs with similar audacity, refusing to be held back by what others may think.

AFTER CLASS, I HEAD to the women's washroom where I find Hana reapplying eyeliner in front of the mirrors. She stops when she sees me in the glass and turns with a smile. The fluorescent light blanches her face and my reflection in the mirror.

"You're coming to my birthday party on Saturday, right?"

"Yeah, sure. Where?"

"At my place." She reaches into her shoulder bag and withdraws a notepad and pen. She scribbles down an address and a time and rips off the sheet and hands it to me. I glance at the paper. She lives just off Commercial Drive, the counter-culture hub of East Vancouver where many immigrant Italian, Portuguese, Vietnamese, Latino, and African families have settled amongst the vegetarians, environmental activists, hemp lovers, punks, and lesbians.

"I work at La Grotta restaurant," I tell her, watching as she turns back to the mirror to touch up her lip gloss. "I've been thinking of moving into the neighbourhood. How do you like living there?"

She shrugs. "I like the community." She drops the eyeliner and lip gloss into the zippered compartment of her bag.

Silence falls between us. "I should probably tell you," she starts then stops. She digs a cigarette out of her purse and lets it hang unlit off her bottom lip. The corners of that lip slide toward her jawline like heavy wool coats about to slip off their hangers. She seems all of a sudden fragile, as if made out of glass.

"What?" I squint down at her, my eyebrows drawn together.

She sighs. Removes the cigarette from her mouth and blows her hair out of her eyes as she picks up her shoulder bag. "It's just that . . . there might be a speck of drama. My partner and I are in the midst of another breakup. She's been sleeping around on me again. Just so you know, as everyone else already seems to. I don't want you to be the only one at my party who doesn't know what's going on. Anyway, I'm determined to have a good time no matter what."

"Okay." I turn to watch her go. As the washroom door swings closed behind her, in that instant, as the door clicks shut, my certainty begins to crumble. What if Hana's life and the lives of all the others I've stamped as privileged—James's, Christine's, Matthew's—are difficult lives, are desperate lives? What if within each is buried a tragedy, waiting to be unearthed, lurking beneath the surface, patiently leaking its poison into the ground soil until its moment is ripe?

Laughter and Forgetting

The address Hana gave me leads to the main floor of a brightly painted purple-and-yellow heritage house. I press the doorbell. After a while, a tall blond wearing a tube dress opens the door, her hair a flaxen shawl on tawny shoulders. The bass of a blues song escapes from deep within the house as she stands there, hand on her hip, leaning into the doorframe. Past her silhouette, I catch a glimpse of a crowd in the kitchen.

"Here for the big birthday bash?"

I nod, hugging myself as I rub the goose pimples breaking out across my arms from the fall chill in the air. "This is Hana's place, right?"

"Uh-huh. Mine too." She turns and I step into the house after her. Setting down my bag in the hallway, I bend over to pull off my flats and add them to the pile of shoes in the open closet.

"Helene!" Hana materializes through the archway of the kitchen. Her breath is warm on my neck and smelling of alcohol as she hugs me. She shuts the door behind me, takes my hand, and leads me into the kitchen, shouting during a momentary lapse in the music, "It's my party, and I'll cry if I want to." When a new song starts up, she introduces me to her many friends and acquaintances from the theatre department and Vancouver Film School. Nodding and waving and shaking some hands, I make my way through the throng after her until we are stopped at the refrigerator by a certain Jean-Pierre from Quebec, who drapes his arm over our shoulders and leaves out his H's: "*appy birt'day 'ana.*"

Slipping out from under his arm as he engages Hana in a conversation about an upcoming play, I peek my head through the second archway into the darkened living room. As my eyes adjust from the bright light of the kitchen to the low light given off by the bottle-green glow of the aquarium on the coffee table, I make out an occupied futon sofa and a couple of mismatched armchairs, as well as three tall paintings on canvas leaned up against the wall.

"Hana?" I ask, interrupting her conversation by pulling on her arm. I point to the nearest dizzying display of fabric and paint. "Are they yours?"

She shakes her head. "Sandy's the painter." She tilts her head toward the blond who answered the door and then turns back to Jean-Pierre.

I leave her then to crouch before the nearest canvas, a wild arrangement of buttercup yellow and strips of orange taffeta. Edging along on my heels, I work my way to the second, on which I make out in the dim light a whorl of blue pointed ovals, shaped like eyes, within each of which are painted even more ovals, each set growing smaller and revealing more within. "Amazing," I say to no one in particular, reaching out to stroke the raised texture of the dried acrylic paint as I inch my way toward the third. "It's like looking through a—"

"Kaleidoscope?" offers Sandy as she waltzes past me, pausing in the archway of the kitchen, further dimming the light.

Forced to abandon my study of her paintings for lack of light, I twist on my heels toward the aquarium, where people are passing around a joint. Beyond their silhouettes, sliding glass doors open out onto a veranda. Standing, I recognize Hana's friend Amani out there in the dusk, leaning into the railing.

"So do you paint?" Sandy asks, setting a bottle of beer on the floor as she kneels in front of the stereo.

"N—n—no," I stutter, startled by this question. "I mean, not really."

"So you're an arts enthusiast?"

"Something like that." Disappointed with my answer but determined not to let it show, I tell her, "Your paintings are great. Are you taking classes?"

"Uh-huh." She flips through a case of CDs.

"Where?"

"Emily Carr."

Emily Carr Institute of Art and Design, one of Canada's foremost art schools. I wander over to the sliding glass doors. Through the spaces in the patio railing, I make out the train tracks that lead down the Cut toward Pacific Central Station. The skyline above the tracks has brightened with the reflected light of the city night, and at their far end, the Science World globe flashes like a giant golf ball on the horizon.

All at once, the loudspeaker beside me lets out a gurgle of trumpet notes like the pitter-patter of mouse feet running up piano keys, and I recognize the opening to a song by Count Basie. I turn back toward the kitchen, longing for the status of artist, overwhelmed by this jealous need to create, fearful I may never display canvases of my own. Or that if I do, it will be to discover that I have no talent after all.

"You remember Laurent?" Hana asks when I return to the kitchen.

The French guy from our philosophy class holds out his hand. "*'elene*, right?" He pronounces my name the French way, silencing the H the way I imagine my father would do. "I remember you, mademoiselle," he says, taking my hand. His long fingers, quilted in furled black hairs that climb out over the length of his spider-leg knuckles, wrap around my palm to curl up over my wrist.

I withdraw my fingers from his lingering handshake and point back and forth between Hana and him. "So how'd you two meet?"

"I volunteered this summer to be paired with an international exchange student as a local contact," Hana explains, placing her hand on her hip to stare up at Laurent. "But I won't be signing up for someone new next semester," she turns to tell me, "because babysitting him has turned out to be a full-time job. I mean his English has improved *a lot*. I couldn't understand a word he said at first."

"*Babysit* who? *Moi?* The problem is she always talks too fast," Laurent tells me. "Come." He beckons me to accompany him into the living room. "She is boring you too, no?"

I glance questioningly at Hana. She gives a wave of her hand to indicate I should follow him. He points out a spot for me on the futon and settles next to me, even though the other side is empty. Across from us, cuddled up in an armchair now, Amani is necking with a girl with a short red bob. Between kisses, she takes hits from a joint. I wave hello from my side of the aquarium and she waves lazily back, her long braid trailing down into their laps. The music changes to something slower.

"'*elene* is a French name, no?" Laurent asks, leaning into me. He smells like laundry detergent and lemon soap. "Do you speak French?" A certain irritation takes hold of me: why he is staring at me? Why is he leaning in so close? Why are his fingers, with their soft black hairs, brushing down the length of my hand a whisper of a second too long?

"What's wrong?" he asks when I lower my eyes from the tight locks that adorn his light brown eyes and long straight nose, a Roman nose, to the boyish line of his shoulder under his red T-shirt and down the length of his pale, woolly arm—

"Nothing," I murmur, trying to hide my discomfort with his easy invasion of my personal space.

The telephone rings behind us. Laurent reaches over the back of the futon to lift it from the table. "*Allô?* Yes, a moment please." He holds the phone aside and shouts, "'*ana!*"

Hana saunters in from the kitchen; then, seeing the telephone, she steps more quickly, whispering as she takes it from his hand, "Who is it?"

Laurent shrugs and turns back to me, reaching forward to grab his beer off the coffee table. As he bends back to finish it off, I drink in his exposed neck, his pointed Adam's apple rising and falling as he gulps. A glance back at Hana shows she is still on the phone, her pinkie in her ear to block the din of the party. Pulling a pack of cigarettes from her pocket, she wedges a fresh stick at the side of her mouth.

Laurent plonks down the empty can on the table. "Canadian style," he says, laughing. A goldfish in the aquarium swims toward the can and bobs against the glass.

"What?" I ask him.

"The way I just drink my *brewski*."

"Oh." I chuckle and lean back into the futon. He follows suit, resting his head next to mine. His hair smells windswept, like fresh laundry hung to dry in a breeze.

I let my gaze wander around the room to where Sandy sits cross-legged in the bedroom doorway, massaging the shoulders of an earthy granola type. Laurent leans in to ask me in a lowered voice, "Do you know Sandy and . . . *merde,* that other girl? I forget her name."

I shake my head. Before I can respond further, Hana lets out a whoop behind us. The murmur of conversation pauses, someone softens the music, and faces peer in through the archway of the kitchen. "Guess what?" Hana gushes as soon as she has everyone's attention. "Bard on the Beach, here I come!"

Cheers break out and I look to Laurent for an explanation. He reaches for Hana's hand and gives it a firm shake. *"Félicitations!"* he says. Catching sight of my bewildered face, he explains what seems obvious to everyone else, "She received a part in the Shakespeare Festival."

A FEW HOURS LATER, I wander into the kitchen, empty now except for the dirty glasses and bottles that line the counters. Sandy waltzes in from under an archway and, whipping open the refrigerator door, stands there indecisively. Her granola friend pads in after her, slipping an arm around Sandy's waist. I rinse two wine-stained cups under the faucet and watch as Sandy pulls out a bag of green grapes, offering a bunch to her friend. She pours the rest into a bowl and disappears through the archway, but her friend lingers, watching me sift through the empty bottles on the table until I find a few ounces of tequila near the back.

The girl stands there watching me as I pour the remainder of the tequila with some orange juice from the fridge into two glasses. "Love dies without chemistry," she remarks. Not sure how her comment concerns me, I glance up. She gazes back at me like a doe staring into headlights.

I shrug. "Maybe you have to work at it sometimes."

Her doe eyes continue to search me out, expectant, nervous. "Of course, if there was passion in the beginning, that energy must still be there now," she whispers. "Nothing in the universe disappears; it's only transformed."

I shrug again and, tucking a half-empty bag of corn chips under my arm, make my way back to the futon. Laurent slides over to make room for me. I hand him one of the tequila sunrises. Sipping our drinks, we watch Hana dance on a makeshift stage of two chairs pushed together under a disco ball strung from the light fixture on the ceiling. The ball flashes silver droplets of light around the room as she shimmies her skirted hips in time to a lament in Arabic.

"Her belly dancing is improving," Amani pronounces from the far end of the futon, knotting her black braid back in a bun.

"Yeah, because you've been giving her private lessons," her friend teases, flicking aside rust-red bangs to reveal a bindi. "It represents my third eye," she explains, when she catches me staring. I nod and pop another corn chip in my mouth.

Amani stands and claps her hands in rhythm. She moves in to circle Hana, tying her T-shirt in a knot under her breasts to bare her stomach. They dance together, Hana above on the chairs, Amani below on the carpet, their tummies rippling and swaying above pulsating hips, their shoulders writhing over heaving breasts, their hands clapping in time to the music. Hana's skirt falls a little lower, revealing a turquoise G-string, and Amani begins to sing undulating vowels that beguile the soul as she harmonizes with the singer.

Suddenly the music stops. Hana glares down at Sandy, who has turned off the stereo. "Telephone," Sandy says, her blond hair sweeping down her back and falling across one arm as she turns sharply back toward the bedroom. "It's your mom," she calls over her shoulder as she pulls shut the bedroom door.

Hana climbs off the chairs and picks up the receiver. I check the clock on the wall: a quarter to midnight. My eyes do a quick sweep of the nearly empty house; Amani and her friend start gathering up their things. I'm thinking I should do the same, but I'm too lazy and cozy in the deep embrace of the futon.

Hana throws the handset across the room into the empty armchair. We all turn to watch it bounce off the cushion with a thud onto the floor.

"She's insisting now that I see a psychiatrist," Hana says. "She's even found one on the Internet—"

"Come." Laurent pats the futon between us. "Sit down."

"—here in Vancouver. That's what she phoned for: to ask when I'm going to stop disgracing her family. It happens every couple of months. She's fine until someone asks if I have a boyfriend, or someone else's daughter gets married, and then she has to have a freaking nervous breakdown."

Laurent pats the futon again, but Hana only gives him a tired, cynical look before starting to collect the empties from around the room. I push myself up off the futon to help her.

"It's my party and I'll cry if I want to," she shouts toward the closed bedroom door, kicking an empty beer can up against it as she makes her way to the kitchen with an armload of bottles.

Following her into the kitchen, I lean back against the table and watch her fill the sink with hot water and dish soap. "My dad is the only person I've ever been able to count on," she says as she collects the dirty cups and glasses from the countertops and slides them one by one under the soapsuds. I hand her more glasses from the table. "He phoned me while my mom was out earlier to wish me Happy Birthday. That's all. None of her closed-minded bullshit." She pulls out a brown paper bag from between the fridge and the counter and begins to fill it with empties from the table.

"Here, let me do that." I take the bag from her and clear the table.

When she has finished the dishes, she bends down to reach deep into the cupboard under the sink. She emerges with an unopened bottle of red wine. "My secret stash," she explains, twisting off the cap and filling two wineglasses. She hands me one and we clink our glasses together.

"So how'd you meet Sandy, anyway?"

"At a poetry slam."

"You write?"

"No, Sandy does. Beautiful lines. *Cold, crisp stanzas with metallic finishes.* At least, that's how they were described in a recent review." Hana takes a rag from behind the faucet and wipes the table. "She's been published in quite a few journals too, but no book yet, except for a chapbook."

I watch her pull the rag across the tabletop, starting at the back. "How long have you been together?"

"Two and a half years, living together since the second month. I should stop caring. I should fall out of love with her poetry, her paintings. I should get on with my life. I'm not cut out for an open relationship, but there she is in the bedroom, *experimenting* again. At next month's poetry slam, she'll be telling the audience all about it."

I move our wineglasses to the table so Hana can wipe up the countertop. "Maybe she does it on purpose, to make you jealous," I suggest.

"Whatever her reason, I can't do it anymore. No matter how open she may be about it, I still feel betrayed each and every time."

Laurent waltzes into the kitchen, catching the tail end of Hana's sentence. "You know what we say in French? *L'amour rend fou*—love drives one mad."

Hana chucks the rag into the sink. She pours a third glass of wine and hands it to him. "Then here is to putting an end to the madness," she says, holding out her glass.

"Cheers to that," I say, clinking my glass with hers and then Laurent's.

In the Wee Small Hours

Sometime after midnight, after the last of the other guests have gone, I'm nestled into the crook of the futon's arm listening to Laurent explain the fear in Paris of an attack on the American Embassy. He is seated at the opposite end, with Hana in between us, her feet propped up next to the aquarium and an empty wine bottle on the coffee table.

Laurent explains that the *gendarmerie*—the French equivalent of the RCMP—has removed all the garbage cans from metro and train stations and replaced them with clear plastic bags hanging in metal skeletons. Public bathrooms have been boarded up against dangerous citizens. The national slogan is *Vigipirate*—a plan of vigilance against attack.

"I imagine a politician got bored at lunch, drew some pirates on his serviette and, *voilà*, invented this meaningless slogan," Laurent says.

Paris. So far away it's not real. I finish off the rest of my wine and set my glass down on the coffee table. I can see Laurent and hear his thick accent; aren't they proof enough of the country my father allegedly left for Canada? Yet what is this tale of police, bombs, and terrorists? That is not the Paris of my imagined homeland: a city where poets and artists commingle in cafés, their trails of perfume and cigarettes wafting through the streets.

While my thoughts have trailed off, Laurent has moved on to the war in Afghanistan. "*Et ben*, the bombing, you know. I am against it completely. It is so detached to push a button from high up in the sky. One does not have to see the carnage that way."

"Well, Bush would lose popular support for his War on Terror if there was any risk to American life, wouldn't he?" Hana says. "So the U.S. Army uses cluster bombs to ensure American soldiers don't get killed on the ground. Those rare few that do get immortalized in a full spread in *Time*."

"Yes, but what I find exasperating is the complete lack of objectivity in North American news reporting. It is more like a propaganda machine for what we call *impérialisme*, the new imperialism of gas and oil."

"What do you mean?" I ask Laurent.

Hana answers for him. "Afghan women have been fighting for basic human rights for years, but it's been virtually impossible for them to get coverage of their struggle. Some of them risked their lives to film the public executions of women in football stadiums and to distribute this footage to Western broadcasting stations. It was never aired." She takes a sip of her wine and continues, "Now, to bolster support for the American invasion, this footage is suddenly popping up everywhere—"

"Because, you see," Laurent cuts in, "the American government is exploiting the grief of its people after September 11 to bomb a pathway for its natural gas pipeline from the Caspian reserves through Afghanistan to the Arabian Sea."

"What?" I ask. "Now, you've really lost me."

"Yes, the Americans call their bombing *stratégique*. French journalism explains this *stratégie* quite differently than the news in North America. A new book just came out in France, written by two intelligence analysts, which explains this war was planned back in July, before September 11, by the Bush administration as a way to push through their pipeline project if the Taliban refused to comply with their plans."

"Well," Hana says, rolling a joint, "that would explain the bizarre series of articles I saw in *Time* last year, which basically tried to sanitize the Taliban rule. I can remember one in particular called 'Still No Place for the Ladies' that reported on the Taliban's authorization of an International Women's Day celebration. I remember thinking it was such a joke in terms of accurate reporting, as I had been following the Amnesty reports, and the use of *ladies* in the title particularly pissed me off. I mean it was so freaking patronizing. . . ."

She pauses to light the joint and exhales with a cough, before continuing: "Now Afghan women are again pawns of powerful men's interests. It all came together so easily, this invasion, and that's what sickens me. I don't know if I'm for or against it—I mean, life can't get much worse than under the Taliban. All I know is that the West could have intervened years ago and didn't, which shows how little concern there is in power politics for whether or not a woman can exercise her basic human rights. It also shows a disregard for democracy and freedom because, you see, the USA touted Kuwait as a democracy during the Gulf War even though Kuwaiti leaders, all men, voted *democratically* to deny women the vote. I'm sure that, similarly, the current American administration will turn a blind eye if discriminatory laws prevail after they *democratize* Afghanistan." She hands me the joint.

I toke and exhale slowly. "But what can we do when that's the norm in our world?" I ask, reaching over her to pass the joint on to Laurent. "Especially now that, for many people, s*sh*afety has become more important than rights. . . ." Hearing the slur in my words, I let my sentence trail off, the mix of what we've been drinking and now smoking catching up to me.

Dragging myself up off the futon, I attempt to march straight but lurch instead with heavy steps down the hallway toward the bathroom, where I douse my face with cold water. Staring into the mirror, I wonder, *Who inhabits this face? What does she signify?* Long before my imbibed brain can come up with an answer, my attention wanders over to a stack of photography books perched on the back of the toilet. I pick up *The Ballad of Sexual Dependency* by Nan Goldin and flick through raw colour photographs and autobiographical shots of drag queens and addicts, of copulating and violence. I move on to the next collection, a compilation of black-and-white portraits by Mary Ellen Mark of unfamous people living on the periphery of urban prosperity. This book falls open in my hands like an overripe fruit. I find myself staring down at "Lillie with her Rag Doll" in Seattle, a portrait of a runaway smoking and clutching at a last remnant of innocence and living on the streets and maybe it's a joint in her hand. I find myself staring down at Lillie's portrait, which is really *my* portrait, the photograph somebody forgot to take of me when I arrived in Vancouver and was sleeping in a lumber-yard on Kingsway, and I lower the toilet lid and sink down onto it, the cold glass edge burning the back of my thighs where my T-shirt dress ends.

WHEN I RE-EMERGE FROM the bathroom, the bedroom door is still closed. Hana is explaining to Laurent that she would never commit suicide. I settle onto the edge of the futon, feeling like an eavesdropper and won-dering if I shouldn't go home. "But what's the point of it all?" she asks Laurent as she pours herself another glass of wine. Glancing up, she be-seeches me with a fierce, soulful look. "*Revolt,* Camus says, but isn't that rather vague and unsatisfying?"

"This is called an existential crisis, *'ana*, a completely normal stage in the development of our identity as young persons." Laurent leans back into the futon and closes his eyes. "When I return to France, I will have to decide what career to pursue: the one that impassions me or the one that my family expects."

"Laurent, I'm not talking about a career choice here! I'm talking about . . . about . . . why do we exist?"

He stands up and digs through his jean pockets. "The meaning of life is to forget the search for the meaning of life," he says, withdrawing a lighter and then a flattened pack of cigarettes. "Just live, kid, no ques-tions asked." He shakes a cigarette forward in the pack and extends it toward her.

"Oh, you're so infuriating," she says. "Later," she adds, shooing away his offer of a cigarette. "You go ahead."

He offers me one in turn. I shake my head, which is spinning enough as it is without a nicotine rush. Laurent pulls out the cigarette for him-self, and some loose tobacco escapes and falls into the aquarium. A blue-and-white striped fish puckers up its lips to nibble at this new food, working quickly to clean the water's surface before the goldfish arrives.

To know yourself, or *to seek beauty in its many forms,* or *to experience this world*. . . . I think of the many possibilities I could offer Hana in answer to her question, but I remain silent because all of them fall short. Instead I watch Laurent pull open the sliding glass doors and disappear out into the darkness on the patio. I turn to Hana and propose, "Five minutes each to sum up our life stories—are you up for it?"

So NOW WE SIT cross-legged on the futon, face to face, weaving our stories together while taking turns swigging directly from the new bottle of wine that Hana has pulled out from under the kitchen sink and managed to open, after searching high and low for a corkscrew, by pushing in the cork.

"My last year in Windeal, I started failing most subjects and completely skipping *ssh*ocial studies class, slouching around town with these two geeky metalheads I knew—I mean, if they had pot." I take another swig. "I started wearing only black ..." *Swig*. "... after my best friend Stacy died. Lyle, that's my stepdad, hated the shredded nylons I wore under everything and the big-toothed zippers I sewed into all my jeans, so there were always fights at home. I started puking up my food because I was ... not anorexic, but the other one—"

"Bulimic?"

I nod and pass her the bottle.

"Me too. I only got over it once I accepted I was gay." She chugs and hands me back the bottle. I remember the pamphlet a teacher handed out in class one day, explaining how the strain of repeated vomiting can lead to tooth loss, heart attack, and even death. *Swig*. I realized maybe I didn't want to loose my teeth, maybe I didn't want to die, maybe I could go on living without Stacy after all. *Swig*. Without a father.

Hana takes the bottle back from me, jarring me out of the lonely tunnel of my thoughts. "So one day," I continue, "Lyle quits talking to me altogether. More than a month went by like that until one evening he arranged a family meeting in the living room between himself, Katie —that's my mom—and me."

"So what happened?"

"He said my rebellion—no, no, my *delinquency*—had spiraled out of control, so they were sending me to a group home in Prince George."

"How'd your mom react?"

"Katie? She just shrank into the couch and didn't say anything. I guess he'd already arranged it with her beforehand because she didn't seem surprised."

Hana says she understands. She says betrayal is a knife that stabs you in the chest, cuts out your heart, and yet somehow you survive. She tells me she was seventeen when her mother caught her with her mouth on another girl's breast. She says that what she needed was her mother's acceptance, her gentle hands running their fingers through her hair like they used to when she got scared as a little girl. She needed to know she wasn't a freak, as her first crush had implied. Instead her mother locked her up in her bedroom for two days straight until her father got home from a business trip. It took her father two hours to calm her mother down enough to let Hana out of the room. "I feel lost most of the time," Hana tells me, gripping the neck of the now empty bottle in her lap with both hands. "I get these fleeting moments of illumination when everything seems to flow together and have some sort of direction, but most days I just plough ahead blindly, hoping to stumble upon a compass. Or a roadmap. Or even just a road." She falls silent, staring down the neck of the bottle.

Outside, a light flips on in a neighbour's house, outlining Laurent's silhouette out on the patio, a shadow leaning into the railing. The light flickers off, and Laurent melts back into the darkness. I reach out to tilt up Hana's chin. "Hana . . ." She looks up and I brush the blue wisp of hair out of her eyes. "I believe that life has a meaning and a purpose, even if we are the ones to give it one. Remember Camus? *I cannot doubt my cry . . . I have to at least believe in my protestation?*"

"Yes," she says, closing her eyes, swaying a little as a smile upturns her lips. "Yes, I remember."

I take the empty bottle from her hands and walk over to the sliding glass doors. Outside the night is grey but not as dark as before. I press my nose against the smooth, cold glass. Laurent startles me when he materializes out of the greyness on the other side. I slide open the door for him and he touches my cheek. "Where do you go, *petit ange*?"

"That's what my dad used to call me," I whisper, having forgotten this.

"So your father is a francophone—"

From the corner of my eye, I watch Hana opening the bedroom door. She stands there in the doorway with a hand on her hip. The girl with the doe eyes squeezes by her and vanishes out the front door.

"French," I tell Laurent, planning to say goodnight and catch a cab home. "From Lyon."

"Night, guys," Hana says to us. "Feel free to crash out on the futon." With that, she shuts the bedroom door, leaving Laurent and I alone in the living room.

Standing close to him like this by the sliding glass doors, my head spinning, I can smell the fresh tartness of his skin, lemon layered with nicotine. I take a deep breath and set the empty bottle on the floor. Laurent has uncovered this vulnerable spot I didn't know I had, this memory I didn't know I had of my father holding me to his thickly carpeted chest. It must be the alcohol. It must be the pot. It must be the late hour, or I should say early morning; it must be the first hint of dawn beginning just now to lighten the sky outside the sliding glass doors.

SEATED CROSS-LEGGED ON the futon we have flattened into a bed, I tell Laurent, "What I want is more . . ."

"*Joie de vivre?* Passion for life?" he offers, lying on his back, staring up at the ceiling.

"Yeah, that of course, but more than that. . . . I want more time—time to be an artist." I twist around to jab my finger toward the nearest of Sandy's canvases. "I want time in my life for painting and photography." I pause to reflect, knocking my fists together. "But how do I start? That's what I keep asking myself. What's the first step?"

He rolls onto his side and says, "You need a portfolio. You need to apply to a school of *beaux-art.*"

My distraught gaze connects with his. "A portfolio?"

"Yes. You know, a collection of—"

"Yeah, yeah. I know what a portfolio is, it's just that . . ." How many

142

presentable pieces could I scavenge from the suitcases under my bed? How many more would I need to create? I glance at Sandy's kaleidoscopic canvases. Is that how one becomes an artist nowadays? Portfolio, art school, and *voilà*, you're on your way to becoming the latest artist featured in local galleries? "That's too easy," I insist, running a fingertip along the seam of the mattress. "I mean, without rich parents or a benefactor, I don't see the point of racking up thousands of dollars in debt to go to art school, when I'd probably have to spend the following ten years working at some soul-destroying day job just to pay off that debt, with even less time than I have now to create."

Flopping onto his back, Laurent folds his hands together, as if meditating for a moment.

"On the other hand," I continue, "a career in anything other than the fine arts seems so disheartening." When he doesn't say anything, I divert my eyes to the goldfish swimming circles in its glass dungeon. "So what are you studying?" I ask him.

He doesn't answer until I turn back toward him. Then he says, "Architecture."

"Here?" I ask, not hiding my surprise. "In Vancouver?" My voice is tense and apprehensive. "But aren't there better buildings in Europe?"

"Yes and no." He shifts around on the futon, lifting his feet over the far arm so he can place his head in my lap. "May I?"

I nod.

"While in Canada, I study what I like. To improve my English."

"I see. So what is it that you like?"

"I live for the classical music." He presses the tips of his fingers against his thumbs and wags his hands up and down for emphasis. "I want to apply to the Conservatory of Music in Paris, but my father is architect, a well-known man in Europe. So there is a lot of pressure to follow his path."

Another man from an affluent family. Still, I allow myself to slide a hand into his cherubic curls, combing their light and silky strands through my fingers, watching how, as my fingertips reach the end of a lock, it springs perfectly back into place. "Are you studying music here?"

"Yes, of course. All my courses are in composition, except for the philosophy class."

"Too bad you can't do both. Instead of having to choose."

He upturns his palms in a display of exasperation and closes his eyes.

I study his handsome, boyish face: two outward parentheses at the bridge of his nose sliding into a collection of long brown lashes, rosy thin lips, a clean-shaven, narrow jawline.

He lifts a hand to write imaginary notes on a score, humming as he does.

I take a deep breath and sigh, finding uncomfortable parallels between his dilemma and my own: he wants to compose music; I want to compose pictures. Neither endeavour carries any guarantee of financial or even artistic success. "Sometimes, I wonder if it wouldn't be easier just to suppress my artistic impulse altogether—"

Laurent sits up.

"What?" I ask, unable to match the intensity of his gaze.

He lifts his thumb to the side of my mouth as if to wipe away my words and, with it, any doubt. "Do not worry. Life will arrange itself."

I forget to breathe as he leans into me. His lips are butterfly feet settling against mine as his fingertips brush up my neck. Time translates into pure silence. This kiss is the stillness that comes from within when staring up into a brilliant night sky, forgetting how small you are against the never-ending largeness and melting into that oceanic feeling of oneness with infinity. As Laurent pulls away, my lashes flutter open and I sink, slow motion, into the hazelnut liquor of his eyes. My fingertips follow the line of his collarbone; he slips my dress up over my hair. He fumbles with my bra clasp until I unclip it for him; he cups my breasts in his palms like two freshly plucked peaches, his hands trembling with reverence. I laugh with happiness. At this sound, he presses the flat of his palm between my breasts, to feel the vibrations in my chest. Ever since he first noticed my melancholic eyes, he says, he's wanted to make me smile. This discovery startles me: I have melancholic eyes?

He cups my cheeks in his hands. "Do not worry, *petit ange,* you have beautiful eyes."

We lie down side by side. He takes me in his arms and wraps me tight within them, and after a while, I pull him into me. He's a bit nervous, I'm a bit nervous, so we hold on to each other tighter. He strokes my hair, I rub his shoulders. When we start to move, I lose track of time, I get caught up in the silence, I fear I may see God. A teardrop plummets from his cheek to splatter against my breast, sliding down between our wet stomachs pressed together, and then all tension gives way as we go slack at the same moment into a pool of liquid and skin.

IN THE DAMP WARMTH of Laurent's arms, I discover myself happy. His boyish but hairy chest rises to brush up against my breasts before falling away again as his lungs seek out another breath, each one more drawn out than the one before, until I know he is sleeping. I slip out from under the weight of his arm, careful not to wake him. His naked body lies on its side, a thick hip jutting up, a stray hand upside down by the small of his back. I tiptoe down the hallway to the coat rack by the front door where I hung my bag when I arrived. I dig out my camera and, returning to his side, take a series of photographs. A shaft of early morning light slants in through the sliding glass doors, illuminating the particles of dust that hang suspended in its beam. I stand naked in this ray of light thanking God or the Universe, or whoever might be out there to hear me, for my existence.

Laurent stirs and opens his eyes. I stand there amongst the dust particles an inestimable time, smiling back at him, in a memory of happiness that I will guard forever in some warm and sunlit corner of the universe within me. When I set down my camera by the aquarium and burrow back into our lair on the futon, he presses his forehead to mine. "It is time to sleep. Close your eyes." When I do, he drapes an arm around me, and we sleep nestled together until the autumn sun is warm on our backs.

YELLOW

One must still have chaos in oneself,
to give birth to a dancing star.

FRIEDRICH NIETZSCHE

The Future

December 2003

Flying back to Vancouver, I don't know where home is anymore. Far below this plane is the ocean surface, beneath that surface thousands of metres of water, and still underneath that water the basalt of the ocean floor. Looking down out this airplane window, I feel as significant as a water spider skimming across the ocean surface, over depths and currents that would drown me.

When the roar comes of the engine brake, I clutch my flat case of sketches and photographs to my chest, my stomach balled up into a tight fist with the anxiety of flying and repatriation. After the jolted landing on the tarmac and rude questions from a customs officer, I stare out the bus window at a city that should be familiar but isn't. I step onto Broadway feeling like a ghost on these streets; the person who left here two years ago has vanished, and a foreigner has taken her place.

I ring the buzzer of my mother's apartment on East Eighth and take the elevator up to her third-storey suite. Her sister Lodi is visiting with her two kids, and I meet my aunt and cousins for the first time. I have kept in touch with Katie by occasional email; she returned to church-going and sobriety eight months ago and, more recently, moved out of Windeal to Vancouver, where she found a cashier job at a grocery store and a younger boyfriend at AA.

My first week back, I make plans to catch up over coffee with Hana, whom I haven't seen since late 2001. I arrive before she does at Café Deux Soleils on the Drive, the same place we went for brunch two years ago, hungover the afternoon after her birthday party. I choose a corner booth by the window, where I can keep an eye out for her. The guy in the next booth runs his fingers through dishevelled hair then extends an arm out over the backrest of his bench, rapping his thick knuckles against the wood. He is explaining something to the woman facing him, but his words merge with the general buzz of the café so that I can't quite follow them. What I do catch, however, are the blocky swells of his West Coast intonation, the inflection and emphasis that once came so naturally to me before my accent picked up so many foreign accessories.

On the plane coming back, the Canadian woman next to me asked if this was my first visit to Canada.

No, I grew up near Prince George.

Is that right? You sound French . . . or German.

My hands are moist when Hana finally swings through the door. She doesn't see me in the corner, wiping my palms on my jeans, so she twists around on the heel of her boot, her eyes sweeping the restaurant. I take in her spiky hair, her winter coat already slipped off and folded over her arm, her open-back red top, the yellow sliver of a new quarter-moon tattoo in the small of her neck. She clutches a small purse. "Helene," she says, spotting me.

In Avignon, men call after women in the streets and otherwise behave badly. When caught staring, they don't shift away their gaze but rather move in to strike up a conversation. I thought I hated their constant badgering, their stalking me in the street and purring, *Bonjour, mademoiselle.* But I realize life abroad has changed me, and little by little the strange has become familiar. What is foreign to me now is how the guy in the booth attempts to check out Hana while appearing not to do so, alternately stealing a look in her direction and averting his eyes like a naughty dog.

Hana reaches my table. "How are you?" she asks. I stand up and we hug, and I realize how much I've changed. I'm still tall with unruly hair and sulky green eyes; she's still short and sleek in heeled boots and jet-black hair. Yet there is a distance now, of my paintings and her performances, my travels by TGV train and hours in European art museums, her improv in Montreal and latest romance with a Ghanaian woman from Toronto. Europe's grimness has reformed what little innate North American exuberance I had to begin with into an even quieter reserve, but Hana, it seems, has never stopped lighting up rooms with her easy smile, and she beckons me with it now from across the table. "I've missed you," she says.

I feel like a foreigner.

Except for the new haircut, Hana is exactly as I remember her and, except for some replacement tables, this café exactly the same as I left it. But you, Matthew, *you* I can't remember anymore. I've forgotten exactly how your cheeks crease when you smile, the way the skin crinkles around your eyes, the depth of the hollow that dents your chin. I can't even conjure up your most basic proportions. Those burning sunset curls falling to your shoulders, those freckles coating your skin in brown-flecked honey. What were their shades exactly? What were their textures?

"Helene, are you all right?"

"Yeah. A little jet-lagged, that's all." I sit up straighter, try to appear more alert and concentrate on Hana. We make small talk and I do my best to carry on a conversation, but I'm tired and my attention is elsewhere. What I want to know is, Matthew, have you found freedom? You got my email address from Christine and contacted me earlier this year. You said you had a two-week leave in December from the humanitarian mission in Iraq, and I agreed to meet up with you then. Then late in October you grew silent. Your emails no longer greeted me when I signed into my inbox. Images of the rubble left by the suicide bombing flickered briefly on television screens the world over; the Red Cross has since pulled its foreign staff out of Iraq, alongside a mass exodus of other aid workers. Except, you—*you*—are not amongst the evacuees; you are amongst the casualties. *Matthew, Matthew, Matthew!* You're not supposed to be dead; this short story cannot be all that was written, my beautiful, my restless, my unfaithful, my reckless Matthew. Have you found your cherished freedom?

Hana cocks her head, puzzlement at the corner of her lips. "I've missed you," she mouths. The server comes over. Hana orders a cappuccino. I order a second espresso. "I've missed you," Hana mouths again through the crook of the server's arm.

"Me too," I murmur. I should never have come back. I can't explain the weight of the finality of his demise. I can't bear to pronounce his name. So, dumbly, I watch the server clear away my first cup.

"Laurent's back in France now," Hana informs me. "Did you have a chance to meet up with him before you left?"

I shake my head, distracted by my thoughts. Last night, I started a new journal and titled it *Letters to a Muse*.

Dear Muse, I wrote as the first entry.
I'm dedicating this journal to you because you have inspired me to seek out a life of personal passion and truth in a world of collective tragedy and deception. It was the scepticism you expressed regarding my intentions and ability—which I have felt ever since compelled to discredit—that has since driven me to centre my life around art.

Hana leans across the table to capture my attention. "I have a secret," she whispers. "I've been waiting to tell you in person." Her eyes are lit with a strange light.

I force my thoughts back to our conversation and try to appear curious. "What is it?"

"I'm going to be a mom!" She smiles and her happiness is like a ray of sunlight breaking across the table. "Rose is four months pregnant, and the donor is Japanese—so we're going to have a Blasian baby."

I gawk at her. "Wow, that is quite the news."

"Yeah. I knew you were coming back to meet up with that guy, Matthew, so I made myself wait to tell you, but I've been dying to shout it out in every email."

"Congratulations! Do you know if it's a boy or girl?"

"No, we're not finding out. We want it to be a surprise."

"Well, I'm surprised already. *You*?" I tease her. "A mom?"

"Yeah, I know. Crazy, right?" She laughs as she stands up from the table. "I'm going to order some food. Want something?"

"No thanks." While she orders at the counter, I gaze out at the street. The afternoon has already faded into an early winter night. The server brings our coffees. I fiddle with the sugar spoon at the side of my saucer.

I wish I could allow Hana's joy to transport me to a happier place, but my fear of forgetting is too great; inside me, where a few weeks ago smouldered a renewed hope for a future with Matthew, there is now a smoking, charred hole. I need to be alone to fill it up with my recollections, quickly, before it's too late, before the last of my memories of him slips away.

"You know, I've been thinking. . ." Hana says, returning with a bowl of chili and a side of marble toast. She slides into the booth and butters the bread. "You should move to Montreal. It's a very different vibe there; you would like it. Especially now that you're fluent in French—"

"I'm returning to France as soon as I can get a new visa. I'm going to apply to some art schools and English teaching jobs and see where that gets me."

"But I thought you were coming back here for good?"

"I had planned to, but . . . but you see, in France I'm a stranger. No matter how fluent I may be, my accent marks me as an outsider. It's isolating but also liberating. . . ."

She nods, but I wonder if she can understand, having never lived abroad, the devastating otherness of becoming foreign—the startling discovery that you have become a stranger to your culture and language, and to yourself—but also the exhilarating freedom of shaking off those shackles. Then again, as a visual minority and a lesbian she probably understands better than me what it is to feel like an outsider.

I continue: "The way I see it, my future is a blank canvas. One way or another, it's going to be blotted and stained. I need to believe I have some freedom to choose the colours and composition; I need to believe that my life is my own to design and that, as a result, I am responsible—"

"He didn't show up to meet you, did he?" Hana leans back in her seat and folds her arms across her chest.

"—for whatever self-portrait I manage to sketch out. Because even if this life *is* fated, what harm can it do to believe—"

"You came back here for him," Hana insists, "but he's flaked out on you, hasn't he?"

I give up on intellectualizing my decision then and tell her instead of Matthew's death. I tell her knowing she thinks aid projects are nothing but colonialism and occupation in disguise; I tell her knowing she thinks he was never anything but a self-interested, self-styled bohemian. I tell her because, of anyone I know, she understands best what it is to elevate another onto a pedestal of unrequited longing and to fall, helplessly, hopelessly, under the grandiose spell of that obsession and desire.

An Invitation

October 2001

Slumped over a large coffee and a newspaper, nursing a hangover in a dark corner of Café Deux Soleils the afternoon after Hana's party, I watch Laurent and Hana order at the counter. As Laurent struggles to make himself understood to the server, I picture myself in the same situation in his country, and a wave of apprehension washes over me. I find it hard to re-invoke the rapture I felt this morning when I stood amongst the suspended particles of lighted dust and the answer was clear: I would say yes to Laurent's offer to lend me his family's vacation flat in Avignon until early next summer. I would spend the long winter nights painting and auditing the art school's evening classes, and I would spend the short winter days wandering the streets, taking photographs, and roaming the city's numerous art galleries.

Late last night, Laurent painted my future life in Avignon with such enthusiasm I couldn't help but believe I could become a sophisticated, cosmopolitan artist. Now doubt has crept back. I run my fingers backward from my temples through my hair. The newspaper slips from the table and sprawls across the floor, flopping over under the table to reveal its front-page headline: UP TO 45 WOMEN MISSING FROM THE DOWNTOWN EASTSIDE. I scan the first couple of paragraphs as I pick it up. Police have identified over 600 potential suspects in the slayings of female drug addicts and prostitutes, but still aren't dismissing the possibility that one or more serial killers may be at work in Vancouver. My temples are pounding from last night's alcohol and lack of sleep. I feel I'm confusing everything. It's like the more I try, the less I understand. This morning I melted in Laurent's arms; now already the magic is gone.

Hana dumps a handful of sugar packets on the table and slides into the seat across from me. She's wearing dark sunglasses and reeks of alcohol from clear across the table. "So . . ." she says, lifting her shades to the top of her head as she empties packet after packet of sugar into her coffee. The whites of her eyes are red veined and sallow. "Laurent says you're moving to France."

"Did he?" I glance over at Laurent picking out silverware at the cutlery stand. "I was pretty drunk last night." I take a sip of my coffee.

"So did you guys hook up, or what?"

"Number eighteen?" a server carrying a veggie burger plate shouts.

"Yeah, that's me," I say, grateful for the interruption.

Laurent arrives at the table before Hana can repeat her question. He takes the seat beside me. I keep my eyes focused on the thin layer of ketchup I am spreading over my bun. He takes a sip of his coffee then complains about how diluted it tastes. "You will drink real coffee in France," he tells me.

"I have a job and an apartment here," I snap, still not meeting his gaze. "And I'm enrolled in university."

He spreads his hands through the air as if to cast a spell. "Imagine life in Provence: painting fields of lavender and sunflowers and grapes."

"I can't go. Believe me, I would love to, but I can't."

"Why?" Hana asks. "It sounds amazing."

"For one thing, I hardly speak any French."

"And France isn't the perfect place to learn?"

Laurent leans into me so that I have no choice now but to meet his eyes. "Oh, stop being difficult. You know you need to make a portfolio." He pecks my lips. I draw back, embarrassed in front of Hana.

Hana chuckles. "You guys totally got it on last night," she says, rubbing her puffy eyelids.

I ignore Hana's comment and turn to Laurent, determined to dissuade him. "I don't need to leave Vancouver to make a portfolio. I already have two suitcases full of artwork under my bed."

"What?" Hana demands. "What kind of artwork?"

I shrug. "Pencil and ink drawings, charcoal and pastel sketches, some acrylic and watercolour paintings. I've never tried oil, though, and I mostly paint on paper. Art supplies are expensive."

"What are they of?" she asks, reaching across the table to arrest my arm. "I mean, what inspires you?"

I feel my face reddening. "People mostly. I've done a few weird collages and more abstract compositions as well."

Hana leans back in her chair with a wide smile, and I realize too late my mistake in mentioning the suitcases as she says, "You have *got* to show us!"

I'm about to explain that I haven't shown *anyone* any of the pieces, with the exception of those portraits of Matthew that my mother happened across, when the server arrives at our table with Hana's and Laurent's omelettes.

"Laurent," Hana says, spreading mustard over her toast after the server is gone, "when are you free this week? We have got to go over to Helene's place and check out her stuff."

I shake my head. "No way. I'm not showing anyone."

Hana chuckles as she reaches her hand across the table to shake my limp wrist. "Listen, you shy little closeted artist, no need to get all flustered. What's the point of art without an audience?"

"That's easy for you to say—you're an actor."

"Doesn't make my point any less valid." She lets go of my hand and asks Laurent, "We'll go easy on her, won't we?"

Laurent mumbles something that sounds like a yes through a mouthful of food, and I lose my appetite just thinking of the two of them going through my suitcases. Pushing away my half-eaten burger, I glower at Hana. She folds her hands across the edge of the table. "Or maybe," she taunts me, "you aren't ready to come out of the art closet?"

LATER THAT NIGHT, I spread the front pages of the newspaper over my kitchen tabletop and use masking tape to secure a blank sheet of acrylic paper over the newsprint. I dig out the photograph I took in September of the waif outside the train station from an envelope of recently developed photos. Using old yogurt containers for my palette, I load my paintbrush with phthalo blue and titanium white to paint a quick wash of sky two inches wide. Moving down the paper, I brush in a grassy field under this sky, dragging the green slightly into the lines of the pencil sketching of stone benches at the centre, my replica of the slain women's monument in front of the train station. After I paint in the grey-brown stones, I fill out the dark shadow of the waif at their centre. Then, dipping into a pale skin colour composed of burnt sienna, alizarin crimson, and white, I brush in the lines of her thin silhouette, referring as needed to the photograph. Once this has dried, I smear a red miniskirt over the tops of her skeleton legs, stroke in a transparent, torn blouse, her loose, stringy hair, the outline of her one good sandal, and the broken golden heel of the other lying on its side in the grass.

Standing back, I consider what I've done. I wonder where the woman who inspired this painting is now. Is she amongst the survivors, clasping tight to private hopes and dreams, all the while diminished and degraded to a *junkie* and a *whore* in the public eye, living a fractured and desperate life on the downtown Eastside streets? I close my eyes and say a little prayer that she is not now, and will never be, amongst the casualties to whom this monument's inscription is dedicated: ALL WOMEN WHO HAVE BEEN MURDERED BY MEN.

I drop my paintbrush into a murky jar of water. In the bathroom, I scrub at the paint caked on my forearms all the way up to my elbows. My knees have begun to quake, most likely from too little sleep and too much caffeine. It's nearly four o'clock in the morning. Clasping the towel rack, I unbutton my jeans. Their legs holes collapse into piles of fabric around my ankles, snakes coiled and ready to strike. I run a bath. One foot then another shakes free and climbs over the porcelain edge. *It's just a hangover,* I tell myself as I slide into the water and under a wave. . . .

I remember my mother once perched on our only suitcase, the hotel room otherwise empty. Her smile was easy, her long arms relaxed. She wore a white cotton nightgown with eyelets embroidered into the trim, the bottom edge of which undulated over her bare feet. *I'm running away,* she whispered, sweeping her hand around the room. *All these years of waiting. And for what? For nothing.*

So I ask her now, my words gurgling through the water, distant and remote: "Don't you know you can run, but your memory will follow? Don't you know that no matter how far you flee you can never outdistance yourself?"

I imagine pulling at the sleeves of her flimsy gown, the same as I did that day, except now the fabric rends in my fists as I drag her across the carpet. Except now I am not crying. Looking down I notice my mother clutching her rug-burnt knees, two scarlet stains seeping through the white fabric of her dress where she kneels in front of me, begging for forgiveness. Except in fact, I was the one who begged the drunken woman to stay.

FROM MY BATHROOM MIRROR, cavernous emerald eyes presiding over a resolute jaw stare back at me. The mouth in that jaw opens to whisper: "You don't have the guts to put yourself out there." I realize I've been clutching to my isolation like a ragged old sweater worn for so long it now seems a part of me. "You don't have what it takes to make it." Watching these words form on my mouth of their own accord makes me feel extraterrestrial, like some parts of me are alien, irrepressible, beyond my control.

To escape these dark mutterings, I wrap up in a shabby towel and tiptoe over to the kitchen table. Peeling away the masking tape securing my painting to the newsprint, I set the warped sheet on the kitchen counter to dry. Staring at the sad, emaciated figure surrounded by the oval circle of stones under a pale sky, I wonder what impact this painting will have on Hana and Laurent. Will this piece arrest their attention, make them take notice, whether or not they like it? Or will they find it flat and dull, or worse, amateurish?

I turn back to the table and toss the yogurt containers with their drying paint into the wastebasket. As I begin to roll up the sodden newspaper, I am struck by the irony of its headline, painted over in part now so that it reads: UP TO 45 . . . MEN MISSING . . . THE DOWNTOWN EASTSIDE. In the paragraph under the article, *600 potential suspects* is still legible between splotches of paint.

I sink into a chair.

Like my journal memories made into public property, that piece on the counter behind me has begun a life of its own, out there, outside of me. If I sign my name to it, I become responsible for the statement it would proclaim to the world. But what exactly do I want to say? To what would I give a voice?

A sentence struck me while reading Nietzsche this summer: *Whoever fights with monsters should be careful lest he thereby become a monster. And if you gaze long into the abyss, the abyss will also gaze into you.* Staring down at this sodden newsprint soiling my hands, I can feel the abyss reaching up for me. I crumple the newspaper into a wad, trying to repress the bitterness that washes over me.

What difference can art make, anyway?

I long to tear my painting into shreds, strip by strip, stray globs of still-wet colour smudging together as red and gold and green stains on my hands. Instead, I chuck the ball of newsprint into the trash and wash my brushes in the sink. The first hint of another dawn is lighting up the sky outside my window as I collapse into a fitful sleep before my morning French class.

The God of My Art

Hana and Laurent buzz as I'm pulling cookies out of the oven. I spent the morning going through my suitcases to cherry-pick fifteen or so of my better art pieces to show them today.

"Cute place," Hana says, setting her shoulder bag down by the door. We hug in greeting. Laurent attempts to kiss me on each cheek as I go in for a hug, resulting in an awkward cross-cultural half-hug, half-kiss embrace. He hands me the grocery bags in his hands and asks me to refrigerate their contents for later, except for the two bottles of red wine that I am to leave out on the counter.

It appears they have come prepared to stay at least until dinner: how long do they expect it will take to go through a few sketches?

They pull off their winter coats and boots and settle onto my sofa. I offer them hot chocolate and arrange the cookies on a platter.

"What's up with all the knickknacks?" Hana asks, pointing at my bookshelf.

I shrug. "I liked them as a kid, but my mom hasn't caught on yet that I've grown up."

"Moms," Hana says, rolling her eyes.

"*Miam*, the cookies smell delicious," Laurent says, reaching for one on the platter I set on the floor between their feet. He drops the cookie back straight away, shaking his fingers.

"Wait until they cool," Hana scolds. She sips her hot chocolate, checks out the view from the windows behind the sofa, and turns back to me. "Okay, enough suspense already. Where are the suitcases?"

It's the moment I've been dreading since brunch a couple days ago.

"Patience, 'ana, patience. Let her sit down and drink her chocolate."

I throw Laurent a grateful look and take a seat at the table, pretending to take little sips, but my stomach has decided all of a sudden to refuse nourishment.

"You haven't hung up any of your work," Hana says.

I shrug, glancing at my bare walls.

"Unless ..." she says, noticing the photocopy of my aunt's photograph on the bathroom door.

I shake my head to indicate that it isn't mine.

"So where are the suitcases? We're all ready to go here."

I walk over to the bookshelf and reach up for the stack on top.

"Here," I say, setting the pieces I have selected down on the cushion between them. Then I retreat to the table to watch what they will do, waiting to hear, *Couldn't a child have painted this?* or *What is* that *supposed to mean?* or, worst of all, the silence of their embarrassment for me.

"Is that all you've got?" Hana asks. Before I can confirm, she reaches out for the first piece: the charcoal sketch of my mother. "Oh, this one is very lifelike," she says. "The shading gives great depth to the woman's eyes."

Laurent picks up a second piece, an acrylic self-portrait of myself as a tree. He studies it for a few moments, not saying anything. Meanwhile, Hana picks up a third and fourth, holding out one in each hand.

"Look at this one," Laurent says to her finally. She leans across the sofa. "Do you see how the vertical lines pull your eyes up from the—how do you say . . ." He points to something on the painting that is out of my line of sight.

"*Roots?*" Hana says. "Oh, yeah, I see it now. It's like they're receding, pulling your eye up the trunk into the branches."

As they pore over my painting, I feel as though I am eavesdropping on visitors at an art gallery, the unseen elephant at their backs. They turn their attention next to the set of watercolours in Hana's hands, painted in two variant washes of red, the better of the many I made from memory of Matthew lying on my bed. Hana says, "In both of these, the single colour creates a sense of connection between the man and his surroundings, almost as if these were still lifes rather than portraits."

"Yes, but they feel different because of the temperature, no? One is more warm and the other more cool."

My underarms are cold with sweat by this time. To tune out my visitors and give my nerves a chance to settle, I swirl my hot chocolate with a spoon and take to imagining how I might best arrange its movement into a still life.

"So where are the rest?" Hana asks all of a sudden.

I look up from my lukewarm chocolate to find they have finished going through the pile. "What do you mean?" I ask.

"Oh, come on," she says, unfolding her knee to get up from the sofa. She strides over to where I'm slouched at the table. "You promised us suitcases full. What you've shown us so far has only whet our appetite."

I think of the numerous self-portraits in all sorts of media and states of undress, the battered sketchbooks filled with quick renderings of people in public spaces, the landscapes painted according to tutorials in art books borrowed from the library, the still lifes of everyday objects found around my apartment, and I begin to hyperventilate a little even as Hana reaches out her small hands to rub my shoulders. "Relax," she says. "It's just us—your number one fans."

I take a deep breath and give into the massage.

"Laurent," she says, "I think our friend here needs a glass of wine—a *large* glass."

Laurent gets up, asking me where he can find a corkscrew and glasses. After he has dug them up in my kitchen, he uncorks one of the bottles on the counter and fills a glass to the brim, setting it down in front of me.

"Drink," Hana says.

I take a sip. After all, it's only two thirty in the afternoon.

"No, not like that. Drink it like a shot."

I gulp down the dry burgundy liquid.

"There," Hana says as I return the empty glass to the table and let my shoulder muscles relax. "That's better."

Laurent pours himself and Hana a glass each and sets them on the table. "If I remember well, she said the suitcases are under the bed."

"Oh, that's *right*," Hana says with mock exaggeration.

"Fine." I push my chair out from the table and stand up, the warmth of the alcohol spreading through my core. Hana moves aside to let me pass through the curtain of my bedroom nook. I re-emerge lugging a vinyl suitcase, and I set it down on the floor, in front of the sofa.

"You're still holding back," Hana accuses as she moves toward the loot. "You said *suitcases*, as in plural."

"I'll be back." I disappear through the hanging curtain again and return with the second.

"Is this really everything, now?" Hana asks.

I nod and retreat to the table again, grateful for the wine that has given me a heady courage to bear this out.

She settles into a cross-legged position before the blue-and-chrome luggage, purchased second-hand from a thrift store. Laurent squats down beside her. I don't offer any advice or help as they struggle to pop the antiquated latches, praying only that the cases will refuse to reveal their secrets. Laurent gets his to open first, lifting its lid and effectively blocking my view of the contents. I reach for one of the two glasses of wine they have abandoned on the table and take a good gulp. Hana says, after she manages to open the second case, "Wow, Laurent, we're going to need a system to organize these coherently if we're going to choose the best pieces for a portfolio."

"Yes, there is a lot of work here, isn't there?"

Again, I am the invisible elephant of a wannabe artist at their backs. *Don't worry about me, guys. I'll just get drunk here at the table while you two rummage around the chambers of my sanctum and decide what you will of my testaments.* They spread out my pieces on the floor until there are only thin paths left to navigate between them. They lay out more pieces on the back and arms of the sofa, over its centre cushions; they tie back the curtain closing off the bed and spread out even more over the comforter and dresser. They lay out studies and sketches, complete and incomplete alike, on the table and over the kitchen counters, until every last surface of my apartment is covered in drawings and washes, paintings and collages. All my failures and successes and variants of in between. I remember the recent scrapbook I made of my photography. Without a word, I follow a slim path of floor to retrieve the album from the bookshelf and hand it over to Hana, as if coughing up one more sin to her, my high priestess.

"They're all commercially developed," I tell her, "but I do plan on learning to use a darkroom one day."

She takes the album from me and sets it down by the suitcases. I return to the table; she returns to helping Laurent compile my artwork into some sort of order. I cannot always follow as they confer with each other, whispering, over a particular piece, but by the time I've finished off the third glass of wine on the table, my curiosity overpowers my caution. I wander over to where they stand and hover nearby.

"This is for the portfolio," Laurent explains to me, pointing out a pile with five pieces at most, the top one of which is the sketch of my mother from the Christmas photo. "This pile is for the maybes." He points to a second heap of ten or so sketches and paintings. I recognize, peeking out from the middle, the corner of my recent landscape portrait of the women's memorial and the waif. "This pile is for the no-noes." He wags a finger at a third stack of two dozen or more pieces; the top ones I recognize as drawings from my early teens and later seascape paint-by-instruction attempts. "Hana and I must agree for the portfolio. You can add what you want to the maybe pile." I shrug and let them continue on their own, clearing myself a small space on the bed to lie back and stare at the ceiling.

I overhear Hana arguing with Laurent over a piece she wants to add to the portfolio pile. "It's not *un*finished. This is a self-portrait drawn from the live perspective of the artist—that is why there can be no neck or head."

"Maybe yes, maybe no. But this portrait of a woman eating birds is more . . . more, how do you say, *vivid? Imaginative?*"

"Let me see. . . . Oh, yes, the colours give it an introspective, almost gothic mood, don't they?"

Laurent says, "It reminds me of the style of Frida Kahlo."

I sit up on the bed. "The black crows flying like mosquitoes around the woman's mouth represent her various fears and anxieties," I tell them. "The woman chews one up and spits it out to show her strength—its blood oozing from between her lips serves as a warning to the others not to fly too close or she will devour them too." I realize I'm explaining all this to them with my eyes closed, the sedative effect of too much wine in the afternoon. I open my eyes to find Hana and Laurent staring at me, as if in shock at the wallflower come to life. I give them a friendly grin as I realize that I, too, have chewed up and spit out one of my fears: exposing my artwork to their eyes and criticism.

"I love it," Hana says with a laugh. "It's a shame though that it's done on paper. You should reproduce it on canvas and make it bigger, much bigger." She places the acrylic painting on the portfolio pile then walks over to the door to take something out of her shoulder bag. She withdraws a small box. "Here," she says, giving it to me.

It's a student oil painting set. "Oh, Hana, you shouldn't have." I feel awkward as she places it in my hands—as if in accepting this gift I am also accepting the obligation to become a *real* artist.

"It's from the two of us," she says, looping her elbow through Laurent's arm. "Hopefully we didn't buy complete crap, as we had absolutely no idea what we were looking at, and the wide range of supplies was overwhelming to say the least."

"It's perfect. Thank you guys so much." I get up and hug them, more demonstrative than usual on account of the wine and the thrill of sharing my art.

I let them finalize their decisions about the last pieces in the maybe pile while I open the oil set: there are five tubes of paint—the three primary colours plus black and white. There are also two canvas painting panels, four brushes, a bottle of linseed oil, and a palette knife. Meanwhile, Hana asks me for a sticky notepad, which she uses to mark the photographs in the album that I should consider adding to the portfolio pile.

When Laurent and Hana have finished, I help them stuff the numerous piles of no-noes back into the suitcases. Then we arrange the fourteen pieces from the portfolio stack in front of us on the floor. We consider them one by one. They gift me with their impression and reaction to each while I explain my source of inspiration and what I had hoped to convey. I am surprised by some of their choices—a simple sketch of a child playing in the sand at Stanley Park, the frenzied portrait of a woman combing knives from her hair, the still life of a peach split in half—but they insist that each piece shows a different side of my work and ability, and that each is, in its own way, mesmerizing.

I don't dare argue so long as they are using words like *mesmerizing*, although I see that they have not included any of my red portraits of Matthew in the proposed portfolio set. I don't ask why, inferring from their exclusion that these portraits are, having been painted with neither reference to life nor photo, weak and uninspiring. Still, I can't shake off this involuntary drive to encapsulate Matthew's lifeblood, to supersede what he stole from me with a full exposure of his being. I want to paint him in a magnum opus worthy of a gallery and then deny that he was ever the source of my inspiration, that he was ever the god of my art.

"A lot of these paintings would be more impressive on canvas," Hana says. "You should trust your talent and invest in quality materials once in a while. The warped paper and dog-eared corners detract from the overall impression. The ones you've done on canvas board are much more presentable. You could also try painting on plywood. I know Sandy does that sometimes."

"Or cereal box," Laurent says. "I saw that in a street exhibit in Paris."

"Yes, but Sandy says paintings on cardboard yellow and fade. You should talk to her about—"

"So do you have a portfolio case?" Laurent interrupts her to ask me.

Hana gives him a look. "Oh, never mind. I don't know why I even brought her up." Turning to me, she says, "What you need is a large, flat carrying case. We saw some relatively inexpensive ones today at the art store—the cheapest was around ten bucks."

I gather up the pieces they have chosen and stack them on top of the bookcase, promising to invest in a case soon.

* * *

LAURENT SPREADS THE GROCERIES on the counter: a tray of lox salmon, a bag of sesame bagels, a tub of crème fraiche, and a bunch of dill. He turns on my oven and toasts the bagels. Then he garnishes them with a thick layer of cream and a folded slice of salmon, finishing off with a sprig of dill and a dash of black pepper.

"This is absolutely delicious," I tell him after my first bite. "I could get used to eating French food. What do you call this in French?"

"*Sandwich.*"

"Ha, ha, funny."

"It is a Jewish sandwich," he explains.

"Really? I wouldn't have guessed."

"I know. I am surprised to find that people here often do not know the origin of their food."

"I knew," Hana says. "Sandy was dating a Jewish guy when we met."

Laurent gives her a look as he finishes off his bagel.

"Oops, sorry," she says. "No matter how I fight it, I can't stop finding ways to slip her name into the conversation. Like, yesterday, I was grocery shopping, and I found myself randomly thinking, *Sandy likes green grapes. I should buy some.* Then I remembered she's moving out at the end of the month, which is like, what, in three days? I don't know why I can't stop thinking about her all the time. I'm very good at avoiding her at home, even when she tries to be friendly, but everything reminds me of her in this city. I'll be walking down the street and see a café—just a regular old coffee shop—and I'll think that's where we went for our second date and she ordered a hot apple cider. Why couldn't she have been the one to initiate the breakup? Then, at least, I could be begging her to stay. Why do I have to be the strong one? It's killing me."

Laurent serves each of us a second half bagel then leans over to hug Hana in her chair. "*Chère 'ana,* when your heart is bruised all you can feel is the pain. But try to remember that Sandy is now your ex"—he draws a large X in the air—"for a good reason."

"I feel so pathetic," she says, looking small in his arms. "I can't stop listening to that Melissa Etheridge song, 'I'm the Only One.'" She hums a few bars of the '90s hit. "Every single word reminds me of Sandy. It's pathetic, I know, but I keep playing it over and over in my head."

"You can talk about her all you want," I tell Hana as Laurent refills her wine glass. "We're here to listen. Unless, you'd rather pretend for the night that she doesn't exist. Whatever makes you feel better."

She says, "We played that CD over and over on our trip down to the Oregon Shakespeare Festival this summer. It was like a freaking honeymoon, speeding in the rental car, staying at cheap motels, and then arriving in Ashland, my dream destination. I so hope to get a part on stage there one day. Anyway, we saw *Life is a Dream,* which is one of the better romances I've seen on stage. That was in the Bowmer Theatre. On the outdoor Elizabethan Stage we saw *The Merry Wives of Windsor,* which was the only play by Shakespeare we got tickets for. In the Black Swan Theatre, we saw Nilo Cruz's *Two Sisters and a Piano,* a political piece set in Havana. It was all so freaking amazing. Sandy paid for everything as an anniversary present to me and to celebrate selling her first painting. . . ." Hana breaks off to dab her eyes.

"I like the second option better," Laurent says, refilling my glass and his own. "Let's please pretend for the rest of the evening that she doesn't exist. In France, we say, 'Mieux vaut être seul que mal accompagné.'"

"I imagine that means something like, being alone is bad?" I ask.

"No, no. It means it is better to be lonely than badly accompanied."

"Wow, I need to work on my French. I didn't get that at all from what you said." I glance at Hana to see how she is taking the switch in topic. She gives me a faint smile, her eyes drying up.

"If you learn French," Laurent continues, as if fearful Hana will try to slip Sandy into the conversation again if he leaves her any room, "then you will be able to apply to the National School of *beaux-arts* in Paris or Lyon, or to one of the regional schools of art, like the one in Avignon."

"Yeah, whatever." I wash down the rest of my second bagel with a swig of wine. "Those schools must cost a fortune."

"Actually," Hana butts in, "Sandy looked into it once. She said they're a lot cheaper than our schools but that the entrance exams are wickedly competitive."

"Oh, Sandy, Sandy, Sandy," Laurent mocks her.

"Whatever," she retorts. "Anyway, since we're already talking about her, I can tell you that I do remember that when she applied to Emily Carr, she also applied to three other art colleges here in Canada: one in Calgary, one in Toronto, and one in Nova Scotia. So you might want to check them out too."

"No, no," Laurent says. "Forget all that. First, 'elene must learn French and take preparatory classes of art; then, she will write the entry exams to study with *la crème de la crème*."

"Oh, you're such an elitist French snob," Hana retorts. "So our schools are just crap then?"

"Whoa," I say. "Hang on, guys. Who said anything about me applying to art school?"

Forgetting their squabble, they turn on me as a united front from across the table. "Helene," Hana says, "you have got to believe in yourself and take the plunge. You know you would just thrive in that environment."

"Uh huh. And after the fun and games of an easy, breezy life at art—"

"*Easy*?" Laurent asks.

"—school? What would I do then? With a huge student debt and no guarantee of a career related to the arts anyway?"

"You would paint," Hana says. "You would spend your days making art and using the connections you made at art school to sell it and get noticed. You might live in poverty—but who cares? As Hippocrates said, *Life is short, art is long*."

In this way, she forces my hand, and I can only nod in response.

AFTER HANA HAS WRAPPED herself up in her coat and pulled on her platform boots, and we have hugged her goodbye and she has taken her leave, Laurent and I make love for a second time. As we kiss, I worry I might be complicating things by allowing this to become more than a one-night stand, but the chemistry is still there so why say no to pleasure? Afterward, I take a shower and ask him to leave. He seems surprised.

"You must not regret your life," he tells me. "First you must book a flight to Lyon or Marseille for late December or early January. Then I will help you to make a reservation online for the train to Avignon. *D'accord?*"

I find his persistence exasperating but enticing. I don't want to be persuaded, yet when I gaze at him I see the image of an artist reflected back.

Happiness Is Overrated

I dial Katie's number, cracking my knuckles in time to the distant, intermittent tone.

My mother answers after ten or so rings. "So you're finally calling me back," she says in reference to my hanging up on her last time, when I phoned from the payphone at school.

I'm lying in a patch of sunlight on the floor, twisting the phone cord around my fingers. "I'm only phoning for Lodi's mailing address." I take a deep breath to stay calm. "I plan to write my aunt for advice on starting out as an artist, on art schools, and on career paths. I have a pen and an envelope ready. Can you read it out to me, please?"

My mother answers by telling me that Lyle has come home. Lyle has left the "little slut" and returned to going to church. My mother says she wants to get her priorities right this time. She wants us to be friends again. She says I don't need Lodi, I don't need art.

"Katie, I just want to write your sister a letter. She's my family too, you know?"

"You think I was a terrible mother, don't you? You think I could have done something to stop your father."

I trace the outer circumference of the table leg with my pen. "I don't see what this has to do with giving me Lodi's address."

"You were two, Helene, two. You can't remember."

I hold the receiver away from my ear and sink my head to the floor in dismay. I lift my forehead and bang it down, down, down against the peeling floorboards, over and over again. We've been through this so many times before, whenever I've asked about anyone in her family—why did I believe this time would be any different?

I lift my eyes to Lodi's photograph on my bathroom door, and I realize what a fool I've been. It's like I think the past is mutable. Once I prove myself—as an artist, as a lover, and as a woman—events will be remembered differently, the fractured landscapes of my life will reveal their significance, and everything will come together into a meaningful whole.

"You've made up your own stories, haven't you?" my mother is asking when I bring the receiver back to my ear. "To rationalize what happened."

I want to tell her that these lives of ours are like matches igniting in the dark, flaring momentarily, blazing up the wooden stick, and dying out. As Epictetus, whom I'm reading for philosophy class, so aptly put it two thousand years ago, I am *a little soul carrying around a corpse*, pre-programmed to die, already dying, and every day a little more. I want to tell her I am only trying to burn bright and not to flicker out, trying to etch something along this lifeline of my matchstick into eternity, something of me, of value, into permanence.

"Please, Katie. Just give me Lodi's address."

After a long silence, she says she's tired and that I must be tired and that everything is dragging on. She says nothing ever changes; in fact, life is one disappointment after another. Worse, it is always when you start to believe again that it all goes downhill. She's losing her capacity for hope. She'd like to say there is still a possibility; she'd really like there to be. But he must know where she is. He must know how to find her. She is filled with so many regrets. There were so many possibilities, so why this one? Why did she have to go down this road? She has never known, she says, when it is time to just let go. In any case, she can't imagine how things would be even if he did come back. She says, "I've been waiting too, you know, for an explanation. But I do my best not to think about it."

I shiver. The sunlight has disappeared behind a cloud, and a draft flows in through the window. I tell her I don't know what she means, that nothing she says is rational, and I climb up from the floor to slide shut the windowpane.

Over the past twelve years, the memories of our life in Prince George have blurred to a mishmash of images, some still sharp in their detail, others too hazy for recognition. What I recall now is the exterior neon sign over the entrance of the bar underneath the hotel: the flashing outline of a red skirt lifting and lowering over a slender blue leg and in steady yellow the words HOT LIVE GIRLS. In other words, boys, the girls are still breathing; the women here are vibrant and alive. As if there existed other kinds of bars, where cold dead girls were put on display.

From the receiver at my ear, my mother's voice drifts over the line, but I'm having difficulty piecing our conversation together.

"Well, honeybun?" she asks.

"What?" I demand irritably, staring out the window at the far distant mountains, having lost the thread of what she is saying.

"Do you think your relationships are affected by not having a father?"

"I think—"

"I suppose you couldn't know yet."

What I do know is that lust is a heady cocktail of hormones and magnetism. I know that lust is a woman trying on men's bodies and minds like changes of clothes, searching for a glimpse of self, searching for a style she can call her own.

But love? I want to ask Katie, *Can you please tell me what* love *is?*

Can it be this longing to immortalize on canvas one man's beauty and give him a place in art? Can it be this urge to paint over and over his particular form, each time the result never equal to the ideal, so that the compulsion is to begin yet again?

Matthew: my beloved, my insufferable muse. Meeting him was a special grace; the uncertainty of ever regaining his affections has become my artistic aphrodisiac. When I dredge my memories for a glimpse of his fleeting form and manage to hold it within my mind's eye, for that brief moment the copy becomes the original, the finite infinite, the infinitesimal immense.

Already, sleeping with Laurent has erased from my memory the taste of Matthew's skin, the texture of his hair, the intensity of his kiss, the depth of his voice, the overall notes of his smell. For this, I resist Laurent, although it is no fault of his own.

I don't know if such desire, unrequited, can be called love. Perhaps this emotion is, at its most base, nothing more than a cannibalistic urge to nourish a fine piece of art on his beauty. What I do know is that every recollection of him is like a blinding explosion of colour in a black-and-white world. What I do know is that his absence sounds in me like that hush when the last, lingering note has been played but the musicians have not yet lifted their bows. I am waiting for the encore, I am waiting for more.

"Lyle tried to be a father to you," my mother is saying. "I always encouraged him to be. Do you realize the coincidence of my meeting him the same week I quit working at the hotel and took that waitressing job at the truck stop? I made one small step toward improving my life, and God did the rest—"

"Oh, you mean, it was God who gave you the cheap ring from Zellers and a singlewide trailer?"

My mother sighs into the line. "Why do you always have to lash out like that? Just because Lyle is back doesn't mean everything is fine. He's so wound up, praying and confessing all the time, making lists of his sins, intimate details I'd rather not know. I thought he came back because I threatened divorce. Now I think it was those attacks in New York that panicked him. He says the apocalypse has come. He's not even trying to save the garage from going out of business because he says money won't help on Judgment Day. So we're living off my paycheque from A&W. Katherine says he may be suffering from . . . wait a minute, she wrote it down for me . . . *obsessive-compulsive personality disorder.*"

"See? I've been telling you for years that he's a nutcase." It's the perfect opening, but the sheer weirdness of my mother's account and the obvious fatigue in her voice drive out any motivation to continue with my usual banter against Lyle. "So what does that mean anyway? That he can't leave the house without checking the oven ten times?"

"No, that's some other disorder with a similar name. Katherine explained that what Lyle is most likely suffering from is . . . here, let me just read out the parts she highlighted on the info sheet . . . *preoccupied with following rules to the point of perfectionism, extremely rigid in interpreting morality and ethics, requires others to submit exactly to his or her way of doing things.*"

"Wow. That does describe him to a T. So is it curable?"

"Well, Katherine can't make a diagnosis without seeing him. He might just be suffering from depression. I've invited him twice to come along with me to see her, but he just mopes and wanders around the trailer in his bathrobe. I haven't insisted because I don't want him to get angry and stop me from seeing her too. You know how he always manages to get his way."

"So what are you going to do? Seriously, do you want to spend the rest of your life living in a trailer park? You can still ask for a divorce—"

"Helene! Have you forgotten that Lyle is the one who took us in and got me dry? Yes, he's made a mistake, a huge one, but now it's my turn to care for him. I've forgiven him; he just needs time to forgive himself. All that matters is that he's come home. You can't imagine the nightmare I lived after Richard . . . well, you know. How helpless I felt trying to raise you on my own in that hotel."

"Okay, Katie. *Okay.* Whatever makes you happy," I tell her, giving in, the same way I always do when she brings up my dad. I mean, what if she's right? What if our relatives are so wrapped up in their lives that they don't even think of us? I leave the window, abandoning my plan to write Lodi, and wander into the kitchen.

"Happiness is overrated," Katie says after a short silence.

"What do you mean?"

"Oh, come on, Helene! Quit giving me advice like I'm broken or something. Go sort out your own stuff instead—decide on a subject you will actually stick to studying and go make it happen with that guy you drew all summer."

"Actually, I've met somebody else." Cradling the receiver in the crook of my shoulder, I open the fridge and take out a zucchini, two carrots, and a handful of mushrooms. "He's from France, and he's offered me the free use of his family's vacation flat for the winter—"

"Where?" she asks.

"Avignon. It's in southern France."

"No, I don't mean *where* . . . I mean, what—*what* about your university studies?"

"I didn't say I'm going. It's just an option for now."

"An option for *what?*"

"For time, for a lot of time." I tell her in a low, measured voice, trying to hide my fluster as I begin to chop the vegetables.

"Time for *what?*"

"Time to . . . to work on my art—"

"Oh, come on, Helene. Don't make the same mistake I did, chasing after some Frenchman."

"No, you don't get it." I switch the phone to my other ear. "This guy is studying here in Canada for at least a year. If I go to France, I'll be going on my own." I push the chopped zucchini and carrots off the cutting board into a saucepan and start on the mushrooms.

"Why don't you try instead to get back into that accounting program? Think about it. Do you want to end up like me at thirty-eight, falling asleep with the question, *Would you like some ketchup with those fries?* repeating in your head?"

The fear in her voice throws me off. I stop chopping to stare out my kitchen window at a crow squawking on a pole in the alley below. What if this latest decision of mine is only another ruse for her attention, to prove she was wrong to discourage me from art? "Many artists go to Europe to explore their talent," I offer in my defence as I toss the last mushroom into the pan. "I do have some ability, you know? I can draw."

"Sure, the same guy over and over."

My shoulder tightens around the phone receiver. "Actually, I have a lot of other . . ." I let my voice trail off, wary of revealing too much.

I open a jar of tomatoes and pour them over the vegetables. I give the sauce a stir, remembering how Hana's mother called her on her birthday to remind her of the shame she was bringing the family. *People are al-*

ways asking, her mother said, *when will my daughter have a husband in her life? When is she going to have children? So I make up terrible lies, terrified the neighbours will find out.* In the wee hours of the morning, I remember sitting with Hana on her sofa, telling her about when Lyle confiscated my Iron Maiden cassettes, and Hana holding her sides as tears streamed down her face. *You listened to* . . . ha, ha, ha . . . *I* . . . ha . . . *Ir* . . . *Iron* . . . ha, ha, ha . . . I started laughing with her then as I realized that childhood is only one stage of life. I no longer have to please my mother—what does it matter if she doesn't like me?

"I didn't say I was going," I remind Katie again as I fill a second pot with cold water and a dash of salt for the pasta.

"Good. Stay here, get a useful degree, and find a decent job. Make something of yourself in life."

"Katie," I say, bracing my hands on the stove in front of me to calm down, to hold back the pinching effect, something like panic, in the region surrounding my pounding heart. "I'm going to make something of myself *as an artist.*" Ignoring the fright twisting up my gut and the flush burning up my cheeks, I continue, articulating each word with a forced confidence: "I've dreamed of being a painter ever since I can first remember, so please stop telling me I'm bound to fail. It makes me feel like you're holding me back out of fear that I might actually succeed."

"Do what you want," she replies in that weary voice she always employs when checking out of a conversation. "One day you'll understand that I only meant to spare you disappointment."

Shades of Yellow

I set down my paintbrush. The telephone has been ringing at five-minute intervals for the last half hour. Wiping my hands on a rag, I pick up the receiver. My mother's voice greets me, warbling the last syllable of my name: "Helen-n-ne?"

"What's wrong?" It's Wednesday afternoon. She always works at A&W on Wednesdays. "Why aren't you at work?"

"I'm at hom-m-e," she whimpers.

Home. I wonder what that trailer looks like now, six and a half years after I dragged my single bag across the withered, overgrown lawn toward my ride to the group home.

My mother murmurs something inaudible into the phone.

"What? Speak up. I can't understand what you're saying."

"Lyle's dead. They found him this morning," she whispers, "on the riverbank a little ways downstream from the railroad crossing—"

"Hold on. What are you talking about? Lyle can't be dead."

She responds with an outburst of sobs.

"Come on, Katie. Stop it! You're frightening me."

"They said he must have been trying to cross over the river in the dark and sl-sl-slipped off the icy rails. Because he didn't leave a note or anything," she wails.

I pull away from the handset to stare at it.

"He was wearing his new yellow jacket," she says in a small voice that drifts up from the telephone in my hand. "The one I bought last week because I thought a little colour therapy might cheer him up. That's how he was spotted—the bright canary yellow of his jacket stuck out in the snow at the edge of the riverbank."

"I'm sorry, Mom. I'm sorry." These words are automatic; I can't believe what she's saying as I press my ear to the handset again.

"You know, when he didn't come home last night, I thought . . . Then this morning the police knocked on the door." She sniffs and blows her nose. "He didn't leave a note or anything!"

"It's going to be okay." Again, my response is mechanical. A hush descends over the line. "It's going to be okay, Mom," I repeat. "You're a strong woman. You can get through this."

"The funeral is on Saturday at ten o'clock. The church people are making the arrangements."

"Okay. . . . So do you want me to come up there or something?"

"Yes, of course! You can't leave me alone in this."

"Okay, okay. Saturday, right?" I make a mental list of what I must do beforehand—give notice at work, hand in my last paper, cancel dinner Friday night with Hana and Laurent, pack. "Okay, Mom, okay. I'll be there. Stay strong, okay? No drinking please, Katie. No vodka."

She sniffs and whispers goodbye, leaving me to the solitude of the dial tone.

I PUTT AROUND MY bachelor suite in my slippers, re-pinning the sheet of my makeshift bedroom, piling up stray newspapers into the recycling bin, wiping and re-wiping the table, boiling water for tea. When there is nothing left to distract me from the painting on the floor, I find I can only paint in shades of yellow: a canary jacket; a mellow Naples moon; the last of the autumn leaves in a raw, raw sienna; a sallow face fleshed out with a touch of cadmium yellow.

Then compulsion strikes and I must begin again: a bouquet of buttery lilies on a straw-coloured coffin; a dog pissing sulphur in the snow; the self-portrait of a yellow-bellied artist underwhelmed by sorrow; a still life of a banana, pineapple, and plum; the landscape of a muddied river painted in Indian and umber yellow under the cold sun of a jaundiced winter day.

The Still Life of Street Life

I awoke earlier this afternoon, drowsy and exhausted after a sleepless night spent painting. As I kicked off the comforter and stretched out in a sleepy daze across the bed, it dawned on me that there was someone I needed to find before catching the overnight bus out of here Thursday night. It would be my first time leaving Vancouver since I had arrived six years ago in a trucker's cab, having hitched a ride at a gas station in Cache Creek after the first truck from Prince George had dropped me off there. I remembered those first nights in the big city when everything was shiny and new, full of promise, sophistication and adulthood. Even the downtown Eastside seemed dazzling then, in a gritty way.

Now, as I watch the blocks flash by outside these city bus windows, I can't find promise in these streets anymore. Repressive and overbearing, they constrict their passersby to the sullen grey of their cement. I need movement, new streets, new promises. Why not take up Laurent's offer? Why not live a while in my father's homeland, and what could, by extension, become my own? I feel the stir of excitement, of possibility. Then I remember Lyle is gone. What will my mother do now? If only I could trust her to recover from grief . . . instead I fear the terrible weight of my guilt should she, out of loneliness and for lack of direction, seek solace in the bottle, with no one around this time to pick up the pieces.

In the plastic bag in my hand, I carry a bottle of water and a colour photocopy of my painting of the waif outside the train station. I scour the streets outside the bus for a glimpse of her, hoping to find her in a well-frequented public space where I can safely offer her the copy.

The bus reaches Hastings Street with no sign of her. After it makes a left turn toward downtown, I get out at the first stop in the heart of the Eastside slum. As the bus pulls away, a man with a gaunt face and swollen hands asks for my bus ticket. I tell him I will need it again and tuck it out of sight in the front pocket of my jeans. I glance over my shoulder to see a guy urinating on the cement ledge behind me. Another man with scabs all over his face asks me if I want to buy dope. I shake my head, zipping up my coat against the cold, and start down the street.

I make it a whole block down East Hastings before another man asks if I want to buy drugs. Distracted, I almost step on a man passed out on the sidewalk. My mood shifts from a determined goodwill to an edgy unease. Everything seems to come at you at once here, in an unpredictable and unreliable fashion. I realize that I must stand out with my fed body, clear skin, and clean clothes. Or, maybe, all these street people know each other, and so I am immediately recognized as an outsider.

"Spare change?" asks a man slumped up against a boarded window on a stained piece of cardboard.

"Sorry," I mumble. "I'm here looking for somebody." I realize, as I move aside for a woman pushing her belongings up the sidewalk in a shopping cart, that there are Missing Person posters of women tacked up everywhere along the street.

I make my way down the seedy strip all the way to Victory Park, after which the gentrified area of downtown begins. I make a quick tour of the park but don't see her. With a sense of dismay, I realize that if I am to do a thorough sweep of the area, I will also have to scour the rat-infested and needle-strewn alleyways. Returning up Cordova a block, then right up Abbott Street, I hesitate at the entrance to an alleyway running parallel with Hastings.

The stench of garbage and urine as I take my first steps into the lane is overpowering. I suppress a gag as I pass a first dumpster. Nestled behind the garbage bin is a lean-to constructed out of pallets and cardboard. A red, swollen foot covered in puss-filled sores sticks out of a filthy blanket. I pass on, deciding the waif's foot would be smaller, daintier. Then, doubting my memory, I double back for a second look, catching sight of two miserable addicts who have entered the alley behind me and stand huddled in the alcove of a back doorway. I watch as they exchange a ten-dollar bill for a pill. Deciding the foot is definitely not hers but relieved nevertheless to see the blanket rising and falling, I swivel around again, narrowly avoiding stepping on the shards of a broken crack pipe. When I look up ahead, I am relieved to see the nose of an idling police cruiser parked slightly across the alley at the far exit. I hurry past the last person in the alleyway, a woman squatting to piss behind a dumpster, resolved to ask the first not-too-sketchy female resident I cross if she recognizes the woman in my painting, rather than continue this random searching on my own.

The police car moves on as I exit onto Carrall Street. Half a block up the street is Pigeon Park, where, against a backdrop of graffiti-tagged wall, homeless people loiter on benches and the brick walls of bush planters. It is more of a plaza, a triangle of cement and trees on the corner of Hastings, than a park. I spot a woman on a nearby bench who seems mostly with it, if not a little drunk. Drunk, I can handle; drunk, I know. Litter is everywhere here, and I keep an eye out for needles on the ground as I make my way toward her. I get another offer of drugs from a guy leaning against the trunk of one of the tall, deciduous trees.

The woman sees me coming from afar. "You want to buy something?" she asks when I stop in front of her.

"No, no. I'm just wondering if you might know this woman." I pull out the copy of my painting from the plastic bag. "I know it's drawn from the back, but maybe by her clothes or her hair?"

The woman looks me up and down, squashes her top lip up against her nose as if to suppress a sneeze, and shakes her head.

"Are you sure?"

"Hell yeah, I'm sure," she says in a loud voice. "I'm not a nark, okay?"

"No, no," I rush to explain. "I'm not looking for her like that. I just want to give her this—it's a copy of a painting I did of her."

"So you're another fucking Ken Foster," she says, taking the copy from me.

"Who?"

"Oh, what the fuck." She stands up and shouts at another woman over by the water fountain. "Hey, you seen Eddie? This girl here did a painting of her."

I feel a little uncomfortable as thirty or so pairs of eyes in the plaza turn on me—the self-proclaimed artist—but I do my best to pull back my shoulders and stand tall under the spotlight. A group of street people wander over to look at the copy. Warily, I watch them pass it back and forth between themselves, their fingernails blackened with grime. I soon begin to relax, however, as it becomes obvious that boredom is as rampant as drug use around here and that my showing up in the square with something new to look at serves as a welcome distraction.

The woman by the water fountain beckons me over. I take back the copy of my painting and turn to go to her, but the drunken woman, seated back on the bench now, arrests my arm.

"Welfare sucked last month," she says. "Got a little something for me?"

I reach into my left jean pocket and, careful not to let the slightest hint of a bill show, pull out what coins I have. She takes them from me without thanks, stuffing them into her shirt pocket. I feel like a penny-pincher as I stride across the plaza with three good ten-dollar bills still stuffed in my pocket, and I feel like every single person in the square is thinking the same about me.

Trash and leaves are strewn around the square base of the cement fountain. I step over a paper plate to reach the woman. She takes my artwork, glances at it, and demands, "Why'd you paint her?"

I shrug. "I don't know. I guess I found her beautiful . . . in a way."

She hands the copy back and points me south down Carrall Street. "Try in that lane there. I seen her in there about twenty minutes ago, behind Carnegie Centre."

"Thanks." I turn to go.

"Hey, don't you got some change for me too?"

"Sorry, I gave it all to your friend."

She spits on the ground and shakes her head.

I hurry away up the street, crossing over Hastings and Carrall to turn into the alleyway. On high alert for dirty needles and other dangerous debris, I start up the darkened lane.

I recognize her right away. She is wearing a black pair of leggings, platform sandals slightly too big for her feet, a peach halter top, and a tattered coat with a fake fur trim, the zipper obviously broken. We are nearing the middle of winter, and I can't help but wonder if she is cold. She is tucked between an electrical pole and a graffiti-covered wall, crouched down with a crack pipe hanging off her lips. As I walk up to her, she slips the pipe into her handbag and straightens up. She looks like she weighs ninety pounds at most, her ribs jutting out from under her top.

"Hi, Eddie. I'm Helene."

She stares at me like I'm an alien from another planet. I do feel out of my element, and it does seem like a different world altogether. It smells of rotting cabbage and urine in here, as well as the remaining chemical odour of whatever she was smoking. The air tastes chalky and putrid, and the sounds of the city are far away and muffled. All that can be seen of the overcast sky are the shapes cut out by lines and lines of electrical and telephone wires, leading deeper and deeper into a tunnel of dumpsters and pulled-up fire escapes.

I wonder what I'm doing in this dangerous and dirty place, introducing myself to a skeleton of a junkie.

"I'm so sad today," she blurts out. "It's my daughter's second birthday. I only seen her twice since she was born."

I hold out the copy of my painting to her.

"What's this?" she asks. I can see track marks on the back of her wrist as she reaches for it.

"It's a painting I made of you. I saw you a few months ago in front of the train station. I came here to give you a copy."

She studies the sheet, pinching her burnt lips together.

I'm considering how best to take my leave when she says, "They won't let me see Ashley until I'm clean for seventy-two hours."

I glance behind me at the exit to the alleyway half a block back. I want to ask her why she doesn't clean up then for three days, but I realize

I am out of my depth. I have no idea what addiction feels like nor to what compulsions it can drive a person. Yes, my mother is an alcoholic, but I also saw her recover. So I have nothing to offer this woman, other than my artistic vision of her as seen by an outsider.

"You wonder why I don't do that, right?" she asks. "So I could make it to her party, right?"

I turn back and give a hesitant nod.

"I'm an addict, and I'll die an addict." She gives a faint smile, showing off a top gum line of missing teeth. "You can't imagine the things I do for money. I spend my entire day trying to rip people off. I sell drugs so I don't have to sell my body, but I done that when necessary too. I done just about everything.

"I got clean for a few months last year. I was taking the medicine they prescribed me and doing real good, but then I screwed up and lost everything. I don't expect to see my girl again before I die in one of these back lanes."

An awkward silence falls as she fumbles around in her bag for a cigarette. I catch the sight of needles, a piece of tubing, and a blue elastic armband before she zips it closed again. She lights the smoke and power drags on it. I notice that her pupils are widely dilated, but I can't bring myself to leave just yet as I sense she desperately needs someone to listen.

"I don't want Ashley's life to be wasted. Maybe it's better that she doesn't know me. They say I'm bipolar. That's why I alternate between wanting to kill myself and feeling like a superwoman. I don't want to mess her up like my mother did me. She was a drunk and got me wasted as a child. I gone through six different foster homes in Prince George—"

"I'm from Prince George too," I offer in feeble contribution.

She seems too intoxicated, however, for a two-way conversation. Paying no attention to my interruption, she continues, "I started smoking pot at eleven and ran away with my boyfriend at thirteen. We ended up down here, camped out in the woods at Wreck Beach. But that was too sketchy for me at night when my boyfriend wasn't around because I was still pretty then." She gives a faint smile. "After I got raped, we moved into a rooming house down here. We started doing ecstasy and coke at after-hours parties. That led to meth and crack, and he got himself stabbed to death selling bunk. Ever since I been lying, stealing, and conning my way from hit to hit. I never even seen where they buried him."

"Do you want some water?" I ask, noticing the dryness of her burnt lips.

"What?" She appears thrown off by my question. I am thrown off by the intimate nature of her revelations. I can relate to running away and to after-hours parties, but the rest . . . I am reminded of how I tried ecstasy for the first time at a late-night underground party in a building only a few blocks from this alleyway; I am reminded of how I dared not fall asleep for the twenty-plus hours it took the two truckers to drive me the long road down south to Vancouver. But how does one get from there to here—to this alleyway, to these flimsy, tattered clothes, to this skeleton of a body on the verge of death by injection and starvation?

I hand her the plastic bag with the unopened bottle of water inside. She takes the bottle out, tucks it into her purse, and tosses the empty sack to the ground.

"You can't imagine the things I done," she continues. "Now I'm scared of disappearing. There are so many girls just vanished. That's why I'd rather sell dope than my body. My handler thrashed me black and blue last week over fifteen bucks." She pulls back her hair to point out the remainder of a bruise on her cheek. "But that beats standing on a corner and getting into some psycho's car."

"How old are you, if you don't mind me asking?"

Her body gives an involuntary tremor. "Twenty-three," she says as she reaches up the thin sleeve of her coat to scratch at her arm.

"Wow. We're almost the same age." I start wondering if maybe we hung out together in a past life, at one of those late-night parties. Her gaunt face looks much older though—she could pass for forty.

She shifts her bag to her opposite shoulder, her movements increasingly brusque and fidgety. "I really want to see Ashley again. She's the only good thing to come out of my life."

"You're still young," I tell her, terrified by the defeat in her voice, by the certainty her life lies in the past.

She opens her mouth in a toothless cackle. "*You're* young. I'm an old soul. I might make it to twenty-five, but I won't make it to thirty."

I thrust my hands deep into my coat pockets and shift my weight to my opposite foot. My eyes have grown accustomed to her emaciated figure, toothless front gum line, swollen knuckles, and threadbare clothes. Now, instead of a junkie standing in front of me, I see a scared and lonely woman; instead of a dark and dangerous alleyway, I see a terrifyingly isolated place to die.

"Welfare's not for another week and a half," she says. "Can you spare me some money?"

I reach into my left jean pocket, trying to peel out one bill from the wad of three tens in there. Unsuccessful, I turn slightly to the side to discretely slip one out from the others. Turning back toward her, I hand her the ten.

"Please," she says, "give me that other one too. I've got to get something to eat, a little meat on my bones."

I start to peel away the second ten then stop. "Just a second," I tell her, reaching into my other pocket to check the time stamp on my bus ticket: thirty minutes remaining. Reassured that I have the means to get home, I hand her the two remaining bills.

As soon as she has the money in hand, she slips away as stealthy as a cat up the alley. When she reaches Carrall Street, she turns around for a brief second. "I like the painting," she yells up the lane in a throaty croak before disappearing around the corner.

I exit the alleyway the opposite way onto Columbia Street. Just before I reach the sidewalk, a guy high on something veers into the lane, scratching wildly at old scabs bleeding on his arms. My heart races as he comes straight at me, but then, just as I am wondering who will hear me scream in here, he continues on, unseeing, locked up in the prison of drug-induced psychosis.

The panhandler at the bus stop asks for a quarter.

"Sorry," I tell him, pulling out my pockets to reveal their emptiness.

"How about some beer money?" He smells like he has been drinking mouthwash. I shrug and show him my empty pockets again. The bus pulls up, and I step back into the world as I know it—clean, well-dressed people with clear skin and fed bodies. As the bus turns right up Main Street and into Chinatown, leaving the worst of skid row behind, I remember Matthew telling me that, in this country, we are free to choose our lives. Who, as a child, chooses neglect and abuse? Who, in their right mind, chooses mental illness? Who, in seeking solace and escape, chooses to become addicted? To what extent, I wonder, can people be held accountable for the brokenness of their lives?

My apartment seems decadently roomy and clean when I get home. I lie down on my couch, replaying the events of the afternoon, sketching image after image of the woman in my mind's eye, a whole series of portraits to frame and hang in my mental galleries. Then I spend the rest of the evening packing. Thursday evening, after a full shift at work, I will catch the overnight bus to Windeal. How different my life has been in the six years since I left the North from that of the waif's in the alley. *Why?* What random chance, what roll of the dice, what turn of fortune's wheel has led to me to better circumstances and her to worse?

Odds and Ends

A slushy rain welcomes the Greyhound bus into Windeal, a lonely Northern town nestled between shallow peaks in a wide valley. The freezing rain splatters on my face as I lug my carry-on down the silver steps of the bus and toward the gas station that doubles as the bus depot. I take a seat inside, staring out at the grey snowbanks lining the highway that splits the town in half before continuing on to more exciting places. The double yellow lines of that highway mean *no passing* up here, but down the hill in the trailer park, they've always meant *no trespassing*: down there, on the other side of the road, is the reserve.

I finish my coffee and leave my bags at the table to wander the two aisles of the gas station. All but one of the other bus passengers have been picked up. I slide open the cooler door and select a pail of raspberry yogurt. The woman at the register takes my money and returns to reading *The Windeal Weekly*, the local broadsheet. I take a plastic spoon from next to the coffee dispenser and sit on the bench outside, under the eave and out of the rain.

A beat-up van stops in for gas, its cream colour lost long ago under layers of grime. A blond man rolls down the passenger window. I recognize Jim, six or seven trailers down from ours, or at least that is where he used to live with his wife and kids when I was here.

"Just got in on the bus, eh?"

I nod.

"Need a ride someplace?" The scent of spoiled diapers and stale beer drifts through the rain.

"No thanks." I spoon yogurt into my mouth and suck at the spoon like a Popsicle, licking one creamy layer off another until only plastic remains. I glance up the empty highway for a sign of my mother, praying my old neighbour won't recognize me.

"You sure?" He points to the seats behind him, crowded with care-free adults and vacant-eyed teenagers. "We got lots of room, eh." He holds up a can and grins. "And beer too."

"No, no thanks. Someone's coming for me."

"Home for Christmas, right?"

I stare into my yogurt.

"Okay then. We'll quit bothering you." He brushes away the blond strand that has fallen across his eyes and holds up his beer can in salute. "Have a nice day, eh."

"Yeah, you too. Bye now."

I'm dipping in the spoon again. All around me black snowdrifts are melting under the late morning drizzle.

"SORRY I'M SO LATE," my mother says when she arrives an hour after the bus has left. She is driving Lyle's wood-panelled station wagon. "We're busier than usual because of the holidays, so I had to stay overtime at work." Her orange and brown uniform smells of grease when I hug her.

I can tell she is not used to driving, at least not on snowy roads. After I load my luggage in the back and strap on my seatbelt in the front, I watch the wipers beat back the slush as she guides the car onto the high-way. She steers us onto the main drag, and we crawl past my old high school. Nothing has changed, except the distance between things appears to have shrunk. What was a long walk to my teenage eyes, from the school to the convenience store, is only a few short blocks.

We inch past the library, city hall, post office, and government build-ings. Neither of us seems capable of small talk. We pass the strip mall with the A&W, Credit Union, walk-in clinic, and co-op grocery. Just after Lyle's church, she signals left and turns the wagon down the steep hill past the gas station to where the trailers lie side by side, an assort-ment of melting snowmen and battered cars scattered in between them.

As we pull in the driveway, I shrink from the tin trailer, its familiar one eye closed, that front window with the blind let down. I fight the urge to run, to put kilometres, oceans, entire continents between myself and this place. Instead, I trail my mother up the porch steps to the door.

Katie stamps off her boots on the outdoor mat then tugs them off, sliding her feet into the worn slippers on the shag rug in the entry. I back away from her and lean against the wet porch railing. On either side of this trailer, more tin houses line the street, a few with Christmas trees blinking from inside their windows and many with empty beer returns piling up under their porches.

The sound of a chainsaw carries through the slushy rain. Turning in the direction of the reserve, I glimpse the green aluminum of a new roof poking through the trees—no, wait, make that two new roofs. Over there, on the other side of the highway, across the yellow dividing lines, where you don't go alone, where you don't go after dark. Maybe in the big city somewhere, cultured people of diverse backgrounds are developing a deeper respect for First Nations peoples, for their unique cultures, languages, and art, but down here the othering persists: *Never trust an Indian.* Never go alone to the reserve, never go after dark: these are the unwritten, unspoken rules over here on the white side.

Yet, if anything has changed around Windeal, it would seem to be over there, where as a preteen and teenager I only set foot once. Actually, I didn't even set foot, just stayed in the back of the pickup while we tore at high speeds though the dirt streets, banded together in the safety of numbers. A braver boy stood to shout out, *Nisga'a!* at an old man shuffling down the street, who paused to shake his head at us, a bunch of redneck kids piled into the back of a beat-up pickup. It was only after I left Windeal that I learned that *Nisga'a* wasn't an insult as the teenage boy believed but rather the name of a band living in the Nass River valley on the northwestern coast. The boy also shouted, *Squaw!* at a woman hanging out her laundry and at a grandmother smoking a pipe on her porch, which made us giggle because the lives of these women didn't look so different from ours. Looking back now, I see how afraid we were, our driver burning through the gravel streets as fast as the truck would allow, leaving behind streaks of dust to choke the raven-haired toddlers pedalling in diapers on their tricycles, the rest of us in the back clapping our hands to our mouths to yell, *Ow-Ow-OWWWWW!*

Standing in the rain on my mother's porch, I am astounded by the ignorance in which I grew up. How lucky I am that Lyle kicked me out of here, whatever his reasons were at the time. Staring at the double yellow lines of the not-so-distant highway, I tremble before the power that place has to determine destiny, dealing out the cards of language, accent, upbringing, education, culture, and citizenship. It is with these cards that we play out our lives. For some these givens are a source of pride; for others, like me, they are more a source of shame.

STEPPING THROUGH THE DOORWAY of the trailer, I hang my rain jacket on the coat rack. My mother has changed into a faded pink housecoat and is smoking at the table. "Are you coming in, or are you going to just stand there letting in the cold?"

I pull the door shut behind me and kick off my wet runners.

It seems that time can make even the mundane memorable. As Katie reaches for the crystal bowl overflowing with cigarette ashes and butts on the cluttered windowsill, I am reminded of how in Prince George, before Lyle, she would wake in the afternoon, swing her legs over the side of the bed, and light her first cigarette of the day. When the shadows had grown long and started to darken the room, she would allow me to turn on the lights; she would go to the mirror, then, to paint her lips fuchsia pink and her eyelids sky blue. Back on the bed in front of the television, she would touch up her matching pink nails then lie back on the pillows twiddling a third or fourth cigarette between their razor edges and laugh at *Cheers* until mascara tears streamed down her face . . . and another bottle of vodka had been drained. She was glamorous then, in a destitute way.

I pull out a chair at the table. Despite numerous re-tapings, strands of dirty stuffing poke out of the yellow vinyl; I re-tuck them into their holes before taking a seat. Katie has opened a takeout container of chicken strips on the table. A sense of irritation creeps under my skin as I dip a piece into the accompanying tub of sauce—the fast food, the tatty furniture, the mobile home, the '80s wagon. I watch Katie crunch absentmindedly on a strip, chewing off a bite before dragging on her second cigarette and drifting away from me in her thoughts.

"So," I say to remind her of my presence, "do you know how to get in touch with any of my father's family in France?" She looks at me now but, rather than answer, drops the remaining half of her strip back into the takeout container and stubs out her cigarette. Standing, she wipes the grease off her fingers with a rag from the sink. When she's done, she turns around to lean against the counter.

"They're my family too, you know. I have a right to contact my grandparents, don't I?"

"Helene . . ." she says.

But I don't stop there. "Did he have any brothers or sisters? Do I have uncles and aunties on his side? Maybe I have a whole slew of cousins in France—have you ever considered that?"

She pushes off the counter and shuffles in her slippers over to the couch where she lies down and seals her eyes. I shadow her. I kneel on the carpet beside her and shake open her lids.

"What?" she asks, her voice like the cry of an injured bird, and closes her eyes again.

I inspect her face. Threads of blue radiate outward from her eyelids like fingers of coral, veins pulsating beneath the skin. A larger vessel throbs at her temple, lifting the pale skin before dropping away. Perched in the hollow of her throat, a silver cross. I know she comes from a middle-class Anglophone family in Montreal. She went to an all-girls' Catholic school. Two round bubbles are forming at the inside corners of her eyelids; one slips past the butterfly of arteries, over the bulging vein, to slide into her ear. She ran away with my father when she was seventeen because she was pregnant with his child—me. He died in a motorcycle accident when I was two, or else he overdosed. We remained at the hotel in the wake of his absence; my mother kept taking off her clothes downstairs while I played with my one rat-haired Barbie upstairs until shortly before Lyle rescued us when I was nine. These details I've managed to glean, but what I want to know is what my father was like. What were his dreams? Was he from Lyon, or did I make up that part? My mother has made nothing clear except that he was a scumbag for getting her pregnant two months before her seventeenth birthday, promising her paradise then dumping her instead in that hotel in Prince George.

Her lips move and she whispers, "All this time, I've been waiting for him to come back to me."

I don't want to talk about Lyle. I don't want to think about Lyle, about the body up on the hill in the funeral home, about the last thing I said to his face: *You never even came close to being a real father.*

"Richard was a lot older than me," my mother is saying.

I inch forward on my knees. "How much older?"

"Sixteen years."

I inch closer, my eyes glued to her face. "Tell me more."

Her blue-veined lids drift open. "We met in a restaurant," she whispers, staring up at the ceiling. "You know, the image I have of him that day is still as sharp as a photograph. I was playing hooky from school with a friend—we were two Catholic schoolgirls in uniform huddled over coffees at a corner table. He was wearing studded leather pants and a black jacket. The moment I laid eyes on him, I knew he was excitement and adventure in person. He swaggered over to the counter with his helmet in hand and asked the waitress to fill up his thermos." She closes her eyes again, as if to better savour the memory. "I undid the top button of my blouse, went up to him, and asked for a ride on his bike."

I wait for more, but as usual she has stopped short. "Katie, please..."

At the sound of her name, she opens her eyes into a squint, as if momentarily confused. Guardedly, she asks, "What?"

"Tell me, how did he die?"

When her gaze seeks out mine, I turn to stare out the window. "I have a right to know," I insist, as if that should be enough to coax the truth out of her after all these years.

WHEN A BREAK COMES in the drizzle, my mother throws on some sweats and her outerwear. "I'm going out to buy cigarettes," she says.

"I'll come with you."

We follow our street to the highway then slug up the shoulder to the turnoff to the reserve. A now paved road leads us under the welcome sign that spans two poles and depicts a bear in traditional black and red. The store is a five-minute walk inside the community past a row of weathered totems and the remains of a cedar-plank longhouse. We pass a few houses on the way. A man pauses from salting his driveway to say hello, and a woman waves at us from her porch. Inside the small store, bags of chips and nachos stand stacked in boxes on top of the video display racks. Lined up next to the cash register are open boxes of liquorice, jujubes, and jawbreakers for piecemeal sale. Plastic-wrapped bannock is stacked behind the counter under a shelf of cigarettes.

"No luck today," Katie whispers as she scans the movies. "Ethan's not here. He never charges me tax."

"So sorry to hear about your loss," the woman behind the counter says as Katie pays. "My brother was the first officer at the scene—"

"I know," Katie cuts her off. "He came to my door with the news."

BACK AT THE TRAILER, Katie leans against the windowsill at the table, blowing blue smoke rings into the dim winter light seeping in through the window. I stare up the hallway behind her, the gateway to the rest of the trailer. I don't feel like discovering what they've done with my bedroom. I don't want to revisit the floral wallpaper of my mother's room nor bear the scrutiny of the Jesus picture above the bed. I don't want to smell Lyle, don't want to smell death. I don't want to remember how, the last time I was here, I dragged my duffle bag down this hallway, hesitated a moment or two on the brink of the doorway, and then threw myself into adulthood—if that's what can be called the haze of drugs and booze and sex that followed my escape from the group home.

Katie takes a series of quick drags, flicks neatly into the ashtray, and studies me curiously. "You know," she informs me. "You've always known. I didn't hide anything from you—well, not once you were old enough. You just blocked it out because you didn't want to know."

On the windowsill, odds and ends flank the crystal ashtray: a red stone, a paperclip, all-purpose glue, broken sunglasses, an aloe vera plant, an old penknife. There is also a collection of wooden carvings: a grizzly, a female bust, an eagle, and a foot.

"Who carved those?" I ask to change the subject.

"I did."

I give her a bewildered stare as I stand up to examine them.

"Helene?" She touches my forearm. I jerk away as if her fingers were red-hot prongs. "You're the one who asked," she says as she stubs out her cigarette. "So sit down and listen."

I sink back into my chair.

"Richard was a dealer. When I say a *dealer*, I'm talking a big one, one of the Angels. He once told me that to be a full member you had to have killed someone."

I roll my eyes. "Whatever."

She knits her eyebrows together, sizing me up. "I'm not exaggerating, Helene. The mistake he made was doing the drugs he was selling."

The lone sunglass lens on the windowsill is covered in dust. Somebody should sort through all the junk in this place and get rid of what is not needed anymore.

"Did you know that when I arrived in Vancouver I slept under a bridge for almost two weeks?" I ask her. "Did you know that I had to beg on Granville Street?"

My mother stares out the window, apparently ignoring me. I listen to the pitter-patter of her fingers clattering over the table in search of her cigarettes, *tap tap tap* as if she were blind.

"I could have ended up on East Hastings with my face on a Missing Person poster. So thank your country for its social programs; without them, I would never have finished high school."

Katie's lighter is a flash in the gathering darkness as she sets a new killer aflame. I watch her suck at her fix, exhale in long, drawn-out sighs until the cigarette has dwindled to a stub. She is staring out the window into the cold winter night, and I want to smash everything in this trailer to bits. Because no matter what I say, no matter how ferocious or bold, I never seem able to get through to her.

Look at me! Look at me, please!

"When are you going to stop being mad at me, Helene?" she asks, standing up. Nonchalantly, as if this were an answerable question.

I want to unload my memories on her, make her take some responsibility. I want to tell her how, in the wee hours of my seventeenth birthday, I spilled my guts to a guy I'd just met and whose name I don't remember anymore, both of us flying high on ecstasy. I want to describe that feeling of deep affection and attachment that filled all the deep, empty crevices within me and how that great drug-fueled passion left me wrecked by midday, left my body trembling and anxious. I want her to understand how terrified I was when six o'clock in the evening came, when the guy was gone but my hands wouldn't stop shaking, and I began to imagine the ecstasy had dried up my spinal fluid and put me at risk for paralysis. This was a year after I'd run from the home in Prince George, hitchhiked my way down south, and knocked at Christine's door. I was seventeen but my body felt forty, raw and used. I want to make Katie understand my desperation knowing something terrible was going to happen if I didn't smarten up—AIDS or a bad trip that would leave me psychotic—and how I was going down, down, down, snorting speed and smoking cocaine. I want her to understand how I came that evening to decide, out of fear, to follow Christine's advice to get my high school diploma, not because the guidance came from Christine but because Christine was the only one to offer any.

Now I've supposedly made it. Got myself into university with a scholarship, an apartment in the city, a waitressing job. Except I'm on the brink of walking out on all this because I don't know the answer to the question of *what next?* After years of struggling to survive, *what now?* I want to ask my mother what you are supposed to do once your *real* life begins. Once you no longer have to pretend to fit in and appear normal.

Katie braces her hand on the edge of the table. "Helene," she whispers, leaning into me. "I didn't have it easy. You know he didn't die. I was nineteen with a two-year-old when he abandoned me."

I cut her off snidely. "Does it always have to be—"

"I'm going to lie down in the bedroom."

"—a competition between us? Who's suffered most? Can't you just stop thinking about your own sorry life for once and admit ..." But then, as her footsteps pad with descending echoes down the length of the hallway, I stop in mid-sentence because I've heard what she's said. I've finally, finally heard what she's said.

The Funeral

Katie holds my hand throughout the church service, withdrawing her fingers at times to blow her nose into the tissues she clasps between her knees before gliding her damp hand back into mine. About twenty-five people are scattered on the pews behind us, mostly Lyle's fellow church-goers. His brother and mother have also driven in from Prince George. Elaine, the hairdresser, sits at the very back sporting a swollen belly; Katie pointed her out when we arrived.

At the pulpit, the preacher intersperses details of Lyle's life with tired Bible verses: "We have lost a great man: a son, a brother, a husband, a stepfather, and a dear friend. *Blessed are those who mourn for they shall be comforted.* We are here today to commemorate the life of a man born in Prince George in the late fifties, the first of two brothers. One of his fa-vourite pastimes as a youngster was fishing . . ."

On the wall, behind the pulpit, ticks the same clock from my first visit here when I was decked out in a frilly daffodil dress Lyle had bought me. Like that day, I sit perfectly still, following the ticking hand forward as it counts down the minutes until the service is over. Unlike that day, however, I am not hopeful; I am filled with sorrow. When my mother married Lyle, I was excited at the prospect of having a dad who would live with us and love me; my first memories are of searching for some-one, anyone, to be my father. Here in the future, I can still taste the bit-ter disappointment of that nine-year-old's dream. Soon into that first year together as a blended family, I found myself at odds with Lyle's in-flexible parenting style; I soon realized that, even if the corners of my bedspread were exactly aligned and all my shoes in the closet pointed in the same direction, I would never achieve the level of perfectionism required to earn his affection.

"Lyle will be forever missed, but I also know in time we will meet again," the preacher assures us, as if privy to the answers of life and death. He speaks about resurrection in the New Jerusalem, about gem-stoned roads and walls of gold. He reads from a leather-bound Bible uplifted and open on his palms. He punctuates his words with skyward gazes, and I glance back at the sprinkling of people behind my mother and me. Don't they see through the artifice of this preacher's assurances, slick and honed like those of a salesman's pitch?

I pick up the Bible beside me on the pew. I flick through its diaphanous pages and fall upon the Book of Job:

He that goeth down to the grave shall come up no more. He shall return no more to his house, neither shall his place know him any more. Therefore I will not refrain my mouth; I will speak in the anguish of my spirit; I will complain in the bitterness of my soul.

Everybody in the audience stands. Returning the Bible to the pew, I follow suit. Hushed amens are uttered throughout the church as the preacher leads us to the end of the service with a prayer for resurrection. After all, why not entertain hope? Still, I find my thoughts returning to the passage from the Book of Job, to the words of the doubter, a man for whom rhetorical answers were no longer good enough, who demanded to know the *raison d'être* of human suffering and impermanence.

We line up to pay our respects to the drowned man. First in line is my mother; deification tumbles out of her mouth, her swan song to Lyle's abandoned atoms, a shroud to bury him in. The stooped lady in front of me, Lyle's mother, refers to his expression as one of eternal peace. My turn comes but painting this last image of him is impossible, this blank, white hole in the page, this erasure of being and word.

I stare down at his embalmed face and remember reading a *National Geographic* feature on the autopsy of a two-thousand-year-old mummy. I remember wondering if the security of scientific reasoning doesn't at times desert archaeologists to panicky thoughts, such as, *What if this corpse reaches out a skeletal hand?* Evidence of consciousness two thousand years after death would be terrifying, but wouldn't it also offer a morbid hope? So what a disappointment it must be to unwrap the linen and find nothing but dried skin taut over bone—no spirit, no soul.

I'm sorry, I whisper to Lyle's body, more for my benefit than for that of the deceased. *I'm sorry for the tragedy of your mortality. I'm sorry that, as Marcus Aurelius wrote nearly two thousand years ago,* in a little time all the world will forget you. *I'm sorry that despite my best intentions, I could never love you. I'm sorry if, after I realized you could never love me either, I sought only to oppose you with my insolence and contempt.*

It's drizzling as we leave the church for the cemetery. My mother is too shaken up to drive, so I take the wheel. After the coffin has been lowered into the frozen hole in the ground, the pastor delivers a line or two more from under his black umbrella. Across from us stands Elaine, her bleached hair knotted into a messy chignon, one hand resting on her belly where it pushes through her coat. She stands precariously close to the edge and I imagine her slipping on the slushy grass into the open grave—

My mother's knees buckle, disrupting the flight of my imagination. The preacher has just recited, *"Earth to earth, ashes to ashes, dust to dust,"* and sprinkled the coffin with sand. I manage to catch Katie by the arm so that she is eased rather than pitched to her knees in the snow. Tearing off her gloves, she claws at the grey slush with her bare hands and tosses a handful onto the coffin, as though throwing a plate in anger across the room. It lands with a *clunk* on the wooden lid. The preacher comes around to help my mother to her feet as Elaine, despite her swollen belly, bends down gracefully to form a clump of snow that she tosses in after my mother's.

I wrap an arm around Katie's shoulders and steer her toward the car. Inside the station wagon, we snap the buckles of our seatbelts into place and wait for the idling motor to warm up the vehicle. We watch the other cars pull away as our breath fogs the windows. I steal a glance through my side window at the hole in the ground. A yellow backhoe has arrived to scoop up the clay; another man stands by, leaning into his shovel. A shudder passes through me for the man about to be hidden away in the bowels of the earth. *What purpose did his life serve? What did it mean?* Impatient, I test the station wagon by taking my foot off the gas pedal. It stalls. I turn the key in the ignition again and we wait, watching through an open window as the cemetery caretakers shape the mound. The last of the other vehicles, with Lyle's brother at the wheel and his mother in the passenger seat, leaves for the reception in the church basement.

I tug at the collar of my coat, my throat tight. What will Katie do now? I glance over at her, but her eyes reveal nothing of her intentions, whether they be to remain sober despite her grief or to numb her pain with booze. Maybe it is selfish of me not to move back up here for a while as she begged me to do last night. As I steer the car along the highway back to the church, I watch her out of the corner of my eye as she bites down her nails one by one, looking faraway behind a blank stare.

My Ticket out of Here

The pale winter light seeping through the sea-green curtains wakes me in my childhood bed. I glance around the tiny room, at the pastel striped wallpaper, the floral comforter, and the folding table, all as I left them at fifteen. I dress and, unlocking the bedroom door, tiptoe down the hallway. My mother stirs on the couch. "Good morning," she croaks as though nothing has happened. I pull on my tennis shoes, grab the car keys, and drive up the hill to the library.

Running away again, Helene? Is that all this is?

I'm online when Christine swings in through the library doors in a knee-length down coat and sheepskin boots. She waves, stopping by the librarian's desk to sign up for the computer before meandering toward me up an aisle of bestseller paperbacks, pausing to scan the back cover of one along the way.

"Sorry to hear about your stepdad," she says when she reaches me, leaning in for a quick hug. "I would have come to the funeral, but I had an exam yesterday. I just flew in last night."

I nod as she releases me. With everything that has been happening, I forgot that she comes home every Christmas—home to her mother's holiday baking, her father's latest hunting photos, and the yearly family backcountry ski trip.

"By the way, James flew up with me," she says. "We're going snowshoeing along the path above the river this afternoon. . . ." Christine's words trail off as her eyes scan the travel details on my computer screen. "Are you planning a trip?"

"I might move to France."

She opens her eyes wide. "But classes start up again in two weeks."

"I'll explain later." I point at the computer. "I've only got ten minutes left, and I need to check out ticket prices." I turn back to the screen, suppressing a smile. Is it possible that I've just managed to impress her?

"You know that Matthew is coming back right after New Year's, don't you?"

I glance at the clock behind the librarian's desk, at the red seconds hand inching forward: once, twice, three times. From miles away, I hear my voice asking, "Are you sure?"

Christine is unzipping her puffy coat when I swivel around. "He told James he'd be back for the winter semester," she tells me. "Apparently he broke his ankle climbing, so he's decided to cut his exchange year short."

"What about his girlfriend?"

"I guess they've split up. She got a position in Hong Kong after her doctoral research was a breakthrough for something in biochemistry. You know Matthew—he's got to be somewhere with mountains."

"But he can't climb with a broken ankle!"

Christine shrugs. "Guess that's why he's coming back here, to finish up his degree while he's still a cripple. He and James are planning a climbing trip to South America, so he needs to make sure his ankle heals properly." Pausing, she studies me. I become aware of how tired and drained I must look. "I could have told you this ages ago if you'd bothered to call me."

I glance back at the computer to avoid the strange hurt in her eyes. The itinerary for a one-way flight to Lyon has popped up. "Do you want to select your seat?" blinks the question on the screen.

"You could have called too, you know," I blurt, louder than intended.

She holds a finger to her lips to shush me. "I've been so busy with my master's program and everything. . . ." She glances at her left hand. Following her gaze, I notice the large solitaire on her ring finger, glinting in the overhead fluorescent light.

"Wow. I didn't know things had gotten so serious between the two of you. So you're going to do the whole marriage thing?"

She shrugs. "Why not? James popped the question last week, and I was crazy enough to accept. Now he's up here to meet my parents."

"How's that going?"

She hugs her coat, looking downright panicked. "We got in late last night, so breakfast is all they've seen of him so far."

I lean back in my chair and run my fingers through my hair. My mother got drunk last night. She came home tipsy carrying a mickey of vodka, and we wrestled until I left her the bottle and stomped down the hallway to my bedroom. Once she figured out my door was locked for good and I wasn't coming out, she talked to herself for hours before passing out on the couch and throwing up later in the bathroom. This morning she greeted me with a croaky *good morning* from the couch, as if nothing had happened. I pulled on my runners, grabbed the car keys, and drove up here.

Running away from another drunken Christmas eve, Helene? Is that all this is?

"I'm signed up for the computer after you," Christine says, turning toward the magazine rack, "so I'll let you finish up."

I nod and open up email from Hana.

Hi Helene,

How did the funeral go? I've been mostly hanging out in the basement playing video games with my brothers since arriving here in Cranbrook. My mom's quit talking to me again, so anything she has to say she sends through Dad. With all this lazing about and family drama, I haven't learned a single line for The Vagina Monologues, *which we're performing in less than four weeks. I'm a little panicked to say the least!*

So what have you decided about France? I hope you will take up Laurent's offer. It's so generous of him and would be a great experience. Let's hang out for New Year's in any case. I know of a couple parties on the Drive we can crash. xoxo, Hana.

As I close the email, my heart skips a couple beats: the pop-up is still there, asking if I want to buy a one-way ticket to Lyon for $479, including taxes and fees.

I glance at the clock again. Three minutes. The young librarian gets up to consult the sign-up sheet.

"You almost done?" Christine asks from the magazine rack.

I lean back from the screen and stretch out my shoulder blades.

As the librarian strides toward me, I remember that her name is Misty and that she was in Christine's grade in high school.

"How are you?" she greets Christine, sweeping dark side bangs out of her eyes. "I heard you just got engaged."

Christine nods and shows off her ring. "Yeah, it seems like the whole town knows already."

Christine was popular in our combined elementary and high school. That's why, when twelfth-grade girls in trendy Guess jeans and Club Monaco sweatshirts started calling me *skank* and *ho*, Christine, even as an eleventh grader, could persuade them to lay off me. It started just after Thanksgiving, the year Stacy died, when at thirteen I lost my virginity to a twelfth grader at a weekend bush party. By Monday, the whole school knew he'd bagged an eighth grader. Three girls in his grade were particularly merciless. They caught me by the lockers and snagged their pens through a hole in my grey winter coat, rending it to shreds. Christine arrived in time to save my homework. *Thanks for the great new look*, I snickered as I sauntered out the back door. Once on the shortcut in the woods that led down to the trailer park, I burst into tears. I couldn't bear the shame of Katie and Lyle knowing what an outcast I'd become, so I made as if I had chosen to dress in shredded clothes as a new style and proceeded to slash holes in every black thing I owned.

When Misty turns to me, her tone flattens to one reserved for strangers. "Your half hour is up. We ask that everyone please respect their time limit."

I close the browser and surrender the chair to Christine. Misty thanks me and turns away. It seems she doesn't remember my downcast eyes, my black lipstick, my inverted five-pointed star. Perhaps that teenage Goth isn't someone worth remembering—even I try to forget the angst of that fourteen- and fifteen-year-old, her obsessive sketches of Stacy's likeness and memorization of Sylvia Plath's poetry.

"Christine?" I whisper when Misty is gone. I want to ask if things are really over between Matthew and Yoshiko.

"What?" Christine demands, her fingers a blur on the keyboard.

Oh, Matthew, I imagine her saying. *You should have seen Helene grilling me once she found out you were coming back.*

"Nothing. Forget it." Over the carpeted floor, past the theft detectors and out through the glass doors, I force my sneakers forward one step after another. My body feels like it is splintering into pieces, each part acting on its own: up comes a knee, down goes a foot. Outside, the air tastes slightly metallic with the fresh scent of rain on snow. My fingers twist the keys in the car door; my hips slide in behind the steering wheel.

To no avail, the drizzle struggles to become snow. As the station wagon winds down the steep hill toward the trailer park, its wipers beat back the slush and my thoughts succumb to the gloom. Why bother going to Avignon and learning French when the bastard I was doing it all for abandoned me nineteen years ago? I suffer a twinge of guilt for thinking so badly of him when he isn't around to defend himself, because maybe he didn't abandon me after all—maybe he had to run for his life, or maybe the gang took him out. On the other hand, maybe he's been living high on the hog all this time in Vancouver, Montreal, or France, with a new woman and new kids. Why should I give a damn about his country or language? We have just buried the only man who was ever a father to me in any way. Now, I must also bury that childhood dream of a father's unconditional love:

Daddy, daddy, you bastard, I'm through.

I sit alone in the car parked outside Katie's trailer, watching the first real flakes of snow begin to fall on the window shield. As I recall the lines of Sylvia Plath's poem, I realize that what I am through with is blaming myself for my father's choice, with feeling responsible for its effect on my mother's life, with allowing it to cast the shadow of despair over me, and with feeling, as a result, inferior in all my relationships.

Now Matthew is coming back, and it is not enough.

In the driver's side mirror, I spy flyers peeking out of Katie's mailbox. Getting out of the car, I slosh through the slushy snow over to the mailbox, reflecting on how, on the one hand, I could stay here and take care of Katie for the rest of the holidays—she is, after all, the only family I know. Then, after New Year's, I could return to the university to beg for readmission into the commerce program—it is, after all, my fastest track to a career. On the other hand, half my DNA is from my father, making me half of French ancestry. For years, I have sold myself a lie to avoid facing the question of why: *why* did he leave without so much as a backward glance? Now part of me wants to reject his language and culture to punish him, while another part wants to feel complete by exploring this side of my ancestry. What were his genetic gifts to me? Do I look somewhat French—do I look like him? Is my sense of melancholy, which my mother has never been able to understand, a French trait, passed on from him? What would it be like to reason and dream in French— would this make me think differently of him, would this allow me to finally understand why he left?

I pull back the flap door of the mailbox and let the flyers fall into my hands. Enveloped inside them is a stack of envelopes, mostly bills. Climbing the porch steps, I stamp my wet shoes on the mat and turn the doorknob. No one is home, but Katie has left the trailer unlocked. Inside, I dump the mail on the table. I heat up a pot of milk on the stove and make myself a cup of hot cocoa. The slush has soaked through the bottoms of my jeans, so I strip them off along with my wet socks and dig out a pair of flannel pyjamas from my bag by the door, packed and ready to go should I decide to catch the bus out of here in a few hours.

Katie, I know, will be out until the bars close again, binge drinking her bereavement into oblivion. Although she has been dry for years, it appears that her old pattern has been waiting in the wings all this time for the first opportunity to re-stake its claim on her. She is the kind of drunk who can sober up for a couple of days at a time, sometimes even a week, but once she has that first sip she loses all control. So I know better than to expect anything less than a two-day bender. I also know that she will do her best to hide it from me, staying away from the trailer until she is too hosed to feel shame and then sneaking back in to pass out. Once it is over, she'll act as though it hasn't happened at all and expect me to play along, just as I did as a child.

However, I have another option as an adult: the Greyhound bus leaves at six fifteen, and I know how to call a cab to the gas station depot.

Sitting at the table, sipping on a warm cup of cocoa with marshmallows, I weigh my feelings of guilt and obligation against this overwhelming desire to get the hell out of here. It is then, poking through Katie's mail, that I come across a letter underneath the phone bill. My hands tremble as I grab a knife from the counter to slit it open. A photo falls out: a middle-aged woman in a plain jean dress hugs two sandy-haired children under a Christmas tree. My whole body shakes as I unfold the card featuring a Santa Claus dropping gifts down a chimney.

Dear Sister,

I read about your husband in the obituaries of The Windeal Weekly *online. I'm sorry to learn of his passing. I'd like to call you —would that be okay? Can you send me your number?*

Two years ago, I divorced Martin and moved to Toronto with the kids. I completed a teaching certificate and now teach art at two high schools. As a young artist, I never imagined I'd end up having to teach. Do you ever think about sculpting anymore? You had such talent. Remember how your art teacher bragged you were going to be the new Rodin after that bust you moulded of me in clay? (I still have it, by the way.) I'll never forget the day he came over to tell Mom and Dad about the early scholarship he got for you to Concordia, and then his reaction when Dad said you weren't interested. I don't mean to stir up old wounds. It's just I think about you often. I wish Dad hadn't been so old-fashioned. He grew up in a different generation, one that felt obliged to hide its pregnant teenagers, but I know he regrets it now.

Mom always asks about you, in case I've heard anything. She has arthritis in her fingers and hip, but they've decided against moving to Arizona as Dad had a slight heart attack last spring. I try to take the kids over to visit them in Montreal at least once a month. We are spending Christmas and New Year's with them this year.

How is your Helene? I imagine she's all grown up now. Tim is nine and growing like a weed. Samantha just turned five and loves kindergarten.

We have a spare room and would love a visit. I could pay your way. Mom and Dad are getting older, and I know they'd like to see you again.

I miss you.

Love,

Lodi.

Setting down the Christmas card, I sip my hot chocolate. Lodi, my idol, that sophisticated artist living all these years in that photograph tucked away inside my pillowcase—one day she was going to rescue me from this colourless life. She was going to introduce me to the world of art, get me situated, get me started, get me connected. Yet, if I am to believe the story seeping out from between the lines of this card, rather than feeling successful as an artist, she feels frustrated working a day job that steals time away from her creative impulse.

Is art worth it?

What makes me think I can do any better? Who is to say I won't end up in a similar situation, having to put aside my art to make a living, all the while feeling as though I am squandering my potential and my life?

Why can't I concentrate instead on developing a real career like a normal person?

Why do I have to want to be an artist?

Why can't I just give it up?

On a whim, I tear off a blank sheet from the notepad on top of the fridge. I have no answer to these questions, only this compulsion I can no longer deny.

Dear Aunt Lodi, I write as fast as my hand will allow.
Here is a sketch I made of my mom. I'm moving to France for a while to work on my painting and photography. I would love to get to know you, my cousins, and my grandparents.
Merry Christmas and Happy New Year,
Helene.

Abandoning the note on the table, I scour the trailer for an envelope, finding a large brown one in Lyle's old desk by the living room window. Back at the table, before I can change my mind, I copy onto it Lodi's address and drop in my note. For my return address, I withdraw the folded-up paper from my wallet on which Laurent wrote the address for his family's flat in Avignon. After sliding in the charcoal sketch of Katie, which I brought with me from Vancouver thinking I might give it to her, I slap on a couple of stamps, also raided from Lyle's desk, and dash up the street through the falling snow in my pyjamas and damp runners to the trailer park's street letter box.

The postal box glistens fire-truck red under droplets of melted snow, a brilliant beacon of colour in an otherwise greyish-white landscape. The hatch slams shut behind my hand like thunder. I open it again to stare down the slot, snowflakes pummelling my face and sliding down my cheeks like tears as they melt. Impossible to reach in and pull out the envelope. Impossible to undo what I've done.

Back at the trailer, I call a cab. While I wait for it to arrive, I toss myself onto the couch and bury my face amongst the ragged cushions, inhaling their odours of alcohol and sweat and cheap perfume, and wonder if I will ever make it as an artist.

Sarah Lane was born in California and grew up in British Columbia. After studying international relations at the University of British Columbia and l'Institut d'études politiques in France, she began to write while working as an analyst at the central Bank of Canada. She then went on to receive her master's degree in comparative literature from the University of British Columbia, where she focused on literary translation. Her short fiction and poetry have appeared in *The Antigonish Review*, *Roar Magazine*, and *Quills: Canadian Poetry Magazine*, among other literary journals. *The God of My Art* was a quarterfinalist for the 2012 Amazon Breakthrough Novel Award. In addition to having lived abroad in France and the United States, Lane has also travelled extensively in Cameroon, Mexico, and Europe. She lives in Vancouver with her husband and two children, where she is at work on her next novel.

To learn of author events and new books by Sarah Lane, please visit www.sarahlanebooks.com.